She had *known.*

Even at the instant of acceptance, Friday had known it was wrong to accept Nick's proposal. She *was* guilty. More so now, when chance dangled before her the opportunity to redeem her fault. Set him free, Friday! Now. Do it *now.*

She opened her mouth to speak the fatal words…

Friday
Dreaming

ELIZABETH BAILEY

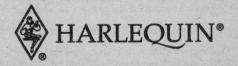 HARLEQUIN®

TORONTO • NEW YORK • LONDON
AMSTERDAM • PARIS • SYDNEY • HAMBURG
STOCKHOLM • ATHENS • TOKYO • MILAN • MADRID
PRAGUE • WARSAW • BUDAPEST • AUCKLAND

ISBN 0-373-30394-7

FRIDAY DREAMING

First North American Publication 2002

Copyright © 1994 by Elizabeth Bailey

Visit us at www.eHarlequin.com

Printed in U.S.A.

ELIZABETH BAILEY

grew up in Malawi, returning to England to plunge into theater. After many happy years "tatting around the reps," she finally turned from "dabbling" to serious writing. She finds it more satisfying, for she is in control of everything—scripts, design, direction and the portrayal of every character! Elizabeth lives in Kent and, in time spared from writing, teaches GCSE and A-level drama at a local school.

Chapter One

Nothing in the air gave warning that fateful afternoon. Stillness held this corner of the big house at Finchamstod in thrall. The drowsy sun seeped his lazy way into the window recess of the library as usual, lighting that favoured spot where a young lady sat in her accustomed place.

The interior of the long room was dim and musty by day, the towering bookshelves that lined the walls at either side cutting off most of the light. Thus it was the practice of its sole occupant to perch on the velvet-cushioned window-stool, her back against one scrolled end and her legs raised up—in a most unladylike and reprehensible manner—so that her elbows rested comfortably against her drawn-up knees, enabling her to bury her nose in a leather-bound volume. Almost literally, as it happened, for Miss Frideswid Edborough's sight was not quite as good as such a confirmed bookworm might have wished.

Even had there been some *frisson* foreshadowing events to come, it was doubtful whether any sixth sense could have penetrated the concentrated absorption with which Friday—as she was familiarly known—was devouring, in the original Greek, the tale of Leda's amorous adventure with the swan. Particularly now, for her mind was fully occupied with the difficulties inherent in this very odd method of seduction.

Could one, she wondered, seriously find oneself attracted to what was, when all was said and done, a large bird? What in the world had possessed the god Zeus to choose such a guise? Swans were admittedly beautiful creatures, with their long necks and elegant bearing. But indeed, decided Friday—with a lack of proper innocence that she knew the average matron would have found shocking—she was at a loss to imagine how Leda might even endure such a coupling.

True, just at this precise moment the maiden was rather half-heartedly attempting to repulse Zeus's extraordinary advances, but Friday could not believe that she might be depended upon to adhere to this resolve. Not, that was to say, if the classical myths were to be believed. For had not this very union spawned the most beautiful creature of the times?

Here Miss Edborough let out a tiny sigh. Ah, Helen! Would that one could even *aspire* to such beauty. At least, one *would,* if one *could,* only to have Paris at one's feet. Not *the* Paris, of course, whose handsome looks had been, along with those of his inamorata, delineated by many hands through the centuries. No, it was her very own Paris whose image filled her inner vision. A Paris whose beauty and manly proportions troubled her dreams not a little. Impossible dreams, of course. She had long accepted that. She was no Helen and Paris was not for her.

Ignoring the faint ache of yearning which long familiarity had enabled her to endure without complaint, Friday buried herself once more in the tale of Leda, and did not hear the opening of the library door.

Not so Bruno, the large liver and white hound, who in the autumn of his days, the excitements of a varied and somewhat chequered career behind him, was content to lie quietly in the shadows, dozing by his mistress's side. At the first scrape of the door-handle, he looked up, alert for any sign of unwanted intruders whom he might feel called upon to repel. At the sight of the gentleman who entered, however, he relaxed, but thought it proper to sit up and nudge at his mistress's side.

Friday did not notice. Nor was she aware of anything other than the contents of her book until a voice addressed her in admonishing accents.

"Friday!"

She jumped violently. Glancing up, she was able to make out only a blurry countenance. The large white blob in its centre, however, together with the frizzy expanse of its full-bottomed wig, enabled her to identify its owner instantly.

"Papa! Gracious, what a fright you gave me!"

Mr Edborough ignored this. Frowning direfully, he delivered himself of an age-old complaint. "How many times must I request you, Friday, not to ruin your eyes in that tiresome fashion? Where are your spectacles? Put them on at once!"

Friday groped on the windowsill to retrieve the offending eyeglasses, but entered nevertheless upon her time-honoured protest. "I do not need them for reading, Papa. It is only faces that I cannot distinguish. And the light is excellent just here."

"Don't argue with me, Friday! As obstinate as your mother, that's what you are."

Undeniably, Friday agreed silently, and a quirk of mirth disturbed one corner of her mouth as she obediently placed the spectacles on her nose. "Better?"

Her father grunted, plainly dissatisfied still. Poor Papa! It was a great deal too bad that he should be saddled with *two* such females as herself and Mama. Though what was on his mind at this moment she was unable to fathom. The spectacles were merely a side-issue, she knew. Although she was perfectly aware that she looked dreadful in them. Not, since she could not see her own face unless she was wearing them, that she had any idea how she looked without them! But she had long accepted her own shortcomings.

Not only had she hair of an indeterminate mousy colour, but she was peppered with freckles across a nose that became a mere button under the huge round spectacles that dwarfed her face. Her mouth was quite plain, and her eyes mere nothings under the thick glass that covered them. Still, she was used to herself, as was Papa. One could not make a silk purse out of a sow's ear. Not that she tried. And Mama certainly did not urge her to do so.

She cocked her head on one side, eyeing her father's disgruntled features that were now clearly visible to her. "What ails you, Papa?"

"What should ail me at such an hour, pray?" he demanded testily. "I suppose it is too much to expect that you might take the trouble to look at the clock once in a while."

Friday's glance flew to the mantel at the other end of the long room. Above it, an enormous wood-encased timepiece declared the hour to be close on five. Her father's annoyance was immediately explained.

"Gracious!" she exclaimed, quickly laying aside her book and swinging her legs to the floor. "I do beg your pardon, Papa. You must be starving!"

"Starving? I?" he rejoined with an air of surprise. "Why should you think so? If I have not accustomed myself in all these years to enjoying late meals of cold meats and congealed gravies that have stood on the table for quite half an hour, then it must be my own fault. Though I dare say in any *normal* household a man might expect to arrive at the dinner-table in *company* with his wife and daughter, in my case I ought to be delighted to be granted even a *sight* of them."

With difficulty Friday controlled a quivering lip. *She* might find it amusing, but Papa's sarcasm could erupt, she knew, into a very real rage at any moment. Normally Papa was such an easygoing man. He usually took in his stride Mama's eccentricities and, it had to be admitted, her own vagaries. But today, for some unexplained reason, it was apparent that he was upset by them.

"Poor Papa!" she said soothingly, tucking her hand in his arm and urging him towards the door. "We are a sad trial to you, Mama and I. She with her family tree and I with my classics. I do not know how you bear with us."

"Nor do I," he said sourly, allowing himself to be shepherded from the room as he added grudgingly, "Though I dare say I may blame myself for that, too. I should never have taught you Greek and Latin."

At the door Friday turned and called to her dog,

reflecting that for her part she was only too glad he had chosen to see to her education himself instead of saddling her with a governess. But it was scarcely the moment to say so.

The hound Bruno, with a realisation as belated as her own, ambled through into the hall and made for the green baize door at the end. A wheezy bark would bring out a member of the domestic staff, and put him in touch with the edible matter no doubt contained in his bowl in the kitchen.

Friday did not dare to suggest that she change her dress, for that would provoke Papa even more. Besides, since both she and Mama quite often dined in day dress if company was not present, it was probably more prudent not to draw Papa's attention to her lapse. In his present mood, she was likely to call down on her head a scold for her poor taste in dress.

Not that there was anything wrong with her plain bronze gown, but she was quite aware that its waist was lower than was presently considered modish and the warmth of its linsey-woolsey cloth more robust than the muslins and gauzes that were currently gracing the willowy forms in the fashion plates of the periodicals meant for ladies of the *ton*. A fact for which neither Friday nor her Mama cared tuppence.

Mrs Sophia Edborough was already seated at the table when her spouse and daughter entered the dining-room. She was a pleasant-looking female of late middle years, dressed quite as unmodishly and plainly as her daughter. But whereas Friday simply drew her hair back away from her face and tied it loosely at the neck in the manner of a man's queue, leaving fluffy strands standing all anyhow about her face, Sophia Edborough wore a cap over neatly banded locks.

Her obsession left no room for fripperies and a logical mind was echoed in tidiness of person.

"You have no idea, Edmund," she uttered to her husband by way of greeting, "how difficult this search is becoming. If I have read one manuscript, I have read fifty! The wretch is nowhere to be found."

Seeing her father's brow darken, Friday hastened to rush into speech. Papa knew perfectly well to what Mama was referring, for they had both heard from her of nothing else for days. A pity that her hunt for some elusive member of the Edborough family tree should not yet have proved fruitful, for Papa was in no mood for this kind of thing today.

"You will find him, Mama, never fear," she said soothingly. "You always do."

Which was quite true, she reflected. Mama's tenacity was proverbial. After all, she had been pursuing her abiding interest in the family history virtually from the hour of her marriage. Indeed, Papa was wont to complain that she had only married him because his ancestry traced back to pre-Norman days. It was true that Mama had chosen her own name of Frideswid only because it was old English.

Her intervention was without effect. Mr Edborough glared at his wife as he took his seat at the top of the table. "For God's sake, Sophy, let me have one meal without a discussion of your infernal family tree!"

"Your family tree, Edmund," she reminded him calmly, apparently undisturbed by his irritation. She was not oblivious to it, however, for she eyed him a moment in silence as he began to ladle servings from a steaming tureen of Spanish green pottage. Then she lifted her brows at her daughter. "What is the matter with your father, Frideswid?"

"There is nothing the matter with *me*," cut in her husband pointedly, handing a full bowl to his daughter to be passed down the table. "And I wish you will not call her by that ridiculous name."

"It is less ridiculous than 'Friday,'" argued Mrs Edborough.

"We are late, Mama," Friday told her mother quickly. "Poor Papa has been dying of starvation."

Sophia Edborough regarded her husband fixedly for a moment or two. Then she picked up her soup spoon and gave judgement. "It is not that. He is quite used to that. There must be something else on his mind."

Struck by her mother's perspicacity, Friday looked her father over as she received her portion from his hands. There was something else. She had herself noted that his mood was uncertain, and Mama was right. It could not be purely on account of having to wait for his dinner. One tended to forget that Mama was so acute.

"Indeed, I don't know, Mama," she said in a puzzled voice. "What is on your mind, Papa? Do tell us."

She was glad to see his features lose some of their unaccustomed colour. He was calming down. With deliberation, he swallowed a mouthful of broth and then turned his gaze upon his daughter.

"You, Friday," he pronounced in a measured tone. "You are on my mind."

"I?" echoed Friday, astonished. "Whatever can you mean?"

Flicking a glance at her mother, she saw that Mrs Edborough was equally amazed. She said nothing, however, but merely waited for further information.

Mama was never one to ask unnecessary questions. It was obvious that Papa was going to speak his mind.

So indeed it proved. "Do you forget that you are coming of age in a couple of weeks?" he asked sternly.

Friday blinked. Her birthday! Gracious, she had indeed entirely forgotten it! So too, it appeared, had Mama.

"Good heavens!" exclaimed her mother, pausing with her spoon in the air. "Are you indeed going to turn one and twenty, Frideswid? I would not have credited it. How time flies!"

Her spouse turned on her. "So that is all you can say, is it, Sophy? Of course it is! There is the matter in a nutshell. Your daughter is on the shelf, and you are not even aware of her age."

"On the shelf?" repeated Mrs Edborough blankly. "What nonsense! Why, I was past thirty when I married you, Edmund."

"Yes, and if I had not been descended from the Saxons I dare say you would have been content to remain an old maid."

"Then by your reckoning, my love," opined his wife calmly, "we shall have Frideswid on our hands until such time as one of Homer's heroes descends upon us to snatch her away."

But Mr Edborough refused to be diverted by the pleasantry. "You know perfectly well what I mean, Sophy. *And* why I am anxious. Who is to look after Friday and the estate when we are gone?"

Friday barely heard him. Her mother's uncannily apt joke had thrown her into confusion. Apprehension began to rise in her breast. She felt herself growing warm and uttered a breathy protest. "But I have no expectation of being married."

"Which is no doubt the reason why you have resisted all efforts to turn you into a fashionable young lady," accused her father. "*And* you have refused every offer for a coming-out season in London."

"It is no use expecting *me* to attend to all that, Edmund," said his wife flatly. "I have neither the time nor the inclination to set about finding Frideswid a husband."

"You have no need to tell me that," snapped her spouse. "All you have time for is delving into the histories of half the noble families in England."

If this was an exaggeration, Friday knew that there was some justification for her father's complaint. Mama had certainly made contact with many genteel landowners in her pursuit of the ramifications of the family, and had been persuaded into producing family trees for others to boot. Much to Papa's chagrin. But for herself, she was all too glad of Mama's involvement. It had allowed her a freedom she might not otherwise have enjoyed, and kept at bay a possibility she had begun to dread.

"Papa!" she broke in anxiously. "Pray believe me! I have no *wish* to be married. At least—there is no one whom I—with whom I..."

Her voice petered out, for into her treacherous mind had already sprung the image of the one person whom she *would* have wished to marry. Only there was no possibility of such a thing. Not in a million years!

Fortunately, Papa did not take her up on her hesitation. "Of course there is no one," he said testily. "How could there be when you have met no young men at all—eligible or otherwise?"

Again, Friday's unruly thoughts betrayed her, as visions of a certain young man—her very own Greek hero, her Paris—crowded her brain. Visions of features so exquisite that females almost fainted at the sight of them—as *she* had very nearly done that far-off day. Features complemented by hair of palest gold, and eyes so green that one fancied one saw in them an echo of the sea. And those *lips*. Sculpted surely by no less than the gods on Olympus! But it was not that alone. Oh, no. She was not quite such a fool as to remain infatuated with a beautiful face. There was also a teasing smile, and laughter. A keen mind. A kind heart and a dear *endearing* trick of looking to her, Friday, for solutions to difficulties about which a female ought to know nothing. He treated her, indeed, just as if she were another boy. But then she was not a female to him. Not at all.

The sharp stab of pain that accompanied this thought snapped her back to reality. What had she said? Had she given herself away? In fact barely any time had passed, to judge by Mama's remarks, although the soup bowls had been laid aside and her parents had begun on the meats.

"What nonsense, Edmund! Not met any young men? She has met any number of them. One in particular, who will do very well. Indeed, I have every confidence that Lydia expects it. Which is why, let me tell you, there is no need for me to bestir myself in the matter."

Mr Edborough stared at his wife, unaware of his daughter's growing unease. "Are you suggesting that *Delamere* wishes to marry Friday?"

Marry *Charles?* Oh, no! He was a dear friend, of course, as well as their closest neighbour. She cared for him deeply. And Lydia, Lady Delamere had ever been kind to her. Naturally, now that her lord was dead and the title had passed to Charles, she must be thinking of his marriage. But not to herself! Charles would not dream of marrying her. Any more than *he* would do.

Here coherence failed her. She must not have this on her mind. Must not—for it was her secret. He must never know. *They* must never know. For it could not be. The very thought was making her heart beat so fast she thought it must choke her. She had never dared to hope—to dream—not in *reality*. She knew he did not think of her in *that* way—however much she herself might feel for him.

"I don't know what Delamere may wish," Friday heard her mother say over her own chaotic thoughts. "All I know is that Lydia has more than once mentioned the matter. She feels the property would round off Delamere's estate very nicely."

"I beg your pardon?" responded her spouse, affronted. "Round off Delamere's estate? Good God! Am I to understand that you, Sophy, the very person who I should have thought would dislike to see the property go out of the family, will support this scheme?"

"I thought it an excellent solution," Mrs Edborough said mildly.

"Yes, for it would save you the trouble of doing anything about it yourself," stated her spouse wrathfully.

"There is that aspect," she agreed tranquilly.

Before her father could explode, Friday quickly intervened, albeit in a shaky voice quite unlike her usual tones, and in a hasty, preoccupied way that drew both parents' close attention.

"Pray don't wrangle! I am quite sure Charles has no intention of asking me to m-marry him. Indeed, I don't think anyone—that is, anyone I *know*—would want to marry me. No one I would care to marry, at all events. After all, he—he says himself I am nothing but a bluestocking. And who, in their right mind, would want to marry one? I don't blame him, truly I d-don't."

The pause that greeted these tumbling words set Friday trembling. Looking from one to the other of her parents, both of whom had paused in the act of serving themselves from the various dishes set out upon the table, she discovered a penetrating stare on her father's countenance, while her mother was looking at her in a fixed manner that was singularly unnerving. Could they read her mind?

Mrs Edborough was the first to speak. "And just who, Frideswid, is 'he'? Delamere?"

"Whom d-do you m-mean?" Friday sputtered helplessly. Gracious, how useless she became when her emotions were touched! Oh, for Mama's calm! Or even Papa's controlled explosions.

He emitted one of them now. "Are you deaf as well as blind, Friday? Your mama is asking—as am I, let me add—just exactly who is the gentleman who refers to you as a bluestocking?"

"Oh, but I assure you I don't m-mind it, Papa," Friday got out, desperate to deflect his attention from that agonising question.

"I am not asking if you mind it, Friday. I am asking for the identity of this gentleman who has apparently robbed you of your intelligence."

Gracious, he had robbed her of far more than that! thought Friday wildly. Only it was not *his* fault that she—

"Frideswid!" Mama's flat tone interrupted her thoughts. "Who 'in his right mind' would not wish to marry you? If you are not speaking of Delamere, then—"

"I was—I was speaking generally," gasped Friday, blinking rapidly under her spectacles as a pricking began at her eyes and her throat tightened.

Concern came into her father's face. Had he noticed her distress? But Mrs Edborough forestalled anything he might have said.

"Of whom are you 'speaking generally'?" she pursued forthrightly.

Close to tears, Friday bit her lip, fighting for control. She *must* not cry. Thank heaven for the all-concealing eyeglasses! Drawing a painful breath, she summoned a fleeting smile. She would have liked to give a light laugh, but she was afraid it would come out as a feeble croak.

"Really, Mama!" she produced, in what she felt to be a poor assumption of ease. "I can't think why you are making such an issue of it. I meant nothing, truly."

"Oh?" This from Papa, still eyeing her with that intent look, although his face had softened.

"Truly," she repeated insistently, taking courage from a deep-seated need to preserve her secret. "It was nothing but a—a poor sort of a joke between—" swallowing on a dry throat and snatching another quick breath "—between myself and...Nicolas."

She was conscious of dropping her voice at the end, barely whispering the name.

"Nicolas?" repeated her mother frowningly, as if she had never heard of him.

Mr Edborough was better informed. "Ah, you mean the Weare boy. *Now* I see. Well, well!"

"Oh, Delamere's *friend*," said Sophia, her brow clearing.

And mine! thought Friday with a rush of warmth at her heart, aware with only a fleeting recognition of her father's rather odd remarks. At least she had that. His friendship. His companionship. Perhaps less often lately, she recalled with a pang. But she must not cavil. If she could not be *happy* in his absence, she was at least content. She had her classics to take her mind away to ancient tales of the adventurous doings of gods and men. And she had her memories. Those *precious* memories…

At fifteen, Friday had felt that Homer's Iliad fell rather flat. It seemed to have lost most of the attraction that had swept her up into a whirlwind of excitement when she had first struggled through it with her father. By now she was able to read Greek with almost the same fluency that she read English, and she was so familiar with the Iliad that she could skim through it in a search for particular passages, hunting down any reference she needed.

Today, however, the usual sensation of apprehension did not attack her as Achilles heard of the death of his friend Patroclus at the hands of Troy's hero, Hector. She read of his distraught rage almost with indifference, although she knew that this would prove to be the turning point in the war. For in his tortured grief Achilles would slaughter Hector, whose death marked the beginning of the end for the Trojans.

She read idly, stretched at her length on the grass, heedless of the crushing to her gown, supported by her elbows, the book close enough to her eyes where it lay on the ground so that she was able—unencumbered by Papa's stern remonstrances!—to remove her spectacles which lay abandoned somewhere beside her. Thus ensconced in her favoured fine-weather haunt on her private hilltop beyond the copse that bordered both the Edborough and the Delamere estates, Friday was able to forget dull reality and allow her imagination to soar.

But her mind was not alive with the images of Achilles and Hector today. Rather it was Paris and Helen that occupied her puzzled thoughts. In the past, she had merely been angry with the two of them for behaving in such a reckless fashion that this whole tragic downfall of a people came to pass. One could scarcely blame Menelaus for revenging himself on the abductor of his wife. Although he might have stopped at killing Paris, Friday had long ago decided judiciously. There was really no need to bring the entire Trojan kingdom into it! Nor to drag his brother Agamemnon, not to mention Achilles and Ajax, and all the rest of the Greek heroes, together with all those doomed soldiers, into a ten-year siege. Really, men were so stupid!

But for some reason this aspect of the matter now paled into insignificance beside the romance of Paris and Helen. What had she that caused him to break all the rules of honour? More importantly, what had he that could cause this woman to destroy all her vows and abandon her husband? According to Homer, her beauty was matchless. According to Friday, Paris must have been equally beautiful.

He must, she thought, have been golden-haired, above a countenance fashioned with a delicacy that would set painters reaching for their brushes to commit it instantly to canvas, each feature a model of perfection, so that together they became a whole so classically pleasing that all who beheld it must have sighed in awe.

She had just conjured up a vision that fitted admirably with these requirements, when a commotion broke out in the copse behind her, wiping the picture from her mind. A ferocious barking that could emanate from only one throat, and a crashing sound as something or someone beat a ragged path through the woods.

"Oh, Bruno!" uttered Friday, annoyed. What was he about now? She struggled up, and had just twisted herself about so that she could see the blurry outline of the copse, when a hazy figure came hurtling out of the woods, closely followed by a loping form that she knew must be that of her misbegotten hound.

Leaping to her feet, Friday flung herself to the rescue, realising as she did so that, even under her abstraction, she had actually heard his growling in the distance together with a vague voice of protest and alarm. Cursing—with a will worthy of Papa's own complaints!—the total abstraction which always enwrapped her when she read, she lifted her cumbersome petticoats above her ankles and made for the dog, shouting imprecations as she went.

"Stop it, Bruno! Bad dog! Stop at once!"

She thought the runner must have heard her, for he slowed and then stumbled to a halt. Her heart in her mouth, Friday saw him reel, and then collapse to the ground just as Bruno caught up, leaping with a triumphant bark upon the prone body.

"Bruno, *stop!*" shrieked Friday, reaching the scene a couple of seconds later, and beating frantically at the animal as she groped for his collar. "*Bad* dog, Bruno! What do you think you're doing? Do you want to get me into trouble? You *dreadful* animal."

Bruno growled his protests as he was dragged away, until a sharp slap to his snout set him whining. Flattening himself to the grass, his weight dragging Friday down on her haunches, he tossed his head and yelped, eyeing his mistress in a deprecating manner that she interpreted without any difficulty. Anger overlaid her fear as she berated him.

"It is no use pretending that you did not mean it, you horrid hound! *I* may believe you were only playing, but Papa most certainly will *not*. And how in the world do you expect me to save you when there is *this* to explain away?"

Flinging an accusing finger at the figure that lay beside her on the ground, Friday turned her head as she spoke. He was deathly still. Oh, dear Lord! She had thought he had merely fallen. Could it be that he was seriously injured?

"Oh, Bruno, what have you done?" she wailed, panic in her voice. Holding the dog off with a firm grasp of his collar, she crawled nearer, and knelt beside the body. Tears in both frock-coat and breeches bore witness to Bruno's assault, and an ominous stain spread down his hand from one reddened lace cuff. Tense with apprehension, Friday bent close so that she might examine his face.

It came into focus suddenly, and Friday froze above it. Her heart seemed to jerk, and stop. Then it began beating again, in a slow pound that built up in her head and threatened to deprive her of her own senses.

Heaven help her, but the face was almost exactly that face that she had dreamed up just a few moments ago! He was very young. Her own age, or but a year or so older. His hair was of palest gold, tied back at the neck. And his features! She had never *seen* such beauty. No, not in the images that graced the walls of any house she had been in. Not in the prints or sketches she had found in books. Nowhere, indeed, did there exist such a face. Except that it *did*. For here it was, lying at her feet, chased here by Bruno just as she was picturing it in her mind. Paris himself!

She shivered, eerily astonished by this odd trick of the mind. It was as if she had dreamed him into existence!

Just then he stirred, and his eyes flickered open, revealing a green gaze that stared up at her in frowning puzzlement for a moment or two.

"Dog...where...?" he murmured vaguely, recalling Friday to a sense of her obligations.

"Yes, I'm so very sorry," she uttered contritely. "He's very naughty sometimes. Are you much hurt?"

The boy seemed to glance over her shoulder, and abruptly brought up a hand to push her back as he struggled up.

"Keep it away!"

"Don't be afraid! I have him safe now," Friday assured him, shoving Bruno behind her. The poor boy must have caught sight of him trying to muscle in again. "He won't touch you while I am here."

The youth had put his hands to his head, evidently still a trifle dizzy from his faint. Friday could not see his face so well now, for he had put a little distance between himself and the offending hound. But she recognised his tone when he spoke again, and saw the eyes spark a little.

"Oh, he's yours, is he? Then why can't you keep him under better control? A ferocious beast like that ought not to be allowed to roam all over the estate."

"He's not ferocious!" responded Friday indignantly, firing up in defence of her pet. "And it's *our* estate, after all."

"It's not your estate," snapped the victim, carefully kneading his brow. "It's Lord Delamere's."

"It most certainly is *not*," argued Friday. "Delamere's estate runs parallel, but the copse is ours."

"That's not what Charles says."

Friday frowned direfully, diverted from the boy's unfortunate encounter with Bruno. "If Charles Delamere is going about saying the copse belongs to his father, then he will very soon find himself corrected by my mama. She can tell you to the inch where the Delamere land stops and ours begins."

The youth dragged himself to his feet, and stood swaying very slightly. "Listen, I don't know who you are, and I don't care who owns the copse. But if we are to talk of correction, you, young lady, are far more likely to find yourself standing before a magistrate on account of your dog's attack upon me." He pointed as he spoke and then caught at his own hand as he saw the red. "My God, he's drawn blood!"

Friday had been about to take exception to the patronising note, but at this she darted forward so that she could examine the wrist where the youth had pulled away the stained cuff of his shirt. Bruno's teeth had indeed pierced the skin. Guilt consumed her.

"Gracious! Oh, dear, that is *dreadful*. I am so very sorry! Pray, let us go to at once my house and I can attend to it."

"Thank you, but I had rather go back to Delamere Place," he responded, a degree less frostily.

"No, no, it is much quicker to ours," Friday insisted, and released her hold on Bruno as she approached.

The young lad backed off hurriedly as the animal showed his teeth, growling. But Friday delivered another sharp slap to his snout.

"You have done quite enough, Bruno. Behave! He will not hurt you, I promise," she added to the boy.

"If your presence is essential to ensure that," he said resignedly, "I suppose I had better accept your invitation. Unless you care to escort me back to Delamere?"

"Of course I will," Friday said at once. "*After* you are patched up. We will drive there in Papa's gig. I don't think you ought to walk too far, you know."

"Good God, I am not an invalid!" he objected.

"But you have been in a faint. I dare say you are feeling a trifle dizzy still. Lean on me!"

Approaching him, Friday moved as if she would support his weight from one side, but he shifted away.

"I am quite capable of walking, I thank you."

"Well, do, then," Friday said huffily, unaccountably hurt by this rebuff. "I am only trying to help. But if you will have none if it, I am sure I do not care."

Unexpectedly, the boy laughed. "That makes twice I've managed to offend you. How many more times will it take, I wonder, before I have revenged myself on you for your wretched dog's antics?"

Friday felt a quiver disturb her mouth, and she was obliged to smile. The hurt evaporated in a warm glow. "I have a sort of feeling you will grossly outweigh the damage Bruno has done to you."

He laughed. "Very likely. Who are you? Mr Edborough's daughter?"

"That's right. I'm Friday Edborough."

"Oh, *you're* Friday," he uttered, staring at her with a new interest. "I've heard a lot about you."

Just exactly *what* had he heard? Friday wondered. But she was not going to ask! "From Charles, I expect," she said as carelessly as she could. "We've known each other practically from the cradle, you see. You must be up at Oxford with him." She sighed, reminded of a familiar grievance. "How I envy you both! They will not let a female at the university. I think it is grossly unfair."

There was a teasing note in his voice as he answered. "Good God, whatever next? We should never know a moment's peace if they let females in! For my part, I would help to barricade the doors."

"Oh, would you?" uttered Friday, falling indignantly into his trap. "Then I can only say that I'm *glad* Bruno bit you, you—you—I don't even know your name!" she finished exasperatedly as he began to laugh.

"Nicolas Weare," he told her, with a tiny mock-bow. "Not terribly much at your service, Miss Edborough."

"Friday," she corrected, retorting, "and I don't need your services. You need mine."

"I suppose I do," he agreed, ruefully surveying the blood on his cuff. "If you're a laundress, that is."

"Don't be silly! Are you coming or not?"

All her discomforts seemed to have vanished. They might have known each other forever. She smiled sunnily and turned for the woods.

He began to follow her, but all at once halted, stretching out a hand. "I hate to own it, Friday, but you were right. Lend me your shoulder, will you?"

Friday turned quickly at the fainter note. Nicolas had paled, clearly unsteady on his feet. Fear came rushing back. She dashed up to him, and his face came into focus again rather abruptly. Her heart jerked. She had forgotten, in all the bustle and argument, about his resemblance to that Paris of her imagination! As she allowed him to settle his arm about her shoulders—he was near a foot taller than she, so he was able to do it quite comfortably—and put her own arm about his waist, she felt an inward tremble attack her and a slight flutter of her pulse.

Neither spoke as they began to move rather gingerly forward, Friday steadfastly regarding the ground. Shyness had attacked her and, with it, a complete absence of attention to what she was doing. As they reached the copse, she almost walked them straight into a tree.

Nicolas dragged her to a stop. "Hey! I'm the one who's injured. What in the world is the matter with you?"

Embarrassed, Friday blinked stupidly. Oh, gracious! Her *spectacles*. She was blundering about like a fool. Hurriedly disengaging herself, she pushed Nicolas at the tree.

"Hold on to that! Wait here!" she commanded roughly, out of a flooding tide of self-consciousness.

"The dog!" he called after her as Bruno came bounding up.

"Bruno, *come* here!" she shouted, so forcefully that the animal halted in mid-stride, glanced from his quarry to his mistress, and, deciding in favour of the latter, dashed after Friday as she sped back to where she had left her book.

With her spectacles once more perched on her nose, she felt much more herself, and her constraint lessened. Until she got a clear picture of Nicolas Weare standing by the tree, awaiting her return, and noticed, as she neared, an expression of amusement on his beautiful countenance. So she looked that funny, did she?

"Now I know what was missing," he said grinning. "Charles described you with those things on your face. That's why I didn't realise who you were just at first."

"Capital!" snapped Friday ironically. "How charming that I am known only as the bespectacled female!"

"And the intellectual one," added Nicolas in a friendly tone. "I'm reminded of my sister's governess."

A governess! It was so little how she would have wished him to think of her that, to hide her hurt feelings, she at once took refuge in a hectoring, businesslike manner that bore out the charge.

"Come on, for goodness' sake! Or you will be falling down in a faint again."

Nicolas Weare was apparently undeceived. As she once more took his weight and they started off again, he said provocatively, "Seeing that I already know you for the offended female, I dare say you will not object to it if I add that description to the one Charles gave me."

"Thank you very much!"

"Not at all. Tell me. Are you planning to make a career of being a bluestocking, or is it merely a phase you are going through?"

Friday glanced up at him and caught the gleam in his eye. Relief flooded through her. He did not *mean* it. He was joking! Warming to him, she entered at once into the spirit of the game, demanding bodingly, "Do you wish me to call on Bruno's services again, Nicolas Weare?"

"No, I take it back!" he cried, laughing. But he eyed the animal consideringly, who was tracking them at a discreet distance to the right. "What do you want with a brute like that, in any event? A stupid sort of pet, if you ask me. Why is he not doing his proper job of hunting?"

"Because he is afraid of foxes," explained Friday defensively, rising instantly to the bait. "It is not his fault. He is a crossbreed—with a pointer. And I did *not* ask you."

"You mean he's a mongrel," said Nicolas, ignoring this last. "I suppose he is afraid of birds, too?"

"Of course he is not. Only Papa would not allow him to become a game dog for he cannot bear gunfire."

"Good God, what a faintheart! And I took him for a very Cerberus."

"Don't be silly! Cerberus had three heads, and he was guarding the gates of hell."

"I could have sworn your dog did have three heads," said Nicolas feelingly. "And if this isn't hell, what is it?"

"Really, you are the most abominable boy!" Friday told him crossly, torn between fury and laughter.

"Why Charles had to invite you here I cannot imagine. He must have windmills in his head! And I wish you will not keep laughing like that!''

"I can't help it,'' Nicolas got out, quite convulsed. "You are the easiest prey of anyone I have ever met. I shall persuade Charles to invite me more often.''

There had been no need, Friday thought, coming back to the present with an unconscious smile on her face, for Nick to persuade Charles of anything of the kind. He must have become sick to death over the years of her incessant plea, "When is Nick visiting again, Charles?''

She discovered that she had finished dinner in a semi-trance of remembrance, and that her mother was just rising to leave her father to his solitary port. They would all meet again later in the evening when the tea-tray was brought in before bedtime. But now she was free to go back to her haunt in the library and indulge herself in daydreams. As long, she hurriedly reminded herself, as they had nothing to do with *marriage*.

She had, she admitted, in those early days, done exactly that. Well, perhaps she had not got as far as marriage. But she had dreamed of a love requited, of a passion as inflamed as her own. But in the dreams she had been a Helen, not a Friday. And although while Nicolas was away she might fashion her dreams after her own inclination, when he was present, with laughter in his face as he caught her—time and again, curse the creature!—in his teasing traps, she could never forget reality. She was plain Friday, a blue-stocking, bespectacled miss. Intellectual—and very often offended, thanks to Nick's jokes!—but in no shape or form even remotely pretty.

Nick's Helen, when she came, would resemble Friday in no way at all. She knew that, for he had already fallen victim, as boys did, to several potential Helens. From his descriptions—ah, how an unknowing heart could wound with unconscious cruelty!—she was as unlike the females his taste ran to as she could be.

She found herself standing before the library window, staring out at the front lawns that led away to the copse and, through them, her hilltop retreat. Nicolas had often found her there after that first day. Afraid of giving away her delight in her face, Friday would always put on her spectacles to greet him. Besides, she could see him better. He had grown more handsome with the years, a man's firm jaw and strength of feature overlaying the delicacy of his youthful looks.

She sighed again, and, remembering the dreadful loss of coherence that had attacked her at the dinner-table, hoped very much that her parents had made nothing of it. She did not wish to marry…if she could not marry Nicolas. And since she could no more marry Nick than fly to the moon, she was doomed to spinsterhood. She did not mind it. She had long made up her mind to it. If only she might be left *alone* on the matter. God send that Papa's sudden interest in her future should wane as quickly as it had arisen!

Chapter Two

"Marry *Friday?*" gasped young Mr Weare, staring at his sire in shock. "Forgive me, sir, but you must have taken leave of your senses!"

"Don't take that tone with me, boy!" barked his father, banging his fist on the arm of his easy-chair. "You'll do as you're told for once in your life."

Nicolas compressed his lips on a sharp retort. He was hard put to it to hold his peace, for had he not performed every task—however little to his taste!—that his father had allotted to him? Had he not come hotfoot from London at his bidding? Slap in the middle of the Little Season, too, as his smart blue frock over buckskins and top-boots bore witness. All were fashionably fitted to his slim form, his cravat tied in the latest mode, his pale gold locks waving above his brow and cropped to rest on his stand-up collar.

He did as he was bid, just as they all three siblings did, in an effort to alleviate the distresses of Lord Weare's life. God knew he understood how trying it must be to be confined to a chair in the prime of life, the victim of a painful complaint. To see only those friends who cared enough to visit. To live alone in this great barrack of a mansion, but for a parcel of servants.

The boundaries of Lord Weare's existence had steadily shrunk to the four walls of the green saloon, with two painful journeys to and from the bedchamber in which his family knew he would some day be wholly confined. The room, furnished in pleasant shades of green upholstery against a pretty striped wallpaper, was as pleasant as it could be, thanks to his daughter's efforts. A large working table held his books near the comfortable chair next to the fire. His position both overlooked the front lawns and faced the door so that he could always see who entered his sanctum.

But it was a dull life, Nicolas believed. Worse since Caro had married and gone to live near Reading. Tony and he had half expected to be recalled to live at home. In fact, Tony had betted him that this summons would prove to be just that.

"Mark my words, old fellow," had prophesied his elder brother gloomily. "He's got wind of your interest in the little Hesket and he intends to keep you safe at home, out of harm's way."

Nick had retorted that if anyone needed saving it was The Honourable Anthony Weare himself. "You don't think Caro's going to let you marry Griselda, do you? Besides, it's far more important who *you* marry. You're the heir."

In fact, Nicolas thought it all too probable that his father had summoned him for the purpose of putting a spoke into his romance. Not that he believed Caro would have betrayed him, no matter how much she herself disapproved. She knew Lord Weare's uncertain temper and would not willingly expose either of her brothers to it. But Lord Weare kept correspondence with enough old cronies of their deceased mama to have found Nick out without any assistance from Caro.

Yes, he had expected a thundering scold. But he had hardly bargained for *this*. Marriage to little Friday Edborough! He could not conceive where his father had come by such an odd notion.

"I beg your pardon, sir," he ventured, "but what put this scheme into your head?"

"Edborough himself," answered Lord Weare readily, and Nick was glad to note that his own calmer tone had smoothed the ruffled feathers. "Came to see me a few days since with a very favourable proposition."

"Favourable!" echoed Nicolas unguardedly.

"Extremely favourable," reiterated his sire with emphasis, shooting him a glare. "And if you're not the fool I take you for, you'll seize your chance and be thankful."

Nick was tempted to retort that he was exactly the fool his father took him for. That he didn't give a damn for Edborough's proposition, favourable or otherwise, and that he would marry none but Hermione—the divinely angelic, *heavenly* object of his adoration, of whom he knew his father would heartily disapprove.

It was the latter thought that held him silent, standing across from his father's chair. That, and a reluctant curiosity that began to burgeon in his mind. Perhaps it was Mr Edborough who had gone mad. He could not believe that Friday might actually wish to marry him. Him—or anyone. She was not that sort of female. It had not even crossed his mind that she *would* marry. Ever. Then why this peculiar mission of Edborough's to his father?

"Well, sir?" he asked briefly.

Lord Weare eyed him from under thick sandy brows. His body might have betrayed him, but he had still all the fire in a handsome face—now prematurely lined from incessant pain—that had attracted the woman who had bequeathed her exceptional fairness of face to her second son. Although the other two, for the most part favouring their sire, were generally accounted good-looking. Nicolas was apt to wonder whether the reminder of his dead mother in his face accounted for the frequent blisterings he received from his father's tongue.

On this occasion, perhaps he felt a softer approach might better serve his purpose, for he refrained from any rebuke at Nick's abrupt tone. He sat back in his chair and took snuff.

"Sensible man, Edborough. Said he saw no reason to expect any romantic flummery. Said his daughter's not that sort of girl. Nonsense, if you ask me. All girls have their heads stuffed with nothing else!"

"Not Friday," put in Nicolas with conviction.

"Pah! Don't believe it. Only have to look at Caroline. Fell in love with that fellow Cleeve at sight, she told me."

"Yes, but Richard was perfectly eligible," protested Nick, recalling his brother-in-law's ample fortune.

"If that's what bothers you, my boy, you've nothing to cavil at there," announced Weare triumphantly. "Marry this Edborough girl and you'll be set up for life."

Nick stared. "What do you mean, sir?"

"Ha! Thought you'd not be so high-nosed when you heard the full sum of it. Edborough intends leaving his entire property to his daughter. Provided he can see her settled with someone who'll look after the place—and her."

"Do you imagine I could be content to live off Friday's bounty?" demanded Nicolas, revolted. "I had rather continue in politics!"

It was a considerable sacrifice, and his father knew it. He hated politics. Hated the necessity to hang around men of affairs and try to curry favour with the nation's governors. He had rather his father had thrust him into the services. Or the church. *Anything* in preference to the dirty world of power-hungry men scrabbling for position. But Lord Weare—after settling the worst of his youthful peccadilloes—had declared that his son showed little aptitude for anything save playing the fool, and decided that he might as well be paid for doing it.

"You may have to continue in it," said his father now, "if you're fool enough to look a gift-horse in the mouth. Good God, what better offer could a younger son wish for? Not as if you don't like the girl."

"Of course I *like* her," Nick cut in swiftly, "but—"

"In any event," went on his father, riding over him, "it is Edborough's intention to settle part of the estate immediately upon the marriage. You will enjoy a handsome competence. Of course, as the girl's husband, in the end everything will come to you."

That was worse than anything. "Capital! So I am to figure as a fortune-hunter and deprive Friday of her inheritance. I thank you, sir, but *no*."

"Lord in heaven, boy, are you a confirmed nincompoop?" demanded his father irascibly. "Manna from heaven drops into your lap, and you spurn it for an insult!"

"Not only to me," said Nick angrily. "What, am I to offer poor Friday Spanish coin? She would see through me in an instant. I won't do it."

"Ah! So now we come to it, do we?"

There was a dangerous gleam in Lord Weare's eye that caused Nick's stomach to lurch sickeningly. He *had* heard.

"I am to believe," pursued his father in a challenging way, "that you do not care for this Friday of yours. If that is the case, perhaps you can explain why you have been living in her pocket for the past I don't know how many years."

"I have not done so," protested Nicolas uncomfortably. "Merely because I have seen her often when I have visited Charles—"

He stopped, recalling how very many times he had left Charles to go and see Friday *on his own*. But that was only because Charles became bored by their incessant arguments about the classical myths, for Delamere had long abandoned any pretension to be a scholar. But Friday, who believed passionately in all the ridiculous stories of the ancient world, was a ready butt for Nick's every attempt to disprove them. He only did it because she rose so speedily to the fly. It was irresistible! She was so funny when she was cross—her little freckled face screwed up under those huge spectacles, that fluffy halo of hair standing out from it in unruly strands. Like a demented owl!

Lost in thought, he began to pace about the saloon, unaware how his father watched him expectantly.

She was a good sort, Friday. Unfailingly kind. Ever ready with a sympathetic word. He had been in the habit of confiding everything to her, as though she had been his sister. Like the time he overgambled his allowance, or when he was caught kissing that pretty little kitchen maid and the wench had chosen to raise the devil of a dust, accusing him of far worse! Friday had urged him to confess the whole to Lord Weare, who had not believed *his* side of the story, of course. But the girl was bought off and that had been the end of it—except that he had found himself in politics. He had blamed Friday for that! Only jokingly. But she had known all about it, and he had taken for granted her acceptance of such matters, for she made so little of it, perhaps because adventures of this sort were so frequently related in the classics. And they *could* talk of such matters because they had never been chaperoned—due, as he knew, to Mrs Edborough's lax control, for Lady Delamere had often grumbled about it. But it had never seemed as if they *needed* a chaperon. With Friday he could talk of *anything,* and fear no evil consequences. She was not like other girls!

He froze up inside. Good God, Friday knew everything about him! All his boyish lapses. How could she become his wife? Wives knew nothing of these things, or pretended they did not. Friday had not an ounce of pretence in her body as far as he knew. He would trust her with his every secret—almost. But *marriage?* No, no. Out of the question. *Impossible.* Outrageous, even to think of it. She would laugh in his face!

Finding himself adrift in the middle of the room, his eyes sought his father and he rushed into impetuous speech. "Yes, I like her very well. Of course I do. She has been a good friend to me. But I *could* not marry her, sir. I assure you, the whole matter is quite out of count."

For a moment his father simply stared at him, champing on an invisible bit, his colour deepening. Nicolas knew these signs and braced himself. But Lord Weare spoke in a voice of grating quiet, more intimidating than a shout.

"Out of count, eh? You don't pull the wool over my eyes, Nicolas, so don't think it! You had not been so against marriage with this precious Friday of yours had you not been infatuated with a creature—yes, I say *creature*—whom any decent man would have used as she deserved and discarded for the next incumbent."

Nicolas was so furious that he dared not trust himself to speak for a moment or two. There could be no doubt that Tony was right. Somehow Lord Weare had got wind of Hermione. But to suggest that he would take her for his mistress was intolerable! Oh, yes, he knew that Mrs Hesket herself came from that sisterhood. But she had turned respectable, and it was unfair to tar his divine Hermione with the same brush. True, Mrs Hesket was putting her daughter up to the highest bidder. He was not so blind as to be oblivious to that.

Besides, Hermione had herself told him that their case was hopeless. Her mama would never consent to her marriage with a younger son. But as long as they were both free there was a *chance,* he felt. He had promised to think of something. He did not know what, although elopement was continually running through his head. But if he was forced into this nonsensical alliance—with *Friday* of all people—all hope would be lost.

He looked his father over and came to a decision. Discretion was the better part of valour. "I do not know, sir, of what you are talking."

"You don't, eh?" said his father grimly. "Then you had better come up with a pretty good reason against the Edborough scheme, or I shall know what to do about it."

It was too much. What was he, a pawn in a game? "Sir, am I to have no choice in the matter? Does my inclination mean so little to you?"

"Inclination! You've said yourself you don't dislike the girl. The whole scheme is to your advantage. Any younger son with a grain of sense in his head would jump at the chance. And you dare to insinuate that I have not your interests at heart? You're my *son*, Nicolas."

There was no escape. His father was determined. It was an appeal he had desperately wanted to avoid, but his tongue uttered it seemingly without his own volition.

"But, sir, I'm in love with *someone else*."

Just as he had feared, Lord Weare exploded. "I knew it! It's that damned Hesket woman's spawn." His fists banged the arms of his chair, punctuating his words. "Do you *dare* to affront me by naming her thus, as if you would make *her* your wife? Great heaven, boy, grow up! Love her, if you choose. It has nothing to do with your future. Mount her for your mistress if you will, but you'll marry the Edborough girl and like it."

"You can't make me," Nick said angrily. "This isn't the Middle Ages, sir."

"Can't make you? We'll see that. Try if you can live without your allowance. For I'll stop it, boy, and I'll bar my doors against you!''

Nick gazed at him, quite appalled. This was beyond all reason. "You *are* mad.''

"Mad? I'll show you mad. Leave this house, and don't come back until you're engaged to be married to Friday Edborough!''

There was a short silence. The truth hit Nick like a blow to the stomach. It was not the match his father wanted. It might be attractive for a younger son, but his allowance was scarcely an intolerable burden on the estate. If Weare had his way, he would take his seat in Parliament soon enough and relieve him of paying it, in any event. No. It had little or nothing to do with advantage. It was a simple trap to prevent him from making what his sire considered a misalliance with Hermione Hesket. Force him into respectable, even advantageous wedlock elsewhere, and he would not be in a position to "play the fool'', as Lord Weare would put it.

Squaring his shoulders, Nicolas gave his father back look for look. His voice was deadly calm, but it shook a little. "Very cunning, sir. But not quite good enough. I'll leave, if that is your wish, but I'll expect to hear from you when you've recovered your senses. I won't be coerced into marriage. With Friday, or anyone else.''

"Damn you, you insolent jackanapes!'' roared his father, plainly furious at his son's penetration. "Get out!''

Nick turned and made for the door, seething. As he reached it, Lord Weare called out to him. "Wait! Wait, Nick!''

Nicolas whirled about eagerly, expecting a change of heart. He was disappointed.

"I almost forgot," uttered his lordship in a much more normal tone. "The girl don't know anything. You're to act as if it's your own idea. Edborough's hand and mine must not appear in the matter. Mind that, for it's a condition of the business. She ain't to know it's been arranged."

Without a word, Nick turned on his heel and slammed himself out of the room.

"And that's all he had to say. Just as if I had nothing else to wish for!" groaned Nick as he raised the glass to his lips.

He drained it, and slammed the vessel to his friend's oaken dining-table with a force that all but broke it. Dinner was long over, but the two of them had sat over their port and then moved on to the claret, talking on until the candles guttered and had to be snuffed, leaving only the one candelabra flickering eerie shadows over their countenances in the gloom. Both young men wore faces quite in harmony with the pervading atmosphere. Doom-laden faces, with downturned mouths.

Opposite Nick, Charles Delamere picked up the bottle and poured more wine with a liberal hand. He was sympathetic to his friend's dilemma. No one could have been more so. Yet he could see all the advantages, and he did not hesitate to name them.

"At least we'd be neighbours," he offered. "And you'd like to have an estate, wouldn't you?"

"I don't want an estate," Nicolas said dully. "I want Hermione."

"Yes," said his friend. "Pity."

"It's not a pity, because I'm going to have her!" declared Nick defiantly.

"There's nothing to stop you," Charles uttered soothingly. "Even your father said—"

"Not you, too! I tell you, I mean to marry Hermione in the teeth of them all. Friday included."

Even as he said it, he was aware, deep down, of the futility of his words. All the way in his phaeton, after he had left his ancestral home in a lather of rage, he had silently ranted and raved about what he would do. And what he would not do. He would *not* marry Friday.

He was enraged more than anything by his father's last disclosure. He did not believe that Mr Edborough could be planning to marry Friday off without even consulting her. Either she knew, and had consented to the scheme—in which case he was damned if he gave her the satisfaction of pretending he *wanted* to marry her—or she had no notion at all. In which case, she would certainly laugh at him. And *refuse* him. Either way their friendship must be ruined.

But his conviction that Friday was bound to refuse him had sowed a germ of an idea in his mind. If he offered, he would both confound his father and obey him—in spirit if not to the letter, because how could he marry a female who refused to marry him? Or he might take Friday into his confidence and beg for her co-operation. She could pretend that he had offered and been refused. Or they might fake an engagement so that he could—what? Run off with Hermione and leave Friday for a jilt, subject to the jeers of the *ton?* No. He could not, would not, do that to a good friend. And something in him balked at enlisting her aid in a project such as this. One thing to ask for advice.

Quite another to drag her into his deception and make her an accessory. She did not deserve that. He would have to offer in earnest, if he offered at all. She would not have him, in any event. He was quite sure of that.

It was a discursion upon which he'd wasted little time, however. For his chest had been full to bursting with indignation at his father's iniquitous plot, and he'd needed more than anything to unburden himself of his wrongs.

Finding himself approaching Reading, he'd toyed with the idea of pouring his heart out to his sister Caroline. Except that Caro was more likely to urge him to accept his fate. She held no brief for Hermione, and had in fact warned him before she left town that he was likely to run foul of their father.

No, Delamere was a far better prospect. Charles was his closest friend. Almost all his boyhood adventures had been shared with him, if not the intellectual excursions he reserved for Friday. In any event Charles would be on fire to know the reason behind the abrupt summons, for he had taken the opportunity to visit his home and see his stewards, travelling up with Nick as far as Oakingham where their routes parted.

Charles would be the first to condemn as vicious a plot as father had brought against son, and would hear him out with patience, as he always did. So indeed it had proved. Although it did not occur to Nick until his friend mentioned it that Delamere Place was in rather too close proximity to the object of his desperate ruminations.

"Think it over," Charles advised, once Nick's rage had boiled off sufficiently to be open to reason.

"Then if you decide to do it you can get it over with quickly and go back to town."

Dark-haired and boyishly slim, Delamere was a pleasant-faced young man, although in looks nowhere near the equal of his friend. But he had a generally sunny temperament and a liberal stock both of good sense and good cellars. Both were placed at the disposal of this companion of his boyhood, and, not unnaturally, the good sense deteriorated with the sinking of the wine.

In his view, the advantages of the proposed match far outweighed the prospective loss of a wench who could only, he felt, be a source of trouble. But to convey this to Nick in his present state of mind was a Herculean task quite beyond his powers. He contented himself with an appropriate word or two in among a plethora of suggestions, which became more idiotic as the dead men gathered at his elbow. Together, they went over all the more impossible alternatives.

"You could elope at dead of night and dash off to Gretna," Charles suggested, fired with the adventure of the undertaking.

"Yes, and afterwards?" demanded Nick sceptically.

"Love in a cottage," uttered Delamere promptly. "Romantic as you please. You can keep pigs and hens and set yourselves up as farmers."

"Don't be ridiculous!" snapped Nick scornfully, enunciating his words with care. "You can't think I would—would expect Hermione to dwell in abject poverty. I don't give a fig for myself, for I could live on love alone." He repeated the phrase, vaguely pleased with its alliteration. "Live on love alone. I could. With Hermione. But—'' raising an admonishing finger that wagged before his friend's face ''—but it is s-scarcely a prospect which a man of honour offers to a delicate young female.''

''Yes, but Hermione ain't d-delicate,'' objected Charles on a hiccup.

''Damn it, Delamere!''

Charles caught the flash of fire in Nick's eye and corrected himself hastily. ''What I mean is, she's probably more at home in a poor environment. Than you, I mean.''

Nicolas was obliged to admit the truth of this. Mrs Hesket had married into the lesser gentry, but her husband's family had been less than generous when he died. Hermione was quite open about it, and had told him—with tears in her gorgeous eyes—that her mama was depending upon her to marry well.

''I s'pose the really honourable thing to do would be to give her up,'' he said gloomily. In his present state of inebriation, this idea conjured up rather an agreeable picture of martyred resignation. He sat up all in a bang, spilling his drink. ''That's it. I'll give her up, Charles.''

''Who, Friday?''

''No, Hermione, you fool!''

Charles sat up too, and raised his glass in a wavering toast. ''Now you're talking like a s-sensible man,'' he said, slurring his words slightly. ''Or, no. Much better, give her up *now*. Have her back when you're married. Just the thing. Yes, give her up—marry Friday. Not, mark you, that I blame you. For not wanting to marry her. Course, I've nothing against her.''

"Neither have I anything against her," said Nicolas indignantly. "Just don't wish to marry her."

"Exactly. I was just going to say. Nice little thing. Good company. But hardly the girl you'd dream of. Not the ideal marriage prospect. In the ordinary way, that is."

Nick, whose gaze was beginning to have a tendency to remain fixed, stared at his friend with his glass held aloft. "I see what it is. You'd *like* me to marry her. Foist her off on to me. Good idea, you think. So Lady Delamere can't make *you* marry her. She's mentioned it several times. Heard her."

"Nothing of the sort," Delamere insisted. "She did have such a notion—at one time. But I told her no. Wouldn't marry Friday with a ten-foot pole. So she gave it up."

"What do you mean, you wouldn't marry Friday with a ten-foot pole?" demanded Nicolas belligerently. "What's wrong with her?"

"Nothing wrong with her," Charles said, repeating his guest's almost exact same words. "Just wouldn't wish to marry her."

"But you don't mind if *I* marry her. What's more, you don't mind if I insult her by making Hermione my mistress."

"Nick," Charles said distinctly. "You're foxed."

"Foxed! So would you be if you had to marry Friday."

"Thought you weren't going to marry her."

"I'm not going to marry her. But I'll have to ask her to marry me. Won't I?"

Under the haze of liquor, he knew that the decision had been taken. The decision he had known all along he would have to take, ever since his father had shown himself adamant.

Charles nodded in solemn agreement and, making a final effort, refilled the glasses, contriving to splash only a very little of the claret over the table.

Nick blinked and forced his eyes wide as he brought his glass to his lips. Then he lowered it again, an anxious look coming into his face. "Charles, you don't think there's the slightest chance that she'll accept me, do you?"

By one of those odd freaks of nature, the day on which Friday attained her majority dawned bright and warm, a final fling of sunshine before winter shivered into view. She woke to a feeling of anticipation, as if something exciting was about to happen. When both parents entered into the room hard on the heels of her maid, bearing gifts, she remembered.

Her birthday! It had slipped her mind again, for Papa, after that one outburst, had not again referred to the business of her possible marriage. Thank goodness! She received all the presents with unaffected delight, showing as much enthusiasm for the necklace of pearls and diamonds—in spite of any hint contained in their being those purchased for Mama's own wedding!—as for the two volumes of plays by Euripides which she happened not to have read before. Papa had also commissioned an artist to paint her portrait—"in whatever fanciful classical fashion you choose," as he put it, much to her amusement. There were other trinkets and letters of good wishes from a number of relatives, and a special dinner of her favourite dishes was promised.

To please Papa, Friday put on one of what she considered her more frivolous gowns, a floral chintz with the customary long, tight sleeves, and a bodice cut lower than she usually wore. For once, she dragged her unruly hair into a topknot, allowing the curls to fall carelessly behind, and did her best—not very successfully, she was obliged to admit!—to contain the front strands tidily.

These concessions did not stop her, however, from seeking her hilltop retreat just as soon as she could without offending Papa, the lumbering Bruno tagging along, and throwing herself down to enjoy the sunshine as she delved into *Medea* from the pen of Euripides.

Absorbed instantly, she did not hear the approach of an intruder until Bruno's wheezy bark made her look up. The spectacles lay abandoned as usual, but the shadowy form standing just a few yards away was so familiar to her in stature and shape that she had no difficulty in identifying it. Nicolas! Her heart skipped a beat, and her mouth curved into a smile of welcome.

Nick Weare observed it with mixed feelings. He had been watching her for several minutes, unable—or perhaps unwilling, if the truth were told—to make his presence known. Until Bruno, who was too old now, he knew, to do more than wag a perfunctory tail at his approach, apparently puzzled by his silence, had done it for him.

As well! The confusions in his head at sight of Friday lying there were almost too much to bear. That she looked so different must be a trick of his mind. He had never noticed before how slim she was, how feminine the slight billowing of her bosom as it rested upon her folded arms. As she glanced up her face, minus the spectacles, seemed altogether alien. It was a piquant little countenance, its sprinkling of freckles not at all unattractive, with two gentle eyes that lit at sight of him. It was hard to believe that they could not see clearly.

"Nick!" she cried joyfully, and, struggling to sit up, groped for her spectacles. "Is it indeed you?"

Next instant the huge round monstrosities were perched on her nose and she was once again the Friday he knew. The Friday for whom he was about to offer—at the behest of his father.

"Yes, it's I," he answered, hard put to it to keep out of his voice the wealth of emotions that surged up on him.

Friday giggled. "Silly! I can see it is you *now*. Have you come especially to wish me happy? That is quite *noble* of you, my dear friend."

"What?" gasped Nick, a quick frown creasing his brow. She knew, then! But nothing was *settled*. Was she making game of him already? "What in Hades do you mean, wish you happy?"

Slight puzzlement entered Friday's features, and her smile wavered. "Why, for turning one and twenty. Isn't that why you're here?"

How oddly he stared! A sliver of distress smote her. What in the world was the matter with him? She got up swiftly to face him, cocking her head on one side. So also did Bruno, growling under his breath until Friday laid a quietening hand on his head.

"Nick, what is it? It's only my birthday, you know."

"Your *birthday?* Today? Oh, my God!"

A wave of disappointment rushed through her, but she did her best to conceal it. He had not known. He had not come for that. But he needed her; that much she could fathom. As a friend. There was something quite odd in his manner. That final groan! Why should it bother him so much that it was her birthday today?

"There is no reason why you should have remembered it," she said soothingly. "Don't concern yourself, pray."

"It's not that," he uttered in a strangled tone. "But why did it have to be *today?*"

A swift smile lit her face. "For that you had better consult my parents. I dare say they had no intention of discommoding you at the time."

Nick was obliged to smile, but he was frowning again in a moment, as he realised the import of what she had said. "Friday, you *must* stop talking of such things. You will set folks in a bustle!"

"Pooh!" she scoffed. "Don't be so stuffy, Nick! As if I have not talked quite freely to you ever since we met. And what folks, pray? You know very well I hardly go into company."

"*Now,* yes," he conceded, "but you never know when it might prove to be—"

He stopped, horrified by the vision that had entered his mind. A picture of himself at a London soirée, Friday by his side, calmly uttering a statement of the kind as if it were commonplace for a young wife to refer to the doings of married couples in their beds!

"Nick, whatever is the matter with you today? If you have not come for my birthday—and there is no reason in the world why you *should*, let me add— why are you here? Don't say you are in trouble again!"

"No, no. At least— Oh, God, I don't know what to say to you, Friday!"

It was plain that there was something very much amiss. Friday's heart contracted, as it always did when Nicolas was in any kind of mental anguish. It was not a matter of whether she *might* help him. It was that she could not bear to do otherwise.

"Let us sit down," she said briskly and, taking his hand, dragged him to sink to the grass beside her. The dog, divining that the intruder's presence was preferred to his own, lay down at a little distance, pointedly averting his head. Friday, intent on Nicolas, hardly noticed. A mischievous smile was teasing him. "It is quite dry, so you will not dirty your fine buckskin breeches, I promise."

"There you go again!" uttered Nicolas, turning on her wrathfully. "*Breeches*. No lady of breeding would deign even to notice my nether garments, let alone *mention* them!"

"Indeed?" demanded Friday a trifle frostily. "Whence this sudden objection to the way I express myself, pray? And how dare you accuse me of a lack of breeding?"

"I did not. All I said was—"

"What is it to you how I speak, in any event, Nicolas Weare? I might remind you, if you choose to take me up on such matters, of all the occasions *you* have not hesitated to mention things to *me* that a female ought not to know about."

"Yes, I know," admitted Nick frowningly, "but the thing is you're so dashed unlike proper females that I—"

"I thank you!"

"—can't seem to think of you as anything other than—"

"A bespectacled bluestocking," Friday finished.

"Yes, I am aware. And just at this moment, Mr Weare, your *other* description of me fits like a glove!"

Nick eyed her, his features taut. "I've offended you."

"Yes!"

"Again."

"Yes."

There was a silence. Then a heavy sigh broke from Nicolas and he lifted his hands to knead at his temples. "I'm sorry, Friday," he uttered roughly. "I had a pretty batch of it last night at Delamere, and my head aches like the devil."

"You mean you were drunk," Friday stated matter-of-factly, adding on a challenging note, "Or is that something else I shouldn't talk about?"

"There's no need to rub it in," Nicolas snapped. "I've said I'm sorry, haven't I?"

"Well, you've ruined my whole mood, Nick, and it *is* my birthday." She smiled suddenly. "I know. You can make amends and come to dinner. Bring Charles. What a pity I did not know you were both here! I might have invited Caro and Dick, too, and made a party of it."

"Oh, no," Nicolas said quickly. Good God, no! He could not stay to dinner. He must just get this thing over with and get away! Besides, he did not suppose she would want him to come to dinner *after* he had done it. Realising by the shade of disappointment in Friday's face that he had been less than polite, he added hastily, "Thank you, but we can't, you see. We have an engagement in town tonight. We only remained here because I had come down from Morton last evening."

"Oh, you've been visiting your father," Friday guessed. "I thought you might have come up for Caro. But of course you must already know her news."

Nicolas blinked. "News?"

"Why, that she is increasing again." She grinned at him. "You will be twice an uncle. Don't say you had not heard?"

He nodded. "I had forgotten. I have had other matters on my mind."

Friday gazed at him through the glass of her spectacles, and her voice softened. "Nick, what *is* it? Don't tell me you are not deeply troubled. I know you too well. Can you not confide in me? You always have before."

Yes, he always had. That was the difficulty. Now he could not do so, because—all of a sudden he saw it, clear and plain!—because he could not hurt her so cruelly. To tell a dear friend that you were suffering so badly because you did not want to marry her! How could he ever have even conceived that such words were possible? There were no such words.

Dumbly he shook his head, not looking at her. He heard Friday begin to talk—of something else entirely. He did not hear much beyond the vague impression that she was referring to Euripides. His mind was too full of the sense of futility that was invading him. What was he doing here? He could not ask Friday to marry him. The best thing he could do was to go away without saying anything at all. Disobey his father. Accept his fate. At worst, he could always take the King's shilling and join the Army. Of course he must lose Hermione, too. Lose Hermione, his allowance, even the political future he had never wanted.

The picture was bleak indeed as he thought of everything he was throwing away. His familial closeness, for he cared deeply for Caro and Tony. The life he had known, his friendships. Charles, who had been more than a second brother. And Friday herself. Devil take it, but it would not do! God, what was life worth then? It was not to be borne!

"I never thought it could be so," Friday was saying, talking in a calm, everyday fashion that she hoped would ease Nick's tension, "but I was very much taken with the necklace." She laughed. "And as for sitting to my portrait, I had not reckoned on the level of my own conceit, for—"

"Friday," interrupted Nicolas, turning to confront her with a determined look on his face, "will you marry me?"

"—I had this instant vision of myself on canvas, looking quite astonishingly..."

Her voice died. Her body died. Or seemed to. Right there, sitting on the ground on her hilltop retreat. Frozen in time, like a stone statue. Devoid of the slightest sensation. Numb.

The thought came hammering out of the blankness that possessed her, thrumming her body back into life. *He could not have said it.* She must have misheard. Aware now only of a prickling sensation that crawled along her skin, she thrust the question up through dry lips that quivered on the words.

"What did you say?" Faintly, like a whispering breeze.

Nick drew a breath. The solemnity of his features did more than anything else to convince her that her ears had not deceived her.

"I asked if you will marry me."

The sun splattered across the heavens, blinding her at the rush of tears to her eyes behind the glass. Her heart swelled until it was in danger of bursting. He wanted to marry her! Nicolas wanted to marry *her*. It was impossible, but here it was. He had asked her. He had actually said the words she had never expected to hear. She wanted to sob and scream. She wanted to leap to her feet and throw herself into the air!

She did none of these things. She sat, staring at him until the grimness in his face penetrated the turmoil of her bosom. The elation collapsed like a pricked balloon. Deflated, she continued to stare. And now the blood in her veins pulsed unevenly. For apprehension outweighed every other thought and feeling.

This was not the face of a man who returned her love. In his eyes was a hostility that she had never seen before. Almost as if he *hated* her. The question flew from her mouth even as it slipped into her mind.

"Why?"

He blinked, shaking his head as if to clear it of a perplexing thought. "What a question!"

Friday held his eyes. "Why, Nick? Why do you ask me?"

Oh, God. The inward groan mirrored the gloom of his features, but he did not know that. He thought only that of course he should have known Friday would react this way. She was far too intelligent to be taken in. For a moment there had been such light in her face. As if she had been given the world! Then it had vanished. In its place a question impossible to answer. Except that he must answer it.

"Suitable," he mumbled inanely. "It would be so

suitable. Friends. We're good friends.'' He tried for a light laugh, but it came out hollow. ''And you know how I detest politics. I could—I could live here with you. You'll have your books. I'll have…'' No. No, he could not say that. If it was supposed to come from him, he must not know about her inheritance.

But Friday was ahead of him. ''You are thinking that Papa will leave the estate to me. Did Charles tell you that? Yes, he must have done so.'' She swallowed. ''Is that—is that what you want, Nick? Is that—is that *why?*''

''Damn it, Friday, for what do you take me?'' he protested angrily. ''Of course that isn't why.''

''Then—''

''For God's sake! Must there be a reason? People marry all the time.''

''But not without *reason*.''

''Well, then, there is reason enough,'' he uttered in a tone of suppressed anguish. ''God damn it, why can't you just answer yes or no?''

Because you don't say you love me, Friday wanted to cry. But she could not. She sat beside him, a sense of unreality invading her mind. This could not be happening. She was dreaming again. Only *this* Nicolas was too unlike that one to be anything but real. Why was he so oppressed? Could it be that he found it impossible to speak of his emotions? God knew, her own tongue cleaved to the roof of her mouth at the thought of revealing to him the true state of her heart. Why should he be any the less nervous of expressing himself? After all, how could he know, any more than she of him, whether his feelings might be reciprocated?

Only Nick did not labour under her own disadvantages. Common sense must dictate that she had been far more likely to fall in love with him than he with her. He could not be unaware of his own attractions. He was not so. He had never been shy of speaking of his emotions about the girls with whom he had been infatuated.

Perhaps that was it. He had shared so much with her that perhaps he should not have shared. Gracious! So this was why he had suddenly taken against the freedom of her speech. As his *wife,* she would have to behave conformably. His wife? To be that, must there not be something more from him? Was he embarrassed to say how he *truly* felt? He was *fond* of her, yes. As he must know she was fond of him. Had it grown into something warmer? She *would* not believe that he could offer for her merely for the advantages it might bring him. But if not that… A hope that she had not dared to acknowledge began to burgeon in her breast. Could it be? There was no way to tell. If only he would look at her!

But Nicolas was incapable of turning his head. More so as her silence lengthened. Why did she hesitate? What was she thinking about? She could not be seriously considering his offer. After the stupid things he had said! She would be crazy to do so. And she was not crazy. He dared not ask again. Oh, God! What was she waiting for? Should he say more? What *could* he say more? Refuse me, Friday! For God's sake put me out of my misery, and tell me *no*.

She ought to say no, Friday was thinking. There was too much uncertainty here. Why in the world did he not say more? God in heaven, was she mad? Why did she even hesitate? Here was her dream come true. Except, whispered a tiny voice at the back of her mind, that it was not true to her dream. But it will be, it *will* be, her heart insisted. And if she let this miraculous opportunity slip away...

"Well, then," she uttered in a croaking whisper, "I will say...*yes*."

His head whipped round. "What? What, Friday?"

Friday swallowed. A smile flickered an instant on her lips, and vanished again. "I said yes."

He went white. A shaft of doubt sliced Friday's chest at the sudden look of glumness in his face. Then he masked it, and in an odd tone he was thanking her, rising to his feet, backing a step or two.

"I had better go and inform your father that the deed is done," he said in a voice of cold formality.

Somehow Friday got to her feet as he walked away towards the copse. She discovered that her limbs were trembling, and she felt quite faint. Without thinking, she rested a hand on the broad back of Bruno, who had materialised beside her, and felt insensibly comforted.

Comforted? Heaven help her, *why?* She had just agreed to marry Nicolas Weare, whom she loved with all her heart. She ought to have been wildly ecstatic. Now she knew what had been the meaning of the anticipation she had felt this morning. It had presaged her life's happiness.

But her life's happiness was teetering precariously on the edge of a dreadful precipice. At any second it might tumble down—and destroy her dreams forever.

Chapter Three

An air of dejection hung about the bedchamber. Charles Delamere, sitting up in the grand four-poster against a bank of pillows, a wet towel wrapped about his aching brow, gazed amazedly at his friend's back where he stood looking out of the window.

"You don't mean to say you've already done it?"

"Yes," answered Nicolas shortly, without turning round.

"But, my dear fellow, it's scarcely eleven o'clock," protested his friend.

"It's her birthday," Nick stated inconsequently.

Charles blinked painfully. "What has that to say to anything?"

"Edborough thought I'd chosen it on purpose. He was delighted."

"Sentiments not echoed by the prospective bridegroom, I collect," observed Delamere sapiently.

Nick turned and shot him a glare. "What do you think? Damn it, Charles, she accepted me. She *accepted* me."

"So you said," agreed his friend, nodding. He regretted the action instantly and let out a groan, clutching at his temples under the towel.

"I don't know why you're complaining," observed Nicolas, eyeing him with dislike. "*You* haven't got to marry her."

"I've got a devilish headache, Nick."

"It serves you out. If you hadn't got me foxed last night, I would've been clear-headed enough not to make such a mull of it. How the devil am I going to tell Hermione?"

"Don't," advised Charles. "Hear of it soon enough when you put the announcement in the *Gazette*."

"Oh, good God!" exclaimed Nicolas. "Have I to endure that humiliation?"

"Not until you've told your father," said Delamere consolingly. "Tell you what. Drive up there and do it at once. You'll be back in his good books, and all well again. *Then* go to town and tackle Hermione."

"Tackle her! You make it sound like a prize-fight."

"Probably will be, knowing her," muttered Delamere under his breath.

"What did you say?" demanded Nick suspiciously.

"Nothing," Charles said hastily.

Nicolas eyed him in a frustrated way. He knew he was being unreasonable, but he needed someone upon whom to vent his ill feeling. The shock of Friday's acquiescence had thrown him into a hideous unreality, where the congratulations of Edborough and his wife—summoned from her eyrie at the top of the house—took on the weird quality of nightmare. He had retained sufficient presence of mind to remain steadfast in his refusal to join them at dinner, thank God! He needed time to master himself before he could face Friday again.

Acute as she was, she would quickly penetrate the flimsy veneer of satisfaction he had mustered for the benefit of her parents. He would end by blurting out— just as he had blurted his offer—that it was all a mistake. He could not do that. For the very fact of her acceptance threw his entire conception of her feelings off balance. He felt as if he did not know her at all! He had been so *sure* of her mind—he thought. Now it seemed as if he was wholly mistaken. There had been all of a sudden such vulnerability in that funny little face. From it, he had gathered the hazy idea that he had the power to hurt her—*terribly*. It was a frightening knowledge. And it had trapped him.

"What *are* you going to do?" asked his friend in a sympathetic tone.

"Blow my brains out!" said Nick gloomily.

"Won't do at all," pronounced Charles, frowning. "Dashed insulting to kill yourself after you've just become engaged. Might as well break it off. Just as dishonourable either way."

"I didn't mean it, you fool!" Nicolas said irritably. "I just *feel* like that. I'd get blind drunk if I weren't still feeling it from last night."

"Don't!" shuddered Delamere. "Devilish bad notion." He held up a finger. "Got a better one, Nick. Remember what we were saying—about the little Hesket."

"Don't mention her name," begged Nick, wincing.

"I didn't mention it," Charles pointed out. "At least, I never said *Hermione*."

"For God's sake!"

"Beg pardon, old fellow. What I mean is, that business of taking her up again. *After* you're married."

"I've told you—"

"Listen, damn it! I know you don't want to *now*. All I say is, pave the way a bit."

Nick frowned. "What do you mean?"

"Your sister!" announced Charles triumphantly.

Nicolas gaped. "Have you run mad?"

"No, listen. Go and see Caroline. If anyone can lick Friday into shape, she can. Complaisant wife, that's what you need. Sensible girl, your sister. She'll see all's right."

Nick's eyes narrowed. "Let me understand this. You are suggesting I enlist Caro's aid to make all right with Friday so that I can take Hermione for my mistress?"

"That's it. Famous good notion, don't you think?"

"No, I do not! Good God, Delamere, what kind of man do you think I am? As if I would insult either Friday or Hermione in such a manner. I ought to drag you out of that bed and knock you back into it!"

Charles sank down into his pillows with a groan, clutching his head again. "Not fisticuffs! Not today, Nick."

But Nicolas was not attending. The idea of talking to Caroline had certain advantages. "As a matter of fact, I will go and see Caro. At least she's one person before whom I won't have to *pretend*."

"Hey, what about me?" demanded Delamere, aggrieved.

"You? With your idiotic advice?" Marching to the door, he opened it and gave a mock-bow. "I thank you, my lord, for your hospitality, and I hope very much that your head remains disgustingly bad for the rest of the day!''

The door slammed behind him with enough force to ensure that his hope was not misplaced. Delamere grabbed his head, groaning and cursing his friend with a will. A second later the door opened again, and Nick's face popped round.

''By the way, Charles, I said you'd be delighted to go to the Edboroughs for dinner. See you in a few days.''

Delamere seized the candle that stood on his bed-side table and, uttering an oath, flung it violently in the direction of Nick's head. It banged harmlessly against the door as he swiftly shut it behind him.

Friday was not quite sure if she relished a visit from her prospective sister-in-law. They were very well acquainted already, of course, for not only had both she and the Honourable Mr Anthony Weare accompanied Nick to stay at Delamere Place on several occasions, but Miss Weare had become, on her marriage, a close neighbour and visits to the Edboroughs—*out* of season—were frequent. Friday liked her very well, and had often, during Caroline's last pregnancy, gone to her home at Hurley to see how she did. But she was Nick's sister, and there was no saying how she would receive the news of the engagement.

Mrs Caroline Cleeve came in like a whirlwind, talking all the time in her quick, high voice as she crossed the morning-room to where Friday had risen to receive her and enveloped her in a swirl of muslin and perfume.

''My dear, I am ecstatic! I declare, I was never so

happy as when Nick told me his choice had lighted upon you, Friday. If you knew the *hussies* I have been obliged to sweep out of his path! What with Mama gone and poor Papa's illness, *everything* has fallen upon me. I have been worried to death, leaving *both* the boys to their own devices, but I have been *so* sickly—just as I was the last time and, though nothing came of it, Dicky would not *hear* of my remaining in town.''

"I should think not indeed," said Friday, answering the last point of this comprehensive speech first. "You should not have come, Caro. I could very well have visited you if you had sent me a note."

"Oh, stuff! I am perfectly well *now*," uttered the pretty creature, settling animatedly on the rose-patterned sofa opposite in a whirl of spotted gauze petticoats, and allowing a handsome shawl of Norwich silk to slip off her shoulders, revealing a buxom figure beneath the fashionably low neckline.

Town or country, Caro Cleeve was not to be seen in anything other than the most modish of gowns, her blonde locks falling in ordered curls down her back from the feathered bandeau that confined them. In the early stage of her second pregnancy she was already putting on a little flesh, but the current mode of high waistlines was admirably suited to her condition.

"I am determined to go back to town in the New Year for I will scarcely *show* in these new fashions," she was saying. "Dicky is against it, I know. But I will be past all sickness by then, and—"

"I thought you said you were well now," interrupted Friday severely, resuming her seat in the armchair upholstered in the same rose pattern that decorated the window drapes. "You are not, are you?"

"No, but it is only the *mornings,* Friday. Which is why I have come at this hour. I could not otherwise have stood the rocking of the carriage, you know."

"It's very foolish of you, Caro."

"Oh, stuff! You don't imagine I could have borne not to *rush* at once to see you after Nicky told me?"

"Where is Nick?" Friday ventured.

She might well ask. Since the moment she had accepted his offer, she had seen neither hide nor hair of him. He had spoken to Papa, for both he and Mama had been waiting for her when she'd finally got up the strength—and *courage,* heaven help her!—to go back into the house. Their reactions—the one so pleased, as if it had been some triumph of his own, the other so matter-of-fact in acceptance that she might almost have been expecting it—had done nothing to ease her doubts.

They were fostered by Nick's apparent refusal to attend at dinner. Charles had come over, obviously still suffering from his potations of the night before, and had looked like a startled rabbit when Friday had enquired why he had not accompanied Nicolas back to town to keep their engagement. Of course there had been no engagement. She had divined that quickly enough from his disjointed reply. Indeed his whole conversation, interlarded as it was with soulful sighing references to "poor Nick", had gone a great way towards pushing her right off that precipice!

She had been ready by the end of that evening to call the whole thing off. But several unsatisfactory letters addressed to Nick to that effect had found their way into the waste-paper basket. She'd slept badly, and wished that Nicolas would only come to see her so that she might straighten it all out in her mind. The next day had brought no Nick. But the day following, a steady stream of well-wishers had come calling. Well-wishers? Or did they come to gawp and wonder—just as she did herself!—at how bookish Friday Edborough had managed to land handsome Nick Weare? She supposed these acquaintances owed their information to Charles, although one could not, in the country, expect to keep anything secret. By the time Caroline arrived, she had grown enough of a skin to be able to conceal her inner disquiet.

But the intimation that Nick might still be in the neighbourhood struck her at once with a mix of apprehension and hurt that he had not been to see her. It was with relief that she heard Caro's reply.

"He has gone up to tell Papa. He remained only one night with us—for you may suppose I would not release him until he had related *everything* and so he was obliged to stay—and set off at once for Morton. Oh, yes, and he wrote to the *Gazette,* as was proper."

"An announcement!" uttered Friday, appalled. "Was that needful?"

Laughter tinkled through Caro's lips. "*Most* needful. How in the world else are people to know of it?"

"There seems to be no difficulty about that," stated Friday drily. "Everyone around us here seems to know already."

"Oh, I know. People are so *vulgar*. They love nothing better than to gossip. I can tell you, I have had my fill of it—what with Tony falling for Griselda Apperley, who is *quite* unsuitable, when here I had brought Julia to the point of *expecting* his offer. Naturally, everyone is saying that she set her cap at him, which is *not* the case. I declare, it is the most nonsensical idea! Lady Julia Kilmartin to set her cap at

the son of a mere baron when she might have *anyone!*
Naturally she is *furious,* as well as she might be, and
I could readily *kill* Tony.''

Friday blinked. ''But if he is in love with someone
else—''

''Oh, stuff! He is no more in love with Griselda
than Nick is with—''

She broke off in a great deal of consternation, her
eyes widening and one guilty hand flying to her
mouth.

Friday's chest felt suddenly constricted, her stomach hollow. She gazed steadily at Caro through her
spectacles. ''With me, you mean?'' she managed
quite calmly.

''No, no, no!'' uttered Caroline on a near shriek.
''Great heavens, Friday, *no!* I meant nothing of the
kind. For all I know, Nick is head over ears in love
with you. I meant someone—*something* quite different.''

Before Friday could take this up, she launched into
a change of subject, jumping up and coming over to
perch on the arm of her chair.

''Now, Friday,'' she said, seizing one of her hands,
''you *must* let me take you in hand. Well enough
when you were content to hide yourself away with
your dratted Greeks and Romans—not that I ever *approved*—but you *cannot* appear in London in this
guise. Indeed you can't.''

''Oh,'' Friday uttered, glancing down at her usual
plain woollen gown. ''You mean my dress.''

''That is *just* what I mean. No, really, Friday—''

''But nothing has been said about London,'' Friday
interrupted. ''I had not supposed I would have to alter
my habits merely because I became engaged.''

"But you *must*. You will not keep him attentive to you else, you know," Caro declared.

Friday looked up at her. Deliberately, she said coolly, "Why not, when I have apparently attached him just as I am?"

Nonplussed, Caroline remained speechless for a moment or two. Then she broke into one of her peals of laughter, which rang a little false in Friday's ears.

"But men, my dear Friday, are the *oddest* creatures. When they have what they desire, they no longer feel any need to flatter and woo."

Flatter and woo! thought Friday. There had been none of *that*. But Caroline was not finished. She squeezed the hand she held.

"A clever wife will keep her husband on his toes. There is nothing like the admiration of other men to provoke a little jealousy—not to mention to keep him from *straying*."

She was away very soon after this, promising, as she enthusiastically kissed the air on either side of Friday's cheeks, to return soon when they might, as she put it, "make some cosy plans together".

Friday was left a prey to suspicion and doubt. The conversation of Mrs Caroline Cleeve had served only to heighten her insecurity. From where had this offer sprung? Not from any emotional attachment on Nick's part, that was clear enough. But he *was* attached. Caro had let that slip. Friday had first thought it a reflection on the unlikelihood of Nick's being in love with her. But Caro's denial had been altogether genuine, she was sure of that. Besides, she had worked as much out for herself. It hurt. But not as much perhaps as Caro thought, for Friday had long schooled herself to that truth. The brief instant when she had glimpsed—or *thought* she had—the faintest possibility that it might be so was not enough to alter her long-standing conviction.

To what, then, had Caro been referring? She did not believe Nick to be in love. That meant he professed to be so. If not with her, then with *whom?* That did hurt. So much that she could scarcely breathe for the actual physical *pain* engendered by the thought. For if Nick was in love with someone else, she could not marry him. And indeed, if he was, *why* had he offered for her?

She was still in this unsatisfactory frame of mind when Nicolas walked in on her unannounced two days later. She was sitting in her usual spot in the library, her feet up before her on the window-stool, a newspaper open on her knee. But she was no longer reading it. She was gazing vacantly into space.

It did not need Bruno's warning grunt to attract Friday's attention. She had turned her head at the opening of the door. Since she happened to be wearing her spectacles, she saw at once who it was.

Her heart leapt, her hands jerked, and the newspaper went flying. She jumped off the window-stool and rushed, accompanied by Bruno's frenzied barking, to retrieve it. Nick was before her, scooping up the sheet and glancing at it while Friday turned to attend to her excited dog.

"Quiet, Bruno! It's nothing. Quiet, now."

Bruno subsided and Friday looked up to find Nicolas eyeing her uneasily.

"You've seen it, then," he stated flatly.

Her glance flicked to the paragraph announcing their engagement and back to his face. "The notice? Yes." A tiny smile crossed her face in spite of her jangling nerves. "Mama is so cross. You should have put Frideswid."

Nick frowned in quick consternation. "God, yes! I never thought of that. I was in such a hurry."

Friday turned away. "I can't think why."

Neither could Nicolas, now he thought about it. Unless it had been the all-consuming desire to put the whole episode behind him. By now, however, he'd had time to recognise that there was no doing that. It was, on the contrary, all in front of him. Except for the hurdle of his father.

Lord Weare had been apparently stunned by the speed of Nick's action. He had evidently expected him to hold out for a good deal longer. Suspicion had creased the lines deeper about his eyes.

"Not trying to outgeneral me, I hope, boy. Some trick up your sleeve? Lull me with false coin, and I'm warning you—"

"Have no fear, sir! I made my offer in good faith. It has been accepted as such."

His father had champed for a while, grunted and given his blessing with a rider attached. "I may be ailing, but I'm still in possession of my faculties. Marriage I said, and marriage I meant. Don't count your chickens till you've been to the altar!"

"Good God, sir! For what do you take me?" Nick had flashed back. "I may be the fool you always call me, but allow me some vestige of honour."

Weare was unimpressed. "All well and good. *You* can't cry off. She can, however. Up to you to see she's no reason to do so," he added meaningfully. "At least not until after the wedding."

Nick could have hit him. Except that one did not offer violence to one's parent. An invalid at that.

Damn him and his insinuations! Rather would he have Caro's outspoken comments, although they had annoyed him at the time.

"Dearest Nicky, I'm *so* pleased!" had uttered his sister joyfully, embracing him with fervour. "Now I shan't have to worry myself to death over your running off with that dratted wench you must needs fancy yourself in love with. Now if *only* I can bring Tony around to accepting Julia, we may *all* of us be satisfied."

Nicolas was not in the least satisfied. It seemed as if the whole world was in cahoots to marry him off, regardless of whom he married, as long as it was not Hermione. Oddly, he felt chagrined on Friday's behalf. She was as much a pawn as he, it seemed. Except that her father appeared to believe it was what she wanted. He had not said it in so many words, but his hints were unmistakable.

"I know you for a gentleman," he had said bracingly, "and I'm ready to swear you'll not do anything to hurt my girl. Fond of you is Friday, my boy. A sound basis for marriage, in my view."

Well, he was *fond* of her, too. But it did not feel like a prelude to a more intimate union. He'd had several days in which to accustom himself to the idea, but it felt still as alien and odd as it had when it was first proposed to him. A sort of numb despair had succeeded the shock of Friday's positive response, and it was in this mood that he came to make a show of attendance on his affianced bride.

Friday had wandered back to her seat in the window, her gaze on Bruno's big eyes as he sat by her, looking up at her with his head cocked in a puzzled way, as if he felt the unease in the room. Nick drew the chair from behind the small mahogany desk that was the only furnishing the room afforded other than its filled bookshelves and the window-stool, and sat down. He fiddled with the newspaper a moment or two and then placed it carefully on the dark leather desktop.

The silence grew oppressive. This was *Friday,* for God's sake! Nick thought desperately. They had always been able to talk freely. If this was how it was *now,* what price the awkwardness of actually *living* together? The more he tried to think of something to say, the blanker his mind became. There was only one thought in his head. A mistake. This was a dreadful mistake. He was almost ready to utter it aloud when Friday forestalled him.

"Caro came to visit me the other day."

"Caro?" he repeated stupidly.

"Your sister."

"I know she's my sister," he snapped.

Friday's head jerked up. She felt sick. It had taken so much to get that one sentence out. If this was how he intended to conduct himself towards her, she wished he would go away again!

"I'm sorry," Nick mumbled.

"It doesn't matter," she said shortly.

"Yes, it does," he argued. "There's no reason to bite your head off."

"No, there isn't."

After a moment, Nick sighed. "Friday, we can't go on like this."

Her glance slid away. "We don't seem to have much choice."

He cleared his throat, trying for a more normal tone. "I'm glad Caro took the trouble to come over."

Friday looked at him. She took a breath. "She seems to feel I ought to smarten myself up. If—if my appearance is a—a problem to you, Nick, then perhaps I *should* alter it."

Nick stared blankly. "Alter your appearance? For me? Are you mad, Friday?"

"Well, but Caro feels I will have to come to London next season and she thinks my mode of dress will not do. Which of course it *won't*, if—if I do have to come to London."

"For God's sake, Friday!" he exclaimed, rising abruptly. "You will do as you choose. As for Caro, it is nothing to do with her, and so I shall tell her." He paced a step or two. "I know what she is at, and I'm not going to tolerate it."

What was she at? Friday longed for the courage to ask. But that would mean she had to ask that *why* she simply could not ask. The sick feeling intensified, but she fought it down.

"Then you don't object to my appearance," she pursued.

"How you look is neither here nor there!" he said angrily. "Caro has nothing to say about it, in any event."

"On the contrary," Friday quipped with an attempt at humour. "She had a great deal to say about it."

But not you, Nick! she added silently, watching him pace restlessly up and down the long room. Not *you*. If he cared, he would say that he was perfectly happy with her appearance, or that he would *like* her to look more the thing if that was what she wished. The sad truth was, he did not care one way or the other how she looked. Of course he did not. He did not care about *her*. Not in the way a man cared about his affianced wife. The words popped out almost without her knowing she said them.

"We are scarcely conducting ourselves like a newly engaged couple."

Nicolas halted abruptly in his prowl about the library. He faced her and forced a smile. "I beg your pardon, Friday. My fault. I'm just—not used to this."

"Nor I," she agreed.

She eyed him a moment. Was this a good time? He seemed less irritable. Her heart was beating rather fast, but she rose and took a pace or two towards him.

"Nick, if—if perhaps you have changed your mind, pray don't let us continue in this way. I value your friendship too highly to—to lose it, and I feel that I *am*. Losing it, I mean."

Nick's features softened at once. He came up to her and grasped her shoulders. "Oh, Friday, forgive me! I never meant it to be like this. We *are* friends. We'll always be friends. Nothing can alter that."

Warmth flooded her, as it always did when he addressed her with such kindness. Her lips trembled into a smile and her eyes glistened under the glass of the spectacles.

"Do you mean that?"

"I swear it!" he uttered vehemently. "This—" he hesitated over a word to express the situation they were in "—ought not to affect the way we feel about each other."

She did not mean to say it. But in the easing of constraint it slipped out on a quiver of laughter. "It is not precisely Paris and Helen, is it?"

A frown of self-reproach entered his eyes. "I'm not doing this very well, am I? Ought I to kiss you?"

Startled, Friday moved sharply away. "*No.*" Then

she flushed, stammering, "Well, if—if you wish to d-
do so, I dare say you m-may. After all, I shall have
to accustom myself to—to doing as you wish."

"Good God, Friday, I am not a monster!" he objected violently. "Do you imagine I will force anything on you? That was no part of the bargain!"

A shadow crossed her face, and an icy draught
sliced through her. "Bargain?"

But Nick's need to disabuse her mind made him
pass over the slip unnoticed. "You cannot think, Friday, that I would burden you with caresses which
must be as unwelcome to you as they would be to—"

He stopped just in time, horrified at himself as the
word "me" hovered on the end of his tongue. But
Friday did not appear to have anticipated him on this
occasion.

"They—they would not be unwelcome to me," she
offered shyly in a small voice.

She was evidently unable to look at him, but Nicolas felt himself at once under an obligation to kiss
her. Awkwardly, he lifted her chin, avoided the huge
spectacles with difficulty, and planted a chaste salute
upon her lips.

The contact was but slight, but the dry warmth of
it set Friday trembling, and she had to grasp at Nick's
arms to stop herself from collapsing under suddenly
unruly knees.

"There, you see!" Nicolas said accusingly, steadying her. "I knew you wouldn't like it. Have no fear!
I shan't do it again."

No, came Friday's thought out of the incoherence
that had attacked her. Because he would not wish to!
Belatedly it had come to her what he had stopped
himself from saying. He would not welcome her ca-

resses. Tears sprang to her eyes and her spectacles misted over.

Seeing it, Nick at once divined her distress. "Friday!" he uttered remorsefully. "I never meant to upset you. I'm sorry. I won't do it again, I *promise*."

Through her tears and the burden of pressure in her chest, Friday could not help smiling. How blind he was! Because he did not *know*. He was moving her to the window-stool, obliging her to sit down. Removing her spectacles, she dried her cheeks with the handkerchief he proffered for her use and handed it back to him.

"Here, give me those!" he ordered, taking the spectacles.

Through a haze, she saw him wipe them off and her heart warmed to the gesture of simple kindness. Oh, if only they could have remained but friends! She was seeking for a way to put this into words when Nick spoke again, sweeping the thought from her mind.

"How long do you think I should kick my heels here? I mean, your father probably expects it. And, for form's sake, I suppose I ought to remain a while. But if you wish to be rid of me, Friday, you have only to say the word. I know you would much prefer to get at your books than dance attendance on a mere affianced husband."

A laugh accompanied these words, and he looked down at Friday's face as he spoke. She was staring at him blankly. Without the spectacles, which he still held loosely in his fingers, her eyes were pools of sheer perplexity in her piquant face. He frowned.

"What?"

She looked away at once, shaking her head. "Nothing.'' She held out her hand for the eyeglasses and quickly put them on.

Nicolas began to feel uncomfortable again, without knowing why. Friday was no longer distressed, but there was an odd tension in her again. He could think of no more to say or do. The ease of friendship seemed to have disappeared. Depression settled on his spirits again and he rose, impatient to get away.

"I'm disturbing you," he said briefly. "I'll go now."

Friday nodded. "Goodbye, Nick."

It sounded forlorn; he did not quite know why. He hesitated a moment, but she said nothing more. Merely sat there on the window-stool, watching him without apparent expression. Nick turned and walked quickly out of the room.

Friday remained just as she was for some little time, willing herself to remain calm. Nausea and butterflies fought for possession of her stomach. He would never know how hard it had been to let him walk away. Everything in her had longed to scream out at him that he must stay. He *must*. Because, as he went, he took with him the remnants of a brief, impossible dream.

Caroline fidgeted with the frothy lace négligé that was draped about her shapely form where she lay on the *chaise-longue* in her boudoir. The pretty pink stripes of the satin cushions were repeated on the walls and drapes, making a fittingly frivolous bower for its occupant.

It was Friday who looked utterly out of place. But Mrs Cleeve had been given no opportunity to express her whole-hearted disapproval of an ensemble that could only be described as *sensible*. Kid boots under the bronze linsey-woolsey dress, a plain beaver hat, and the dark cloak that lay discarded over the back of her chair.

"Caro, *pray* tell me the truth," Friday begged for what must have been the fourth or fifth time.

"But Friday, there is nothing to tell," protested Caroline yet again, wriggling uncomfortably. Her voice took on a petulant note. "I declare, I shall *kill* Mary for letting you in. I am not at all well today."

"Yes, I know, Caro, and I am sorry for it. But you must not blame your maid, you know. I made her allow me to come up, for this *cannot* wait."

"But indeed I don't *know* anything," uttered Caroline desperately, fluttering her hands restlessly about.

"Yes, you do," Friday insisted. "I know it is unkind of me to press you—particularly if you have been sworn to secrecy, as I dare say may be the case—but it is my whole *life* that is at risk."

"Oh, stuff! That is nonsensical, Friday."

"No, it is not nonsensical, though it may sound a trifle melodramatic. I *cannot* marry in these circumstances."

Caroline sat up with a jerk. "You are not thinking of crying off?" she cried in a horrified tone.

"Well, yes, I am, Caro," Friday said apologetically.

"Oh, *no*, Friday. You cannot. Indeed, you cannot! What in the world shall I do with Nicky back in circulation? There is no saying *what* will happen if you release him now."

Friday regarded the anxious features steadily. "Indeed. What *will* happen?"

Caroline prudently took refuge in tears. Friday rose

quickly and went across to perch beside her on the *chaise-longue,* catching at her hands and speaking in a voice of earnest intensity.

"Caro, I didn't mean to upset you, truly I didn't. But pray don't fob me off! I *know* Nick does not really wish to marry me."

"He does! He does!" wailed Caroline. "Or if he does not he *should.*"

Friday found herself smiling in spite of the ache in her heart. "I suppose you told him so?"

Caro snatched at a wisp of lace handkerchief in her sleeve and agitatedly blew her nose. "No, but Papa did so when he told him of your father's visit." Then she uttered a gasp, her hands flew to her mouth, and she groaned a despairing, *"Oooh!"*

Curiously, the impact was not quite as severe as it might have been. Friday felt little surprise. She was even conscious of a measure of relief. It was, then, just as she had begun to suspect. She should have guessed it long ago. She would have done, had she not been so blinded by the shock of it all. There had been hints enough from Nick, even before that last speech of his that had told her what she now knew to be the case. Even when he'd offered, he had almost mentioned her supposed inheritance. A bargain, he had called it later. Then there was Papa. Both he and Mama *had* known—just as she'd felt they did, without knowing that it was so. Small wonder Papa had not continued his diatribe about marriage. He had already arranged the matter!

Tears were trickling down Caro's cheeks and Friday was attacked by a feeling of remorse. She took hold of one of her hands again and held it tightly.

"Don't be concerned! I would have found out in

any event—if not from you, then perhaps from my father or Nick.''

Caro eyed her uncertainly. ''Are you not very angry?''

A rather pathetic little smile wavered on Friday's lips, and she had to swallow on a rising sob. ''No,'' she said huskily. ''The blame is mine. Something I— let fall, inadvertently, is I think what prompted it. Papa is very observant. He must have guessed—recognised...''

''But it's so *suitable*, Friday,'' said Caro persuasively, reviving now that the murder was out.

''For whom?'' asked Friday wryly.

''For *everyone*, don't you see?''

A laugh escaped Friday. ''Everyone? Are we supposed *all* to be marrying, then?''

''Oh, you know what I mean. It suits *me*, for I have Nick off my hands.'' She began to count the items on her fingers. ''It suits *your* father, for he will have the estate cared for.''

''Is that what he said?''

''Yes, and that *you* would be looked after, too.''

Yes, Friday remembered now. She had been too agitated to notice at the time, but it was what he had said when he'd first brought up the subject of her marriage.

''And it suits *my* father,'' Caro continued, ''because it means he no longer has to worry over Nick's future. It suits Nick, for obvious reasons, and—''

''They are not obvious to me,'' interrupted Friday in a sharper tone than she had yet used.

''Oh, stuff, Friday!'' said Caro, laughing. ''You must be quite aware that, if your father intends to settle the estate on you, the advantages to Nick are *astonishing.* It is no use being missish about it. A younger son—and Papa was *quite* right about that— ought to jump at such a chance.''

"In other words," Friday said tightly, "Papa has bought him for me."

Caroline seized her hands. "*Don't* be hurt, Friday! Nick rejected the idea in no uncertain terms, you must know. Papa had to bring *such* pressure to bear as you would not *conceive.*"

Friday pulled her hands away, and rose quickly from the *chaise-longue,* pacing away to the window, and removing her spectacles so that they would not mist over. She spoke with her back to the room, a tremor in her voice.

"Do you imagine that makes me feel any better? Heaven help me, I *knew* well enough that he was ill-at-ease on the matter, even that he *misliked* the notion. But to hear that he had to be *coerced* into making me an offer!"

She could hear Caroline dissolve into tears again behind her, but her own distress was too acute just now to allow her to do anything to help her. But in a moment or two she had herself under control again. The eyeglasses back in place, she turned and came to sit down again.

"Don't cry, Caro," she said gently. "It is none of it your fault. I wish you had not to be dragged into it. But you must understand that I cannot possibly marry Nicolas now."

Caroline was sniffing into a damp handkerchief. "I am only weeping because you are, Friday. I cannot *help* my sensibilities. Especially in my present condition."

Friday smiled at her. "I know. I'm sorry."

Caro tucked the handkerchief away. "It makes no matter now you have stopped crying. But I wish you will think *better* of your decision. It is not as if Nick is not *fond* of you. Besides, a man's feelings, you know, will often animate more deeply towards a woman if they are in close proximity, no matter *how* he begins. There is a warmth of feeling generated between a man and a woman when they share a bed that *cannot* be ignored!"

A hint of laughter sparkled under Friday's spectacles. "Caro, I am sure you ought not to speak of such things to a mere spinster."

"Yes, but the thing is that I *must*—if you are not to remain a spinster."

"I am afraid that is past praying for now."

"No, but only *think*, Friday," she said persuasively. "You would not wish to deprive Nicky of his advancement—and it is no use your pretending that you do not care about that, because I know very well that you like him—"

"Like!"

Caro threw up her hands. "Well, *love,* then! Great heavens, Friday, do you think I do not *know?*"

Friday sighed. "I had hoped not to be that obvious."

"Yes, but I am a *woman,* my love," said Caro in a superior way that amused Friday despite the wound that had been inflicted on her heart. "And for all that Nicky is my brother, I am quite *furious* with him for being so *stupid*. I am at one with Papa, you know. I cannot think he would have been nearly so averse to marrying you if it had not been for that *abominable* creature."

An icy hand gripped Friday's heart. Here it was at

last! She had known it. Oh, she had *known* it. There *was* someone. The question that came out of her own mouth sounded in her own ears like a dreadful croak.

"What abominable creature?"

"Oh, an impossible female!" Caroline said heatedly. "For all she has inveigled her way into Society—or rather, her *mother* has—she properly belongs in the *demi-monde*. Which is where she will end up, mark my words. But Nick has not the wit to see it— yet." She leaned forward eagerly. "But if he were *married,* Friday, there is no question but that he *must* see it."

A laugh was surprised out of Friday. "I can't imagine why you should think so. If he loves her—"

"Stuff! He has no such feeling, although he *thinks* he has. It is but a silly infatuation. Friday, I promise you, it is not worth an *instant* of your consideration. All boys do fancy themselves to be in love with such females. It is a part of growing up, you must know. I thank heaven that Nicky has at least the sense to see *your* worth—for you may believe he would *not* have offered if he did not value you, no matter *what* Papa said—and I am convinced you need never trouble yourself about the affair. You will very soon wean him away from her, I *promise* you!"

She chattered on in much the same vein, but Friday scarcely heard her. Every word made her heart sink lower. Yes, perhaps there was consolation in that the duress under which Nick had offered for her had been necessitated more by his involvement elsewhere than his reluctance to marry her. But infatuation? Was it not just such an infatuation that had started the Trojan War? Had not Phaedra's infatuation with Hippolytus led to both their untimely deaths? Heaven help her, there were enough examples in the stories she had read of the dire consequences of simple infatuation!

It was clear enough that *Nick* did not regard it so lightly. Abruptly she recalled those odd words of his about Caro—that he knew what she was at and he would not tolerate it. What she was at, of course, in trying to smarten Friday up, was holding her out as a lure to wean him from his attachment.

It was laughable! How could *she* wean him from his affection? Unless it was really true that the girl *was* so ineligible. In that case, whispered a tiny hopeful voice in her heart, would it not be a *kindness* to marry him? Quite apart from the advantages she was able to offer, her love could bring him happiness. Oh, it *could*—if he would only give it a chance!

Caroline's words began to penetrate, falling on fruitful soil. "*Now* do you see, Friday, the advantage of taking some care with your appearance? I can help you, *indeed* I can. My worst enemy cannot say of me that I don't know fashion!"

Which was indeed true, Friday conceded. She was not so ignorant of such matters that she could not see that for herself. *Could* she be so changed by modish clothes that Nick might look at her with new eyes? At least she was eligible, even if she was not pretty. And Nick was already fond of her. Perhaps Caro was right. She drew a breath.

"Very well, if you wish it, Caro. We can but try."

Caroline beamed. "Then you will come? Famous! On the first morning, then, that I am well, we shall go together to Reading. I have an excellent dressmaker there who can…"

She was off. There was no curbing her enthusiasm and Friday wisely did not attempt it. Besides, her fighting spirit had been roused. Or perhaps, she thought honestly, she just could not bear to put an end to her engagement. If there was the slightest chance that it *might* end in her favour—if she could find some way to attract Nick's interest on a *different* level—then she would try. Perhaps—unlikely though it seemed—she *could* win Nick away from this "impossible female".

A very few days later Caroline sent her carriage to fetch Friday, and together they drove into Reading. They stepped down in front of the door to the salon of the modiste to whom Caro had chosen to take her, and the carriage moved on to await them down a side-alley.

Caroline was in fine fettle, and had just seized Friday's arm and was about to drag her into the shop when she caught sight of her brother a few yards up the street. She stopped dead, staring.

"Great heavens!" she exclaimed in a faint voice.

Friday looked in the direction of her fixed gaze. She was not wearing her spectacles—Caroline having snatched them from her face at sight of her, saying that her dressmaker would faint with shock if she saw them—and could see only three figures standing there. That two were male and the other female was as much as she could immediately judge.

"Nick! Oh, the *wretch!*" came in an angry undervoice from Caroline. "How *could* he?"

"Is it Nick?" asked Friday quickly even as she recognised the shape and stature of one of the gentlemen, who was now coming towards them.

"How do you do, Mrs Cleeve?" uttered the female in a breathy voice as they came up.

"Very *badly,* I thank you!" answered Caroline grimly.

"Caro! Good God! What are you doing here?" asked Nicolas in an appalled tone. "I mean— shouldn't you be resting?"

The second gentleman's voice and outline was just as well-known to Friday. "How do, Caro?" He coughed, as if he was embarrassed.

"I am at least glad to see *you,* Charles." Caroline's tone was even higher-pitched than usual, and the note of fury was evident under the over-polite tones. "I am come, Nicky, to help *Friday—*" laying undue emphasis on the name "—to choose some *bride* clothes."

"Bride—! Oh, God!" uttered her brother disjointedly. "Friday, why now? Why *Reading?*"

"Because my dressmaker happens to be here, Nick," said Caroline severely, answering for her. "And I might also have a *why* to put to you!"

Friday was groping for her spectacles in the basket she carried. The tension was tangible, and the now familiar sick feeling had already attacked her in Nick's presence. More importantly, in the presence of this strange female whose hand, she could now see, rested possessively in the crook of Nick's elbow.

Charles Delamere was hanging back, plucking at Nick's sleeve. "Er—beg pardon. Mustn't keep you. Matters to attend to, you know."

Caroline seemed to come to a decision. She seized Friday's arm in a vice-like grip. "Come along, Friday. *We* have *important* matters to attend to."

"Wait, Caro," Friday said, not even looking at her as her fingers closed about her eyeglasses and she drew them forth.

She noticed Charles edging away. She felt Caro give her a nip with her fingers, and try to drag her towards the door of the salon. She ignored her. Peering at Nicolas, she addressed him in a calm tone that wholly belied the turmoil in her breast.

"Are you not going to introduce me to your friend, Nick?"

"No, no!" whispered Caro frantically.

Nick coughed. His voice was hoarse. "This is Hermione—or rather, Miss Hesket."

The spectacles slotted into place as Friday turned to look at Hermione Hesket. An enchanting face came into focus. Eyes of cornflower-blue, a tip-tilted little nose, and a dainty bow of a cherry-red, full-lipped mouth, surrounded by a halo of rioting golden curls.

Friday took in the vision, and withered where she stood. She was exquisite. She was peerless. Helen of Troy in person.

Chapter Four

Thoughts tumbled chaotically through Friday's mind. "Abominable creature". This was she? And with Nick. *Very much* with Nick. Gracious, how to get *away* from here? Heaven help her, but she'd no notion of—of a female such as *this!* Wean him away? She, Friday Edborough? Almost she laughed out. What was Caro thinking of? She must be mad. As mad as she herself would be, if she did not leave this place on the instant.

But her feet seemed rooted to the ground, her gaze fixed on the lovely features whose shocking advent had set the seal on her determination. For there was no possible hope now that she could go on with this farcical betrothal.

She became aware of a tugging on her arm and Caro's voice. "For heaven's sake, Friday, come on, do!"

Rescue! Come? Come where? For the moment, Friday could not recall where she was or the purpose of her being there. It did not matter. Wherever Caro wanted her to go, she would follow. Anywhere,

please God! Anywhere but here, with "Helen's" face
to tear the heart out of her bosom.

As her eyes, perforce, were wrenched from the dis-
comfiting image, they flickered fleetingly to Nicolas's
countenance and registered there dismay and morti-
fication, feelings she at once felt more greatly than
her own. Compassion pierced her.

"Never mind it, Nick!" she cried out quickly, just
before Caroline dragged her into the dressmaker's salon, and she found herself vaguely taking in a sea of
interested faces in an elaborate décor of gilt, mirrors
and green and white striped wallpaper that began to
waver before her eyes.

Mrs Cleeve had barely shut the door before turning
on her prospective sister-in-law in a wrathful whisper.
"Never mind it! Never *mind* it? Have you taken leave
of your senses, Friday?"

"No," Friday murmured, all at once conscious of
the import of the spots in her vision, the buzzing in
her ears, "but I am just about to."

"So I should think! Of all the— Oh, heavens!"
ended Caro, taking in the younger girl's whitening
features. "*Don't* faint, Friday!" She looked wildly
around, encountering the stares of two customers and
a bevy of hovering female assistants.

To these she addressed herself in a near shriek,
grasping at Friday, who was swaying precariously, to
prevent her from falling. "Here, quickly! A chair. A
stool. *Anything*."

With great presence of mind, one of the seam-
stresses thrust a gown she was holding at a colleague,
and leaped forward to help guide the afflicted cus-
tomer to a gilt-edged chair near the counter.

Friday sank down as directed and, obedient to the

pressure on her back and the insistent voice, allowed
her head to fall forward over her knees. A moment
later, an acrid aroma assailed her nostrils as Caroline's fingers waved her own open bottle of sal vol-
atile under her nose. It made Friday's eyes water, but
in a moment or two the sickening sensation of diz-
ziness began to subside. A trifle feebly, she raised her
hand to push away the smelling salts, and gingerly
raised her head.

"Don't try to get up!" Caro warned. "Sit still.
There is nothing more guaranteed to have you
stretched at your length on the floor than a too pre-
cipitate rise."

Friday had no intention of trying to stand up. Her
legs would not have supported her in any event. She
was grateful nevertheless, for Caro's prompt action
had prevented a full swoon. She leaned back in the
chair, putting her hands to her head.

"I am sorry to be so s-silly," she muttered. "I
can't think why I did that."

"Well, I can," declared Caroline, from her tone
evidently still seething. "I am only astonished that I
did not swoon myself."

A tiny smile flitted across Friday's lips. "At least
you have a legitimate excuse."

"Stuff! *Anyone* might have fainted. That, or been
provoked beyond endurance. I wonder you did not *hit*
the wretch. I promise you I had a mind to do it myself. When I next see Nicky—"

"Oh, don't, Caro," Friday begged. "Not now. Not
here."

Caroline glanced about, recollecting herself as she
noted the interested ears pointedly *not* listening.
"Yes, but what is she *doing* here?" she nevertheless

pursued, although in a lowered tone. "That is what I should like to know."

It was not a question that had occurred to Friday. But it did so now, and with considerable force. What *was* the female doing here? Had Nick sent for her? No. He would not be so foolhardy, let alone being far too much the gentleman to risk just such an encounter as had occurred. Then she must have come on her own account. Of course. She—Hermione, was it not? Even her *name* was beyond competition!—had read of the betrothal in the *Gazette,* and come perhaps to find out the truth of it. No, she must know it was true. It would not else have appeared. What, then? Had Nick not warned her of his intention? Had she come, risking perhaps the humiliation of his rejection, to find out why he had deserted her for another?

Friday shivered a little at the thought of such a confrontation. In the girl's place, she could not herself have faced it. Hermione must love him very much, she reflected. The thought brought fresh pain to the still raw wound. But it only strengthened her determination. She must set Nick free. And the sooner the better.

She looked about for Caroline, and discovered her to be deep in conversation with a middle-aged female dressed in a suitably modest gown that yet managed to convey an aura of quiet elegance. This was undoubtedly the dressmaker—whose services, Friday thought wryly, she no longer required.

She discovered that one of the assistants was proffering a glass of water, and took it with a murmured word of thanks. Her eyes, however, were on Caroline Cleeve, and it was with some misgiving that she contemplated the thought of informing Caro that she had changed her mind—irrevocably.

Nicolas, meanwhile, had been galvanised into action by that one single statement from his affianced bride.

"Never mind it, Nick!"

But he *did* mind it. Very much indeed. For the look in her face, when she was hit with the impact of Hermione's identity, left him in no doubt that his sister's fiddlestick of a tongue had made sure she knew precisely what the name meant. He could not have wished for a worse way for Friday to discover the truth, and wished very much that he'd had the courtesy—not to mention the courage!—to lay bare to her the whole matter in the first place.

He had been himself much startled by Hermione's suddenly announced presence in the vicinity, and had come here to meet her today—with Charles in tow to lend the encounter *some* respectability—expressly to beg her to return to London. As luck would have it, they had chosen the direct route from the over-public George where they had met, and where Charles and Nick were too well-known to escape remark, to a less conspicuous sanctuary at the Green Man at the other end of the high street. It was but a curst mischance that Caro—the meddling busybody; he had meant expressly to charge her to leave Friday's dress alone—had chosen that precise moment to bring Friday to Reading.

Too shocked to do more than stutter the desired introduction, he had stood like a fool while his betrothed had made the acquaintance of the woman he had wanted to marry! And she had then thrown him into even more acute embarrassment by attempting to offer consolation. "Never mind it". Typical Friday. Always trying to ease everyone else's burden.

The remark made him seize Miss Hesket's arm and move off at a great rate, dragging her with him, his thoughts so thick that he did not even hear her breathy complaints until Delamere forcibly stopped him in his tracks.

"Hold hard, man!" urged Charles, firmly grasping his arm. "Devil ain't after you, you know. Poor girl's about to trip over her own feet."

Glancing down at Hermione in some consternation, Nick saw that she was panting a little. Remorse consumed him and he forgot Friday for the moment.

"I beg your pardon, my lo—I mean, Hermione," he uttered, correcting himself hastily as he recalled that he no longer had any right to address her by such a tender endearment.

"Whatever—is the—matter with you—Nick?" she gasped, round-eyed.

He shook his head. "Nothing. But we must get to the Green Man as soon as may be."

Miss Hesket had a hand pressed to the fullness of her still heaving breasts, but her gaze remained steady on his face. "I have been—thinking, Nick. Why do we not go back to my cousin's—*alone*—" with a glance at Charles Delamere of which the message was clear "—and then we can talk?"

Nicolas was frowning a little, still too shaken by recent events to think soberly. "What cousin?"

"Did I not say? Mrs Bemerside. I am staying with her."

"Thought you were staying at the George," put in Charles, echoing Nick's thought.

"Oh, no. I could not stay there alone. My ma would never allow it."

Nick blinked. "Do you tell me your mother *knows* you have come here?"

"Oh, no," said Hermione, trilling with laughter that set her golden curls dancing under the bonnet and lit her eyes to a glow. "She knows nothing at all about it. But she would be very cross if I stayed at an inn."

Nicolas felt that her mama was likely to be "very cross" to know that she had come here at all, but he could scarcely say so. He found that Charles was nudging him.

"Seems to me you'd best escort her, Nick. I'll wait for you at the George."

Miss Hesket looked much pleased with this suggestion, but Nick was less than enthusiastic. He frowned at his friend.

"How are we supposed to keep this innocent if you slope off?"

Delamere snorted. "Too late for that. The thing is blown already. Might as well face it."

"Oh, God!" groaned Nick, reminded of the disastrous encounter with his affianced wife.

As he hesitated, Hermione set her fingers on his arm. "Come, Nick. It is only a step. We will be there in a trice."

Too distressed to argue further, he allowed himself to be drawn down a side-street and did not even notice the absence of Charles Delamere. If tongues were already wagging, it mattered very little *where* they chose to talk.

But when they reached a modest little cottage some few minutes later, and he belatedly recalled Mrs Hes-

ket's origins, he was rather less happy. It was scarcely
likely to improve matters if he was seen visiting a
beautiful young girl in the house of one of Reading's
solid citizens! Yet he found himself unable to refuse
Hermione's plea that he enter.

"Only for a moment or two," begged the breathy
voice plaintively, eyelashes fluttering above the blue
of the large eyes.

Mrs Bemerside proved to be a disapproving matron
of dour aspect, who greeted the arrival on her doorstep of the stunningly handsome escort with a suspi-
cious glare.

"And does Nancy know as how you take and bring
gennelmen home to visit?" she enquired sourly.

"Ma is very well acquainted with Mr Weare,
Cousin," Hermione said blithely. "I assure you she
would not object to him."

"I will not stay above a moment," Nick assured
her, annoyed by the implication contained in the
woman's words. Hermione could hardly be held ac-
countable for her background! It did not mean she
was of the same cut as her mother. Although *that*
female would heartily object to his visit—on very different grounds, however. The whole business was singularly ill-advised, confound it! They should have
gone to the Green Man as he had intended.

Mrs Bemerside had, however, grudgingly stood
aside to allow them to enter, throwing open the door
to a tiny parlour, but declining to remain.

"None o' my concern, if she chooses to travel that
road," she said, sniffing. "Though I'll thank you to
pick some other place next time. I'm a respectable
woman, I am—in despite of my *connections*."

The last was thrown so blatantly at Miss Hesket as

to rouse Nick's anger, so that he slammed the door behind her instead of leaving it open as he had half formed the intention of doing. But as he turned he was unprepared for the assault of Miss Hesket's body flinging itself at him.

"Oh, Nick! Oh, Nick! How *could* you?" she cried out pitifully, throwing her arms up to clasp about his neck.

"Hermione, what are you doing?" he uttered, appalled, grabbing at her wrists and forcing her away from him. "Matters are bad enough!"

Her eyes blinked up at him and tears gathered within them, making them glow. There was sadness in her tone. "You've made me so unhappy."

Nicolas felt himself weakening and squared his shoulders, moving away from the door towards a narrow fireplace in order to put as much distance as possible between them.

This, in a room so modest, was not a great deal. There was space only for an all too cosy little sofa, two neat chairs and a small table set in the slight window embrasure. Chintz drapes matched the sofa coverings and a landscape print and a mirror, aside from two candle-sconces, were the only adornments to the white-painted walls.

Miss Hesket looked quite out of place in her highly fashionable pink velvet pelisse over the usual white muslin gown, topped by an attractive bonnet beribboned in the same soft shade. But, while her beauty disturbed Nick's senses, his consciousness of the clandestine nature of this meeting—which in itself constituted disloyalty to Friday—would not allow him to give in to the baser instincts prompting him to take advantage of their situation. On the other hand, he owed Hermione an explanation.

"I am sorry that I did not warn you, Hermione," he said stiffly.

"Oh, yes, and I have been so unhappy," she repeated. "How could you become betrothed, Nick? How?"

He turned and faced her, all his resentment rising up and colouring his voice. "I had no choice. My father *forced* it on me."

"But how could he?" she asked in a bewildered tone.

"Very easily," Nick said heavily. "He threatened to cut off my allowance and bar me from the family home."

Miss Hesket's eyes widened. "You mean you would have no money at all?"

He nodded. "That is it exactly."

The idea appeared to strike the lady dumb. Her mouth fell open as she stared at him. Then she drew breath. "That is *horrid* of him. What would you do without money?"

He laughed shortly. "You may well ask. Take up some gainful employment, I suppose."

The lovely countenance went blank. "You can't mean—work? Why, you are a *gentleman*."

"But only a younger son."

Her face fell. "Yes, that is the pity of it." She sighed. "If only you had been the one destined to become Lord Weare, I am sure Ma would have made no objection at all."

"No," agreed Nick shortly. "And I would not have found myself engaged to be married to Friday."

"Friday," repeated Hermione, suddenly intent.

"You mean *that* is the female? The one we met in the street? That one with the spectacles? Oh, Nick, *no*."

Nicolas was conscious of a stirring within him—of annoyance. But he could not be annoyed with Hermione. Could he?

"What do you mean?" he asked evenly.

She came a step closer, her eyes big with pity. "Oh, *poor* Nick. How *dreadful* for you. Why, she is quite the plainest creature I have ever seen. Why in the world should your father think of *such* a female for you?"

Nick now discovered that he could be singularly annoyed with Hermione. More than that. He was able to express it to her. Quite forcefully.

"Don't speak of her like that! She happens to be a very good friend of mine."

Hermione stared. Then a tiny frown creased her brow. "You do not *like* her, do you?"

"Like her? Of course I like her."

All at once, Miss Hesket's eyes filled again. "Oh, Nick! And you said you were forced to marry her. I thought you cared for *me*."

The tears softened him at once and he moved towards her. "Don't weep! I *do* care for you. You know I do."

She looked beautiful despite the tears. Even because of them, for they did not disfigure her with ugly red blotches. Her eyes became luminous, and her cherry-red lips pouted adorably. Nick could not help putting an arm about her and giving her a quick hug.

"Hermione, forgive me! You're the one I *wanted* to marry. But this came up—there was no time to tell you, or I would have done. It is a great reproach to me that you felt you had to come here—at such *risk*."

Two teardrops rolled down her cheeks. "But the announcement made me so unhappy, Nick. Even though we could not marry, you *said* you cared for me."

"And so I do. But I cannot help this wretched business, Hermione. Friday is heir to her father's estate, you see, and my father—"

"Oh, I see!" she interrupted, the tears clearing like magic. A joyful expression transformed her countenance. "You mean to say it is an advantageous match?"

"Yes, exactly. Naturally I would have given anything to marry you, but—"

"Yes, yes, but it would not *do*, Nick," she interposed again. "You have no money and no title, and Mama would not hear of it."

"Nor my father," he agreed gloomily.

The unfairness of it all overcame him suddenly. Here he was with the woman he wanted above all others, and circumstance forbade any kind of union. Hermione was altogether too lovely, too enchanting with the recent teardrops still sparkling on her eyelashes. She was looking at him with a glowing warmth that sent his senses reeling. He lost his head.

Pulling her to him, he kissed her. She did not resist. Rather she returned his embrace with a fervour that registered surprise somewhere in the heady fog that the close feel of her body against his own engendered in his brain. The sensations evoked by her response were in fact so pleasurable that he squeezed tighter. Upon which, Miss Hesket very properly struggled a little and he had to release her, conscious that he had done very wrong in kissing her at all. She had every right to reproach him, and an apology was forming on his lips even as he braced himself to receive her anger.

To his astonishment, she merely uttered calmly, "Do mind my bonnet, Nick! I am *so* uncomfortable. Only let me remove my pelisse and you may kiss me again."

Nicholas hardly noticed the provocative smile that accompanied the words. A feeling he could not identify succeeded his surprise. An uncomfortable feeling that he did not wish to associate with Hermione Hesket.

"You don't mind?" he asked in a bemused tone.

She tinkled. "Mind? Of course not. Why should I?" The smile became dazzling. "You have proved to me that you *do* care."

"Care?" he echoed, irritated without knowing why. "My God! I'd have done *anything,* Hermione." His voice became ragged. "I would even have borne the poverty, for my father swore he would turn me out penniless if I married you. For me, Hermione, just to be with you would have been enough."

If he expected a like response, he was disappointed. "Yes, but not without any money," Hermione returned, busy tidying the offending bonnet, which had become a trifle dislodged during the recent embrace.

Nick frowned, the irritation deepening. "Is that all you care about?"

Her eyes came up, and widened piteously. "Well, but I *could* not live without parties, and pretty clothes," she said in an excusing way.

She smiled again, and her radiance drove away some of the irritation, afflicting Nick to not a little degree, so that he was hard put to it to refrain from kissing her again. This he was determined *not* to do. For he was betrothed to Friday and it was not right. Perhaps Hermione had not quite grasped that. What she had grasped became all too clear the next instant.

"But there, Nick. You are only marrying for advantage. There is nothing at all to worry about."

A deep sigh escaped him. "Except that this must be goodbye, Hermione."

"Goodbye? Oh, no, Nick. Why?" she cried, the clouds gathering again in her eyes. "You *care* for me. You said so. You *kissed* me."

"Yes, and it was very wrong of me, but—"

"Wrong? Oh, *no,* Nick. A little kiss! In any event, it does not make any difference *now,*" she uttered persuasively.

"How does it make no difference?" Nick asked, uneasy all at once. Why could she not see that they *must* not give in to their mutual emotions?

"I am talking of your marriage," she explained. "There can be no need of sacrifices. After all, I may also be married soon. But that need not concern us. We can still be *together.*"

The implication behind her words suddenly hit him. The impact was blinding. He felt as if he had received a blow to the stomach. His eyes narrowed, and he asked in a voice of dangerous calm, "Just what exactly do you mean by that, Hermione?"

She fluttered her lashes at him, moving closer. "Don't you see? Marriage is for *advantage* only. For me, too. But what is marriage, after all? It need not be a barrier, Nick. We will have to wait a little, to be sure, but I can bear that. If *you* can."

Nick did not want to believe what he was hearing.

She *could* not be saying it. No, that was ridiculous. She *had* said it. Desperate to thrust away the suddenly tarnished image of innocence in that adorable countenance, he sought in his mind for excuses. She was very young. She did not understand. It was not *his* Hermione speaking, despite that wonderfully exciting voice that hovered always on the edge of seduction— God, what was he *thinking?* There was nothing deliberate in the way she spoke. She could not help it. No, this was not the real Hermione. This was the voice of her "ma". Of course! It had to be that. She made this appalling suggestion in good faith, not because she was in any way depraved, but because she had no notion that it *was* depraved. The blame must be laid at the door of her upbringing. It was not her fault!

He took her by the shoulders, saying gently, "You know you don't mean that."

Her brows snapped together. "You don't want me?"

"Of course I do. But not like *that*. You cannot know what you are saying Hermione. What you suggest is intolerable. To have you when you are another man's wife! And for you to advocate that I should betray Friday—"

Miss Hesket pushed away from him and stamped her foot. "You *don't* care for me!" she accused passionately. "You have more regard for this horrid Friday than you have for me!"

"I have not!" snapped Nick with sudden heat. "And don't call her 'horrid.' But good God, Hermione, if your positions were reversed—if you were Friday and she you—could you tolerate such an arrangement then?"

Miss Hesket's beautiful features puckered, and then

the tears gathered in her eyes again. Avoiding the question, she uttered protestingly, "But you care for me. *Me*."

"That is quite beside the point," he said quickly. There was nothing for it. She was too naïve to understand that what she proposed could never be. He must be strong for both of them. Better a quick, if painful, break now than a protracted term of regret and longing. He drew a breath.

"Hermione, it is all over between us. This is—it *must* be—the end. You must go back to London, and we must never see each other again."

She stared. "You can't mean that."

"But I do. I said it before and I say it again. This is goodbye, Hermione."

The swimming blue eyes gazed at him in disbelief. "No, Nick, *no*. You cannot cast me aside!"

"I am not doing so. But we *cannot* continue—"

"Don't say that, Nick!" she shrieked, catching at his lapels with urgent fingers. "You *can't* mean never to see me again."

"Hermione, *hush*."

She battered at him with curled fists as her tears began to fall. "No, Nick, *no*. No, no, *no!*"

"Hermione!"

"You cannot do this to me, Nick," she wailed, bursting into sobs. "How can you be so *horrid?*"

Conscious of the unseen presence of her relative somewhere outside the little parlour, Nicolas put his arms round her and tried to quiet her. But Miss Hesket was not to be comforted. A storm of weeping protest was shrieked into his chest, and Nick found himself clutching her tighter as if he would smother the noise. But it was only when her questing lips found his that quiet descended on the parlour, and Nick thankfully sank with her on to the small sofa, giving his own principles up to the only way there seemed to be of calming her hysterics.

Curiously, although he was conscious of the strongest feeling of compassion as he held her—warring, it must be said, with even stronger feelings of guilt!—her outburst only strengthened his resolve. Just before the heady sensation of this close embrace overtook him so that he could not think at all, the treacherous thought passed through his mind that she was going to prove to be a confounded nuisance.

Friday awoke heavy-eyed and very little refreshed by what rest she had managed to gain in a night largely spent tossing on her pillows. Despite every argument she had advanced, Caroline had not managed to undermine her resolution. It was not that, not *solely* that which kept her awake. For the tiniest seed of doubt *had* been sown. Caro had categorically denied that anything worthwhile dwelled under the beautiful countenance of Hermione Hesket.

"Mercenary, that's what she is, I give you my word. She has no thought of anything but marrying for money."

"Then why is she here?" Friday had demanded. "She must love him very much to embark upon such a journey."

"Stuff! She loves having him about her because he is so well-looking, that is all."

Friday found that difficult to believe. "It does not explain her rushing up here to be with him."

"That, Friday, is a remark that only *proves* you know nothing of the world," declared Caroline. "*No* lady of breeding would chase after a man, *whatever* the circumstances. At first I thought it must be Nicky's doing, but on second thought I see that it is *far* more likely to have been her own idea. Her *mother* has no principles at all, so why should you suppose that *she* might have them?''

It was tempting, after this, to fall into the way of believing that one had a *duty* to rescue Nick from his own folly, Friday thought. But a duty that must guarantee her a life of daily anguish, knowing that Nick's heart was engaged elsewhere, was not one that she could contemplate with any degree of compliance. Besides, by what justification could such a duty fall to her lot? By her *love* for him? *No.* For *that* instinctively urged her to release him, that he might enjoy true happiness. It seemed incredible to Friday that this Hermione could come here—braving God knew what consequences!—merely because she coveted Nick's beauty, and wished to keep him in her court of admirers. No one could be *that* stupid.

No. What was really exercising her mind—and heart, if the truth were told—was the manner in which she could do the fell deed. Over and over into the small night hours, she rehearsed endless speeches to Nicolas—discarding them, one after another, as each began quite simply and became rapidly too convoluted to be eligible. For what *reason* could she give?

Too petty to break off her engagement merely because she had been introduced to Helen of Troy! What in the world could she say, without revealing the full extent of her knowledge? For Nick believed she knew nothing. Every method of putting forward her objections began to appear melodramatic.

''Nick, I know everything. I cannot marry you.''

''Nick, I have decided to do the honourable thing and release you from your obligations.''

Heaven help her, but she would sound like some play-actress from the stage!

In the end, she achieved a measure of calm only by deciding that she would go over to Delamere Place in the morning, accost him, and trust to the inspiration of the moment.

The morning, however, brought a singularly unnerving letter from Lady Delamere. It was full of delighted congratulation and an offer to hold a betrothal party for the couple at her home as soon as she returned from London for the Christmas period. Friday's need became all at once urgent, throwing her back into panic.

Since this unwelcome missive was on her breakfast tray, Friday was obliged to pass on its contents to her parents, although she could not of course express her desperate hope that by the time Lady Delamere returned the notice of cancellation would already have appeared in the *Gazette*.

''Betrothal party?'' said Mrs Edborough, raising her brows.

''It is customary, my dear,'' said her spouse drily.

''Then I wonder you did not think of it, when you know that I would never do so,'' retorted Sophia.

''Lady Delamere says it is to save you the trouble, Mama,'' Friday put in quickly.

''Yes, because she knows well your mama would not bother with such an event. And I dare say she is delighted because she does *not* wish Charles to marry Friday, as you suggested, my love,'' he added, not without a touch of satisfaction.

Mrs Edborough remained unperturbed. ''Very

likely.'' Her gaze moved to Friday, and there stayed. ''Frideswid, you do not appear highly elated by this offer of a party.''

Friday flushed and looked down at her plate, avoiding the instant bearing of her father's eye upon her own countenance, for she knew she looked hagged. Trusting that her spectacles would conceal the worst ravages of her sleepless night, she improvised quickly.

''Well, you know me, Mama. I am as little partial to parties as are you.''

Her father was frowning. ''Are you well, Friday? You look a trifle peaked.''

''I am perfectly well, thank you, Papa.'' She managed a smile and retired quickly into her coffee-cup.

Fortunately, Mama's preoccupations did not permit her to waste more time than was absolutely essential and the family breakfast party broke up shortly after this. Friday, feeling that if she delayed any further she might lose her nerve altogether, put on her cloak and sallied forth to make the short walk to Delamere Place.

It had not occurred to her, as she'd re-rehearsed possible phrases to the dog Bruno, accompanying her in his ambling fashion through the park, that she might find her quarry absent. Dismay attacked her when the butler informed her that only Lord Delamere was in the house at present. Don't say Nick had gone off! But where?

''Has Mr Weare gone to London, perhaps, Tattenhoe?''

''I could not say, miss,'' responded the aged servitor very correctly.

Friday was sorely tempted to turn on her heel and

go home again. But she stood her ground. She *must* do it. As soon as possible. Only if Nick *had* gone to London— Well, she would just have to write to him, she decided, shrinking inwardly at the thought of penning the words she must say. They sounded bad enough spoken. Heaven send he had not left the vicinity! Charles would know.

"Very well, then, I shall see his lordship," she said with decision.

Leaving Bruno to wander desultorily about the grounds, she entered the Delamere mansion. Tattenhoe bowed her into the yellow saloon opposite the ballroom. As she waited for Charles to make his appearance, she reflected that never had these well-known surroundings seemed more formal and alien.

The straw-coloured Chippendale sofas, the daffodil print of the wallpaper, the gilt ornamentation to the mouldings and the curlicued mirror above the mantel had always been pretty and warm. Today they looked coldly fashionable, symbolic of the world with which Nicolas was familiar—and she was not. For if she had been she would have known all about Miss Hermione Hesket and she would *never* have accepted a hand that had been offered only under pressure, when it truly belonged elsewhere. And she would not now be in the hideous position of having to reject that hand— when everything in her cried out that it was *hers* by right. For she loved its owner!

So that is it, Friday Edborough! she admonished herself sternly. She did not *want* to break it off. Fool! Did she not realise how dreadfully unhappy she would be with him?

Not as unhappy as she must be without him, whispered a traitorous little voice in her mind. She was engaged in sternly banishing this subversive when Charles Delamere walked into the room.

He was looking excessively embarrassed. For a moment, Friday could not think why.

"Charles, whatever is the matter? I have only come to find Nick, you know. Where is he?"

Delamere's flush deepened. "Ah. Um—not here just at present."

"So Tattenhoe informed me," agreed Friday, coming up to him. "He has gone to London, has he? Or to his father?"

"No, no. Still here all right and tight. Thing is, had to go out."

He was unable to keep his eyes on hers and Friday, remembering, divined the cause of his discomfort. Her heart lurched and she spoke her realisation aloud, unthinkingly.

"He has gone to see her!"

Charles winced and nodded. "Wasn't going to tell you."

Friday's bespectacled gaze considered him. The initial shock was fading. Of course she had been stupid not to think of that. Nicolas was bound to spend as much time with his inamorata as he could. Perhaps it was just as well he was not here. For Charles must know a good deal about it all. Now that the matter had been mentioned, perhaps she might probe a little.

"Why did she come here, Charles?" she asked in her direct way.

"Saw the notice," said Delamere uncomfortably. "Hadn't known anything about it, you see. Mind, I knew she'd kick up the devil of a dust. But I never thought it would happen on your own doorstep! Sick as mud over the whole thing, is Nick."

It was a fresh barb, although Friday already knew it. Nick had been "sick as mud" from the moment he had come to offer for her. She managed a tight smile.

"Well, he need not be so any more. I mean to release him."

"What?" gasped Charles, the horror in his voice almost worthy of Caroline. "You mean to break it off? Friday, you can't!"

"I *must*, Charles," she uttered on a frantic note. "The situation is quite intolerable."

"No, it ain't. Dash it, Friday, he's giving the wench up! Doesn't that *show* you?"

Friday shook her head. "I don't wish him to make that sacrifice for me. He *loves* her, Charles."

"No, he don't," argued Delamere vehemently. "The girl ain't worth it, Friday, I give you my word."

"What has that to say to anything?" she asked in some exasperation. "You are as bad as Caro, Charles. I cannot marry Nick when his heart is given to another. That is all there is to it."

Charles stared at her, dismay writ large in his countenance. "But Friday, you haven't *thought*. You don't *know*. Worst thing you could do, I'm telling you."

"Why is it the worst thing I could do?" Friday demanded almost crossly. Why could no one see the sheer impossibility of her situation? But Delamere's reply struck her dumb.

"Because if you do old Weare will cut Nick off without a penny and bar his doors against him."

For a moment or two, Friday thought she could not have heard aright. No one, *no one* could be that revengeful. Only because his son would not marry the female of his choice?

"Pooh! I *don't* believe it," she announced, finding

her tongue. "Not even Lord Weare could be that medieval."

"Well, that's what he said," Charles told her firmly. "And you ought to know as well as I that he's a man of his word. Good God, hasn't Nick told us endless tales to prove as much?"

It was true. Over the years, there had been quite enough proof of Weare's severity. She had thought it needlessly cruel, after the episode of the kitchen wench, to thrust poor Nick into a profession he patently loathed. And if it was true that he had made such an issue of Nick's marrying herself—

"What exactly did Lord Weare say to Nick?"

"Ordered him to offer for you in the first place," Charles said without hesitation, for in his view nothing could be more disastrous than a breakdown of the engagement at this point. "Swore if he didn't he'd cut off his allowance and bar him from the family home—just like I told you. Even after Nick had offered and you'd accepted him, Weare *still* didn't trust Nick. Said he'd better make sure you'd no reason to cry off, or he would know what to do about it."

Despair gripped Friday. All her instincts were telling her to finish this as quickly as she could. Now here was Charles informing her that if she followed her instincts she would be condemning the man she loved to a life of poverty and degradation. What in the world was she to do?

Delamere might have read her mind, for he said urgently, "Tell you what. Go home now, Friday. Dashed embarrassing for Nick to find you here. He's been to see Hermione. Feels bad enough. Now here's you. What the devil is the poor fellow to say to you?"

Friday was less concerned with what Nick might

find to say to her than with what she could possibly say to him—now. She hurried towards the door. "Yes, I had better go."

"I won't say you were here, never fear," Charles assured her, moving to open the door for her.

Friday stepped into the hall and halted. Too late! Nicolas was back. He was just closing the front door. Gracious! What should she do? Hide?

She stepped back as if she would return to the yellow saloon. But Delamere, emerging, bumped into her. Nick heard the slight commotion and turned his head.

"Oh, my God!" he groaned. "Friday, not you as well!"

"As well as what?" she demanded out of the instant intensity of emotion that washed through her at these unwelcoming words.

Nicolas sighed strongly and, removing his hat, threw it on to the hall table. He came up to Friday, quite failing to understand the frantic signals Charles was making to him from behind Friday's back. When he spoke, it was in almost the normal manner he was accustomed to use with her.

"I beg your pardon, Friday, but I am sorely beset." He frowned in perplexity at his friend. "What *is* the matter, Charles?"

Friday glanced round, to find Delamere shrugging with assumed nonchalance.

"Nothing," he uttered innocently.

Oh, gracious! Charles was trying to warn Nick. And he had promised to keep silent! She felt her cheeks grow warm and she brushed past Nick. "I must go."

He detained her with a hand on her arm. "No, wait. Why did you come? Did you wish to speak to me?"

Through the spectacles Friday scanned his face. He looked worn, poor Nick. How he must be suffering! Her lips wavered on a smile.

"I did, but—but it no longer—I mean, I *can't*— Oh, Nick, it is of no consequence."

Nicolas was conscious of a tug of emotion that he did not recognise. He had just had the most appalling scene with Hermione. Worse, if anything, than yesterday. The last thing he wanted was another hysterical female on his hands. Only Friday was anything but hysterical, he reminded himself. Although she was distressed. He could tell that much. Or discomposed, at least. And she had not come here to pass the time of day with Charles.

"Stay a moment!" he uttered impulsively, and slipped his hand about hers. He looked at Delamere. "Forgive us for a space, Charles."

Next instant, Friday discovered that she had been drawn back into the yellow saloon, with the door shut, and was facing Nicolas, her fingers still tingling from the touch of his even though he had released them.

"Friday, I can explain. I mean about what happened yesterday. I should have done so before, but—"

"No!" she cried out. Then again, more calmly, "No, Nick. Don't try. I—know."

He bit his lip. "Yes, I thought you might. Caro?"

Friday nodded. "She did not mean to, Nick. But you know how it is with her."

"Her tongue runs like a fiddlestick and she does not realise what she says. Yes, I know."

He turned away and crossed the room slowly, wondering what he should say. He could not at this moment assure her that he would never see Hermione again, for, although he had managed to extract a promise from her that she would return to London today, he'd had to agree to meet her there to get it. For himself, the liaison was over. He had given to Friday the rights Hermione might have had, and he had no intention of violating them, whatever violence the wrench did—*was* doing—to his feelings.

"Friday—" he began, but she interrupted him.

"Nick, don't speak of it, pray," she begged quietly. "There is no need. If—if we are to go through with this, then let us obey the adage and say as little as possible."

His head turned and a frown was directed at her. Friday felt the puzzlement behind it as suspicion.

"Why do you say 'if'?"

She drew a painful breath and met his glance squarely. "Don't you feel there is some question about it?"

Nick could not imagine why he suddenly felt as if a great gaping hole had opened up under his feet. He was unaware of the rasp in his voice as he spoke. "That is what you came for, isn't it?"

Friday could not answer. She was conscious of the most unjustified sense of guilt. Heaven help her, what had *she* to feel guilty about? Nick's *emotions* would suffer nothing at all on her account, even if his personal situation was at stake. Had she offered for him under false pretences? No, she had not. Had she been coerced into taking the proffered marriage? No, she had accepted in good faith.

Oh, no, whispered the voice of conscience. She had *known*. Even at the instant of acceptance, she had known it was wrong to accept. She *was* guilty. More so now, when chance dangled before her the opportunity to redeem her fault. Set him free, Friday! Now. Do it *now,* she urged herself.

She opened her mouth to speak the fatal words. But all of a sudden from the hall came loud voices raised in argument, and the words died on her lips.

Barely had both occupants of the yellow saloon turned their heads towards the sound when the door burst open. In the aperture appeared a monstrous sight. A dame of large proportions, dressed in a travelling cloak that broke apart across a massive bosom, revealing a highly unsuitable muslin gown beneath. Under a feathered beaver hat, a round countenance, mottled with red patches of anger, directed a glare at Nick's astounded features.

"So!" boomed the creature in a formidable voice. "I find you, do I, Nicolas Weare?"

She advanced into the room, eyes snapping. Behind her, Delamere edged in, throwing up his hands in an eloquent gesture of helplessness.

"Just barged straight in, Nick. Couldn't stop her. Didn't even knock or ring the bell!"

"Knock? Ring?" echoed the extraordinary female, as if such matters of simple courtesy were unheard-of. She turned her embattled features upon her unwilling host. "I know you high and mighty folk and your country ways. Doors always unlocked. Not the same in town. And I know butlers. He wouldn't have let me in," she admitted with a candour that confirmed her words, and her gaze found Nick again. "But I want a word or two with you, young Weare, and I'm going to have 'em."

"What is it you want, Mrs Hesket?" asked Nick on a frosty note.

"Don't come that tone with *me,* you young jackanapes," rejoined the dame belligerently. "I've just come from the Green Man, my lad, and what I want to know is, *what* have you been doing to *my girl?*"

Chapter Five

The question rang round the saloon, seeming to bounce off the walls. Friday winced. This very odd female must be the girl's mother. She might be naïve in matters of the world, but Friday knew enough to recognise the type. Now she began to understand Caro's term "impossible"! A wave of compassion for Nick swept over her. How in the world was he supposed to deal with this?

Instead of answering the woman's question, Nicolas was moving towards Friday. He cast a glance at Mrs Hesket as he did so. "You will forgive me, ma'am, if I escort Miss Edborough to the door. After I have done so, I will be entirely at your disposal. Come, Friday."

"So!" burst from the female once again. "Friday, is it?"

To Friday's consternation, the empurpled features turned towards her. With some gratitude, she felt Nick's hand at her elbow, guiding her, and she began gingerly to approach the door, which Charles quickly went to hold open.

But Mrs Hesket shifted, placing her immovable

bulk in the way and holding up one pudgy hand. "No, you don't." She peered at Friday. "I take it you're his betrothed, the Edborough girl."

"Y-yes," Friday admitted hesitantly.

"What's this 'Friday' thing, then?"

"It is for Frideswid," she answered automatically.

"Mrs Hesket!" broke in Nick, trying to move on. "Stand aside, if you please."

The redoubtable dame turned on him. "I will not stand aside, young Nicolas Weare. As for you, ma'am, I'd as lief you stayed put yourself."

"Oh, no, pray!" Friday uttered feebly. "I *could* not."

"Ah, but you ought," argued Mrs Hesket. "Mean to marry him, don't you? Then it's well for you to know how he conducts himself. *And,* what's more, you'd do well to stay and be sure you *are* going to marry him. Because, young Weare—" snapping back to Nick with a threatening thrust of her voluminous chins "—if you've sullied my girl, there's no question but this here unfortunate young lady *ain't* going to be the one to marry you!"

Friday gaped at her, unaware that beside her Nicolas was standing rooted to the spot in disbelieving shock. When he had left Hermione at the Green Man, she had regained a measure of calm and was preparing to go back to her cousin's and pack her bags. Either Mrs Hesket was deliberately lying, or—

"Sullied!" echoed Delamere incredulously, breaking into the hideous thoughts that were flitting through Nick's mind. Charles let go the door-handle and moved into the fray. "Have you run mad, woman?"

"No, I've not, young saucepot—and I call you so

to your face, be you never so much a lord!—and if I've not come straight from finding my pretty in a flood of tears, screaming out her agony and that she's been betrayed, you may call me a Dutchwoman.''

''*What?*'' gasped Friday, finding her tongue.

''It's a damned lie!'' Nick said angrily, regaining his presence of mind. What had Hermione been *saying* to her mother, for God's sake?

''A lie, is it? Do you dare deny you were visiting her a bare minute before I got there myself?''

''I have no idea when you got there, Mrs Hesket, I am not a magician,'' Nick said acidly. ''But certainly I did visit Hermione at the Green Man. But if she has said *anything* to give you a false impression of my conduct—''

''Your conduct, young Weare, leaves a great deal to be desired!'' announced Mrs Hesket boomingly. ''You had no business visiting her at all, let alone scandalising the neighbourhood—which I'll be bound you *have* done, for you can't trust inn servants to keep their tongues—''

''Might point out,'' interrupted Charles, firing up in defence of his friend, ''that it was your girl who came up here after Nick. He was only trying to get her to go home again.''

''A fine way to do so, inveigling his way under her petticoats!''

There was a short silence. Friday began to feel unreal, as if this was not actually happening. It was an odd sensation whereby she was able to think clearly, but could feel nothing at all. It led her to behave with a calm that was far from the true state of her mind.

''You must be mistaken, Mrs Hesket,'' she said

quietly. "There is no possibility of Nicolas conducting himself in such an ungentlemanlike way."

"Thank you, Friday," Nick uttered gruffly, but his eyes were on Mrs Hesket. "I do not know, ma'am, what Hermione has said to you—"

"Said? *Said!*" reiterated the dame, setting her arms akimbo as she glared at him. "There was no making out anything she said, I'll have you know. Burst out crying fit to bust herself the second I stepped into the room. Couldn't make head nor tail of it—except that *you'd* been there, betraying her and all."

"If she used the word, ma'am," Nick said with some relief, "you may be sure she did not intend you to take it the way you have done. Good God, I have only seen her twice, and that scarcely above a half-hour!"

"Time enough, my lad, time enough," said Mrs Hesket. "But I can soon find out whether you've done the deed or no, and if I find—"

"Keep your tongue, Mrs Hesket, in the name of God!" begged Charles desperately, coming up to her. "Lady present, you know. Innocent ears!"

Friday almost laughed out. Inside her, the numbness was cracking, with little slivers of pain jutting through here and there. But she could still be amused at Delamere's assumption of her inability to cope with the woman's insinuations. Did he imagine she had no notion of what she meant?

"Don't concern yourself, Charles," she put in calmly, and then addressed herself to Mrs Hesket. "I am confident that your investigations will prove Nick's innocence, ma'am. You forget that he is engaged to me. I cannot think that he would commit so dishonourable an act in these circumstances."

"Easy to say," responded the woman grudgingly, adding with a lightning change of front, "but I'd say his lordship's in the right of it—you ought *not* know of such things! However, since you've mentioned it, I'll make no bones about saying more. You're bound to make the best of him, situated as you are, but *my* knowledge of men, ma'am, don't lead me to trust any single one of 'em, and that's a fact!"

"No doubt!" snapped Nick suddenly, drawing her fire. "How *dare* you come in here and make these insinuations in front of my affianced wife?"

"Nick, don't!" uttered Friday warningly, seeing the fat cheeks, in which the colour had died a little, flare up again.

"I beg your pardon, Friday, but it is quite intolerable!" he declared furiously. "I will not have you subjected to this all on my account." Seizing her arm in a grip made fierce by his own emotions, he turned on Mrs Hesket. "We will finish this with the gloves off, ma'am. *After* I have escorted Miss Edborough out of here."

"Hear, hear!" shouted Charles, and, taking Mrs Hesket unawares, grabbed her arm and tugged violently so that she was pulled sideways, out of the way.

Leaving the woman grappling with his friend, Nick dragged Friday to the door and wrenched it open. Too soon for a bevy of servants, who were crowded around, half bent to listen at the woodwork. Nick glared at them as they quickly moved away.

"Lady Delamere shall hear of this!" he threatened.

"Hush, Nick!" Friday begged in an urgent whisper. "Pray be calm, I beg of you!"

Nicolas ignored her plea, striding with her towards the front door which the butler—who had stood off, despising the practice of listening at keyholes, yet either unable or unwilling to prevent his juniors from so doing—was moving to open. As he did so, a hand thrust at it from the other side, and Hermione Hesket hurtled into the hall. By this time, Mrs Hesket, managing to rid herself of the frail barrier that Charles had set up, was just marching into the hall behind the departing couple. Thus it was she who made the first utterance.

"So!" she burst out in the usual way. "You hussy, what are you doing here?"

Brought up short by the sight of her mother advancing upon her, Hermione set up a whine. "I knew you would come here. Oh, I *knew*."

"Tattenhoe!" roared Delamere from the doorway to the yellow saloon. "What the devil is the entire domestic staff doing in the hall? Get rid of them, damn it!"

Upon which, there was a general scattering, the rest of the embarrassed principals herding back into the saloon as fast as they could. Mrs Hesket came last, driving her daughter before her with a series of whacks to her posterior.

"Get in there! Get in there, my girl, and look to your reputation!"

"Ma, don't!" wailed the girl protestingly, running ahead to evade the heavily avenging hand.

Friday, escaping from Nick's slackened hold, went away to the wide French windows and kept her back to the room, overcome by a reprehensible—and, she admitted, highly inappropriate!—fit of the giggles. She hardly realised it herself, but it was an inevitable reaction under the excessive strain of the past minutes. Behind her, she heard the argument rage on.

"Now then, my lad, look my girl in the face and tell me you ain't done nothing to ruin her chances?"

"Ask the girl, that's what I say," came from Charles. "Ask her!"

"Hermione, what have you been telling her?"

"I'll tell you what she's been telling me—"

"Ma, do be quiet! You're the one ruining my chances. Spoiled everything coming here, you have."

"Oh, I have, have I?" Mrs Hesket said ominously. "Let me tell you, my girl, I've come here on your behalf. You're to marry a lord and behave decently. I *won't* have you sullied."

That word again! thought Friday, her laughter quenched. So *ugly*. As if Nick *would*, no matter how much he loved her. Or would he? Her heart skipped a beat and she found herself listening hard to the conversation that had continued on. What had she missed?

"—must think I'm a fool, Ma," Hermione was saying. "I *know* how to do. If only you will *let me alone.*"

"Hermione, will you please inform your mother that I am innocent of the charge she is laying at my door?" Nick demanded irately. "You may quarrel as much as you choose with her later, but at this moment my honour is in question."

"Well?" Hard and cold, from Mrs Hesket.

Friday found that she was holding her breath, waiting for the reply.

"Well—well, no. I mean, yes. Nick is quite innocent."

Mrs Hesket exploded. "Oh, he is, is he? Then what do you mean, you brass-faced hussy, by telling me he'd *betrayed* you?"

''He has! He has!'' wailed Hermione. ''He means to cast me off only because he is going to be married.''

Friday whirled about at this, to see Miss Hesket moving to Nick, holding her hands up like a suppliant.

''Nick, you didn't mean it, did you? You didn't *really* mean it? I know you didn't! You *can't* have.''

''Hermione,'' Nick said sighingly, ''you know perfectly well I meant every word. You *promised* you would go back to town.''

''Yes, and you're going to come and see me there. You *said* so.''

''Oh, no, he is not!'' intervened Mrs Hesket, grabbing at her daughter's sleeve and confronting Nicolas. ''You'll leave well alone, young Weare. I don't trust you an inch! You might have curbed yourself this time, but there's no saying what might happen if you see her again. So you keep away! Understand?''

Before Nick could respond, Hermione had turned on her mother and begun to batter at her, her fists bounding off the rolls of flesh without apparently having any effect whatsoever. ''You let him alone, you! Let him alone!''

Mrs Hesket dealt her a slap, and she left off hitting out and wrenched away, moving to Nick. ''Don't heed her, Nick! You *can* see me. You can!''

''Oh, he can, can he?'' demanded her redoubtable mother, moving back into the fray. ''And what do you suppose his betrothed will have to say to that?''

Hermione's eyes looked wildly round and found Friday by the windows. Her gaze halted, and tears welled up, her features crumpling piteously.

Charles was heard to mutter, ''Oh, lord!'' and Nicolas took a step towards the girl, saying swiftly on a warning note,

"Hermione!"

But Miss Hesket's lips trembled into speech. "You won't begrudge me one *little* visit? Only one. There is—" hiccuping on a sob "—so much to *say* still. *Please.*"

"Oh, this is quite outrageous!" came from Nicolas suddenly as he recalled the callous way in which Hermione had spoken of a liaison between them *despite* Friday's possible feelings. How could she now make such a pathetic plea? He could see Friday's soft heart responding, and it sickened him. Desperately, he turned to Mrs Hesket.

"Ma'am, if you have any decency in you at all, you will remove from here and take Hermione with you. Anything that may need to be said may be said at some future time. This is no fit subject for the ears of my betrothed. Surely even you must see that?"

"What do you mean, *even* me?" demanded Mrs Hesket, a frown descending on to her brow which had just begun to lighten at the early part of this speech. But she advanced on her daughter nevertheless. "Come along, you!"

Hermione gave one last fluttering sigh at Friday, and then turned at her mother's urging and, flinging out her hands towards Nicolas, uttered brokenly, "Oh, Nick!" and burst into noisy sobs.

Delamere covered his ears, grimacing, and the incensed Mrs Hesket took her daughter strongly by one arm and one ear and began to drag her towards the door, muttering direful threats as she went.

Friday, her heart wrung, glanced quickly at her betrothed. "Nick, you *can't* let her treat the poor girl like this!"

But as Mrs Hesket opened the door it was clear from the sound of scattering footsteps that the servants had been regathering around it. Nick, who had taken a step or two forward with some thought of intervening, recognised the sound and turned away. Groaning, he sat down on the nearest straw-covered chair and dropped his head in his hands.

Charles Delamere uncovered his ears, and shouted for his butler again. "Tattenhoe! Escort them *out,* do you hear?"

Mrs Hesket could be heard alternately haranguing the unmoved butler and her daughter as she made her way down the hall.

"Wonderfully entertaining for you, eh? You see, you little minx, what you've done? Looked your fill, have you? Shut your noise, girl, do! *I'll* give you something to cry about, see if I don't!"

The sobs and complaints were abruptly cut off as the front door shut behind them. Friday was still benumbed, gazing dumbly at Nick where he sat in that dejected pose, when she felt a hand on her arm and looked up to find Charles beside her.

"Best go home, Friday. I'll escort you."

She blinked and shook her head a little as if to get rid of the cobwebs that appeared to be fogging her brain. "There is no need for that. I have Bruno—if he has not wandered away."

Allowing him to draw her towards the door, she glanced at Nicolas again and found him looking up at her. He rose quickly.

"Friday, we have to talk!" he uttered fretfully.

She shook her head quickly. Not now. She could

not possibly talk now. She might say what she might regret!

"Tomorrow, Nick. Come and see me tomorrow morning."

"Quite right," approved Charles. "Calm down. Think it all over. Talk then."

The last glimpse of Nick's face almost overset Friday, and she was obliged to fight down a lump in her throat. He looked so pale and harassed, so acutely distressed. Poor Nick. What a dreadful time he'd had!

As she left the house with Charles, she became aware of a faint resumption of those dreaded Hesket voices and, looking up, she saw the open carriage carrying them away, the heart-rending sobs of the girl echoing back to her.

Caro Cleeve swished up and down the length of the Edborough library at Finchamstod, animadverting bitterly on the dreadful consequences of yesterday's débâcle.

"To think that I had to sit and *listen* to those females, who did *not* believe me when I said it was all a nonsensical exaggeration, no matter how much I tried to laugh it off! I declare, I was never more furious with Nicky in my life!"

"It was not Nick's fault," Friday repeated tiredly from her window-seat for what felt like the fiftieth time. "He did his best to avert talk, you know."

"Avert talk! How could he possibly do so when there, apparently, was Mrs Hesket shouting all over the Green Man that Nick had *seduced* her wretched daughter? And all this before no fewer than three chambermaids, the landlady, the boots and—if my so-called *friends* are to be believed—even an ostler or two. Oooh!''

Friday began to think that Caro was the more put out by the fact that she had been obliged to endure the indignity of being unable satisfactorily to refute the gossip of her social inferiors, for the two females thus mentioned—the rector's wife and a young matron just barely genteel—were friends merely on a local basis.

''And if this was not enough,'' pursued Caroline crossly, ''some of those wretches in service at Delamere Place must needs report on all the goings-on in the yellow saloon, saying that *you*, Friday, did battle for Nick and *won*, sending the Heskets off with Hermione having screaming hysterics.''

''Well, *that* is at least true,'' remarked Friday feelingly. ''She made no bones about her distress, I admit. In fact, I can find it in me to pity poor Nick if he *does* marry her.''

Caroline paused in her pacing and turned a frantic eye upon her. ''Marry Miss Hesket? Oh, Friday, what in the world are you at now? You cannot—oh, you *cannot* mean to desert him now. If ever he needed you, it is at this moment.''

Friday winced. ''I knew you would say something of the sort. But you are wrong, Caro. Whatever he needs, it is not being betrothed to me. That has only complicated matters.''

''Friday, that is nonsensical! It is the best thing that could have happened to him.''

''No.'' She got up and came to Caroline, taking her hands in a warm clasp. She must try to make her understand. ''Can't you see, Caro? If he remains betrothed to me, how is he ever to feel confident that it is *right* for him? He must be allowed the freedom to *choose*. Not that I suppose—'' She broke off, dropping Caro's hands, and turned away.

Caroline frowned. ''You don't suppose he would choose you, is that it? I declare, Friday, you are enough to try the patience of a saint! You *have* him now. Why in the world must you risk your happiness by letting him go?''

''Because I am *dying,* Caro!'' broke from Friday, whipping round. Her lips trembling, her eyes, even under the huge concealing spectacles, showing dark with distress.

''Friday, don't talk nonsense!'' Caroline said sharply, but there was doubt in her face.

Friday shook her head. ''I don't mean literally. One does n-not actually *die* of love. But I *feel* as if I am dying. Inch by inch. Whatever the outcome, he *loves* her. And she him.'' A shiver shook her slim frame. ''I th-thought I could live with that, Caro. But I can't. I *can't.*''

It was at this inopportune moment that there came a knock at the library door. From outside, a voice spoke.

''Friday? Can I come in?''

''Nick!'' uttered Friday in an agitated whisper. ''Heaven give me strength!''

''Will you not think about it for a little while, Friday?'' asked Caroline urgently. ''*Don't* make a hasty decision.''

Friday shook her head firmly, taking a breath to steady herself. ''It's no use, Caro,'' she uttered low-voiced. ''My mind is made up.''

''Oooh!'' uttered Caroline frustratedly, and, going to the door, dragged it open, glaring into her brother's face as it appeared in the aperture. ''Well, you have what you wanted, Nicky. I trust you are satisfied. Whether Papa will be so is another matter altogether!''

Then she brushed past him and marched off down the hall, calling to the footman, who had accompanied her under the orders of her husband, for her carriage. Nick looked after her for a moment, and then came into the library and looked across to where Friday was standing, her back to him, apparently gazing out of the window.

Nicolas quietly closed the door, his eyes on his affianced bride. If he read Caroline aright, that was not likely much longer to be a correct appellation, he thought ruefully. Well, if that was Friday's intention, he could scarcely blame her for it.

He had spent an uncomfortable night. Even a liberal application of a hoped-for remedy from Delamere's cellars had not helped. In fact it had left him stone-cold sober, and deeply miserable. Much as he cared for Hermione, her behaviour had very much displeased him. Bad enough when he had visited her at the Green Man that she had subjected him to another wearing scene, extracting precisely the promises he did not want to give. But to approach *Friday!* To cry at her in that ill-bred way! It would not have angered him so much had Hermione not already made it abundantly clear to him that she cared *nothing* for Friday's feelings. True, she was very upset, and perhaps in that state she might be pardoned for not being able to wear another's shoes. But when he had seen her moving towards Friday he had been attacked by the most dreadful sensation. He had literally wanted to *kill* her. He could not understand such a feeling in himself! And towards Hermione, for whom he cared so greatly.

Later, talking it over with Charles, there had been a small crumb of comfort. For Delamere had offered a simple explanation.

"Tell you what. It's a close-run thing, this business of love, my mother says. Too akin to hate for comfort. Love one minute, hate the next. That's what she says."

It did not ring particularly true to Nick, but he supposed it might be so. In any event, it occupied very little of his thoughts. What troubled him the most was the thought of what Friday would do now. He could not rid himself of the conviction that she was almost certain to break off the engagement.

A week or so ago, nothing could have delighted him more. Why, then, did he find the idea so unpalatable? It was not as if he *wanted* to marry her. It was not even as if the betrothal had been in any respect happy for either of them. They had lost the ability to talk freely. They could barely look each other in the face! Surely to break off would allow them to recover the ease of their former friendship. So why in Hades did he dread the thought of Friday telling him it was all over?

Seeing her standing there, deliberately not looking at him—for she knew he was there, confound it!—brought all his dread to the fore again. Was this the way she intended to punish him? With a cold shoulder, a dignified silence?

"Friday?" he uttered hesitantly.

She turned slowly. To his utter astonishment there was a smile on her face. A very sweet, gentle smile.

"Hello, Nick," she said, moving forward and holding out her hand to him.

Mesmerised by her extraordinary manner, he moved forward, taking the hand and bringing it unconsciously to his lips. It felt cold to the touch, and he thought a quiver disturbed her countenance. A slight frown came to his brow.

"Are you all right?"

"Perfectly," she said, gently withdrawing her hand from his hold. She smiled again. "Come, Nick, don't frown! I have been thinking, you know, that we should all have been living on Olympus yesterday. I was reminded of nothing so much as the antics of the Greek gods."

A short laugh was surprised out of him. "Oh, indeed? And who am I supposed to be? Zeus of the ever-roving eye, I dare say?"

"Which would make me Hera," Friday pointed out. "The jealous goddess."

Nick's brows snapped together. "Are you jealous? You need not be."

"Oh, I think I should have to be," Friday said lightly, "if you were to conduct yourself like Zeus."

Did she mean *not* to end it, then? He felt quite at a loss, disorientated. She should be angry, upset. Instead she was treating the whole affair as a joke. Or was she? He scanned her face. The spectacles hid the truth of her eyes from him, for the light hit the glass and kept them partially obscured. Was there a tightness about her mouth? The freckles must disguise any paling of her countenance. It struck him suddenly that, for all their long friendship, he did not really *know* Friday.

She moved away a little as if his searching scrutiny

disturbed her. The faintest of tremors sounded in her
voice when she spoke again.

"I have been trying to think which of the classical
creatures I am reminded of by that dreadful female."

"Mrs Hesket? Oh, a Gorgon," he said instantly.

Friday cocked her head on one side. "Medusa?
Yes, she might turn anyone to stone, I should think."
She managed a laugh. "And poor Charles, trying so
hard to be a Perseus."

"And there you had better stop," warned Nicolas,
mock-severe, "before you start fancying yourself An-
dromeda, and saddling me with some equally fatuous
identity chosen from your endless stock of idiotic
characters that never existed outside the imagination
of your fanciful Greek poets."

It was a remark calculated to arouse Friday's indignation. She began indeed to respond in the usual
way. "They may not be *quite* true to life, but to suggest that it is all…"

Her voice died as it struck her how reminiscent this
exchange had become of former times. That teasing
note was back. Oh, how long it seemed since she had
heard it last!

"Oh, come, Friday! The word is 'myth.' You ought
to consult Dr Johnson's Dictionary, I believe, for you
have evidently not properly understood it."

Friday quickly removed her spectacles, for tears
were pricking at her eyes. But she must *try* to follow
it up. "*Believe* is precisely—" Her voice gave out
and she quickly turned away.

"Friday!" uttered Nick in quite a different voice.
He took a hasty step towards her and, taking her
shoulders, jerked her round to face him, cursing as
she looked up involuntarily. "Confound it! I *knew*

you were distressed. Why are you trying to conceal it from me?''

Friday pulled away. ''Because I think we have had enough of scenes,'' she said huskily. ''Let us, for goodness' sake, save what we can from the wreck!''

''You do mean to end it!'' Nick exclaimed, conscious of an odd tightness about his chest. He took a step back, staring into her uncovered eyes, the strain there visible. God! What had he put her through? He reached out unconsciously, and his finger lightly caressed her cheek. ''Poor Friday! I never meant to hurt you.''

Tears stung her eyes, but Friday winked them away, her lips quivering a little as she tried to smile. ''Pray don't concern yourself over me. You are the one in trouble. I only wish I had released you before—as I promise you I wanted to do.''

''Did you?'' He sighed heavily. ''Well, you have every right, I can't deny that. I am only sorry it has come to this.''

Friday replaced her spectacles, saying in a firmer tone, ''It must always have done so, Nick, given the circumstances. And I am sure you will not rue the day. Once you have got over all this dreadful embarrassment, you will be happier with your freedom.''

From behind the safety of the eyeglasses, she looked for relief in his face. It was not there. He was frowning at her, the beautiful features more solemn than she remembered to have seen them.

''And you?'' he asked, with a hard edge to his voice. ''Will you be happier, Friday?''

''I—don't know,'' she managed, although she felt as if the swelling grief in her chest must choke her. ''I *think*...yes.''

Something flashed in his eyes, and was gone again. His face softened and he came closer, taking up one of her hands and holding it between both his own.

"Forgive me, Friday, but I *must* ask you this. I can't help but suppose—I mean, your father must have had your best interests at heart. He would not have—he must have *thought* you could be happy with me."

Friday glanced away. Gracious, what could she say? Of course Papa had thought it. But he had not known—*could* not know—how deep her feelings went. She drew a breath and brought her gaze to bear on his face again.

"Papa was in *error*. At least, not—not *quite* that, but—it was all a mistake, Nick. He took a notion into his head. He said *nothing* of it to me, or I would have—it should never have happened, and I am sorry for it." She withdrew her hand from his hold, and continued more calmly, "In any event, I believe *your* father can scarce blame you for the outcome."

Nick gave a mirthless laugh. "You don't know him!"

Concerned, Friday looked into his face. "What can we do? Should I perhaps write to him and—and explain?"

"Good God, no, Friday!" He shuddered. "*No*. That would be worse than anything. Oh, don't fear for me." He grinned briefly. "At worst, I shall batten on Caro and Richard. Or Delamere. Besides, though I dare say my father *may* carry out his threat, I cannot believe that he will not come round in the end. He only forced the issue because—"

He broke off, the realisation coming home to him that Friday knew it all. *All* of it, confound it! Every last detail. How could he ever have done this to her? What could be more *insulting* than to know that a man had been made to offer for a woman with all but a pistol to his head?

"Oh, God, Friday, I am so ashamed!" he jerked out. "How *could* I have—that you should have been subjected to such—?"

"Nick, don't!" she begged quickly. "We have been friends for *so* long. It is only natural that you turned to me."

"Yes, but I *didn't* turn to you. If only I had told you it all at the outset!"

Friday shook her head. "You could not have done so. I see that quite clearly. Besides—" she hesitated, her breath catching "—it would have made no difference. Perhaps...perhaps it is all just part of growing up. Or growing—*apart*."

The break in her voice wrung Nick's heart. He watched her fingers come up to remove the spectacles and knew by that how close she was to tears. Did she imagine he could not *tell* why she always did that? he wondered tenderly. She was not looking at him, but she had not turned away. He wanted to put his arms about her, but there was something in her pose that gave him pause. A dignity that distanced him, and yet touched him at the same time.

"I dare say," he began, wanting to offer some comfort and understanding, however small, "that it may take a little while before we can resume our former relationship."

Friday's head came up then, and the valiantly held-in tears seeped from her eyes, reddening her nose and lips. Oddly, Nick felt no repulsion. Indeed he was struck by the stark contrast between Friday's courage and Hermione's conduct in similar circumstances. Her words, therefore, little more than a croak, fell upon his ears with stunning effect.

''Yes, well, that is the reason for my distress, you see. I cannot see *any* possibility of our resuming our former relationship.''

He stared, conscious of a sinking feeling at the pit of his stomach. A faint question entered his voice as he responded, ''Not in the immediate future perhaps, no.''

On a note of flat finality she answered him. ''No, Nick. Not *ever*.''

Chapter Six

Lord Weare eyed his younger son in a puzzled way. He had poured the vials of his wrath upon the boy, but Nicolas had behaved in a most uncharacteristic fashion. He had stood without a vestige of defiance in his face, neither wincing at the verbal hammers flung his way nor attempting to mitigate their weight. It was as if the deluge of words passed over him, touching him not at all.

Running down, Weare stared at him in frustrated silence, champing. At length he could bear it no longer. "Well, boy, well? Have you a tongue in your head?"

"I have, sir," Nick said shortly.

Weare waited. When nothing more was forthcoming, his fists banged on the arms of his chair. "Then *say* something, damn you!"

Nick shrugged. "What is there more to say? I have told you what occurred, sir. I have expressed my regret."

"Regret? Ha! Don't tell me."

"You will believe what you wish, of course," Nick said evenly. "I await your judgement, that is all."

"Oh, you do, eh?" Lord Weare champed again, nonplussed. What the devil did the boy mean by this meek acceptance?

His lordship would have been even more puzzled had he known that Nicolas did not even *care* any more. He would not himself have believed that he could feel so bereft. He'd had no idea that Friday's friendship meant that much to him. But the acute stab of pain she had dealt him with those simple words "not ever" lingered as a dull ache that never seemed to go away.

Out of the instant protest that had consumed him he had thrown a senseless accusation at her. "Is this revenge, Friday?"

She had shaken her head. He had seen the wetness gathering under her eyes in the blue shadows that had been concealed by those infernal eyeglasses. He had wanted to snatch them from her hands and grind them under his heel. Why he did not know, but he had felt quite *savage* about the things.

"Not revenge," she had said quietly, her voice raw with the emotion she was trying to control. "I would not wish to hurt you, Nick. You must know that."

But she *was* hurting him. Only he had not said so. Without knowing what he did, he had taken her by the shoulders and known by her wincing that his grip was too strong. But he had ignored it, wanting to make her *feel* his hurt.

"Then what reason could you possibly have for saying we cannot ever be the way we were together?"

A tremulous smile had pierced him with some unnamed emotion, but before he could identify it she'd thrown him into a worse case.

"A very selfish reason," she had said, and then he

had felt her pull his head down and her lips had been pressed fervently to his own. His loins had sparked and he'd jerked in shock.

Next instant, Friday was gone from under his hands and had run out of the library, leaving him a prey to dejection. And a confusion of ideas that he was still unable to sort out. All he knew was that his life was a mess, and it would make no difference to him now whatever he did. If his father cut him off, so be it.

But Weare did not appear to be in the mood for casting off his son. "I suppose I need not blame you for that Hesket woman's actions," he grumbled grudgingly at length. "As long as you're cured of that foolish *tendre* for as worthless a chit as ever drew breath."

That did draw Nick's fire. He might be upset about Friday, but that did not mean he could tolerate his father's animadversions upon Hermione. But his reproach was couched in far less boyish terms than of yore.

"How you deal with me is as you wish, but I will be obliged to you, sir, if you will refrain from making odious comments about Miss Hesket."

"Be obliged, will you?" grunted his father. "And do you think it's my intention to oblige you?"

"No, I do not," Nick said coldly. "Yet even a man on the scaffold is granted a last request."

"Last request? Last request? What do you take me for, a damned executioner?"

Nick's lips tightened a little. "I wish you will get it over with, sir. Or shall I save you the trouble and take myself off?"

"You'll go when I tell you and not before!" roared Weare. His jaws worked for a moment or two. Then he waved an impatient hand. "Very well, very well. That'll do. But mind this. If you dare attempt to marry that girl, you may count yourself penniless and out-cast."

"Familiar words, sir," Nick said in a steely voice, "which I seem to recall hearing before on account of Friday."

"Damn your impudence!" burst out his father. "Time was a remark like that would have earned you a whipping."

"Time was, sir," retorted Nick, with a flash of his old manner, "you'd have had strength enough to ad-minister it!"

"Ha!" barked his father, surprising Nicolas with an unmistakable tone of satisfaction. "That's more like you! Beginning to think you'd lost your steel, boy."

Nick's eyes flashed. "Do you mean to tell me you have been deliberately goading me?"

"Pah! Nothing of the sort. But I'm damned if I want to see any son of mine knuckle under the blows of fate."

For a moment or two Nick eyed him incredulously. Then his shoulders relaxed a little and a sigh escaped him. He moved across to the window of the green saloon and gazed out over the lawns. Without turning round, he spoke again, a little wearily.

"I do not know, sir, if you take pleasure in indulg-ing in some sort of game with me. I wonder if you have the slightest inkling of the harm that has come out of this sorry mess?"

"Blaming me now, are you?" came Weare's voice behind him on a slightly querulous note. "My fault, I dare say, that you choose to fall for some cheap—

oh, very well, very well,'' he snapped as Nick's reproachful eyes turned towards him. "I'll keep mum for that, since you seem to have *some* sense in your head.'' As his son's eyes went back to the window, he burst out testily, "*What* harm, damn your eyes?''

Nick turned. There was no longer reproach in the green eyes, but Lord Weare could not but be moved—however unwillingly!—by the look he saw there.

"You forced me into *using* Friday, sir. Oh, I don't blame you. I dare say you thought you were acting for the best. But the *outcome*. God, but I'd give anything to undo it!''

"Pah! Nonsense. Both young. Soon get over it.''

"Get over it? Do you think one so easily gets over the loss of a valued friendship? My God! I started out to take advantage of what Friday could offer me in terms of position. Now I have neither that—which I did not want, let me add!—nor the companionship of an intelligent, stimulating and amusing female, with the tenderest heart of anyone I have ever met!''

Lord Weare considered him, his brows rising. "Ain't what you said about your precious Friday when she was proposed as a wife for you.''

"I know that!'' Nick said, snapping all at once. "I was—taken by surprise. I didn't *know* her—not really.''

He meant it. He had never thought of her in the light of anything but just *Friday,* the companion of his youth. But he had been confronted with a woman—a creature of wayward moods and complex emotions, as were all women. No, he had not really known her.

"In any event,'' he uttered gruffly, "it is not as a

prospective wife that I miss her. She was my *friend,* Papa! God, can you not grasp that?''

Weare only grunted in response, but his keen gaze never left his son's face.

Nick turned away again, but his mind's eye showed him a far different picture from the rolling lawns presented to his view outside. A picture of Friday as she used to be: laughing under the owl-like eyeglasses, showering her warmth over him as they sat on her hilltop retreat. And never once—never *once*—had it so much as crossed his mind to take even the slightest advantage of their unnatural freedom. Due solely, as he was well aware, to Sophia Edborough's carelessness of these matters. By rights they should have been chaperoned ever since they met. They had both been quite old enough for an amorous entanglement. But, as God was his witness, until she had kissed him that last ghastly day, he would never have *dreamed* that he could be aroused by little Friday Edborough. He was not. Not really. It was just that she had taken him unawares. Though she *was* a woman, she was *not* sensual to him. She was his *friend.* Had been, he reminded himself disconsolately. That was gone now, apparently forever.

''What of the Hesket girl, then?'' demanded his father suddenly. ''Hermia, or whatever her name is.''

''Hermione,'' corrected Nick, coming to himself with a jolt. Hermione! He had not thought of her in *hours.*

''I warn you,'' pursued Weare. ''Won't tolerate you running off with the wench, or anything romantical of that sort.''

Nick cast him an all but scornful glance. ''Have no

fear, sir. I have had my fill of scandal, I thank you. I am intent now on only one thing.''

''What's that, if I may make so bold as to ask?'' queried his lordship ironically.

''To show my face in town, sir, that my acquaintance have no excuse to call me coward.''

That this disclosure pleased Lord Weare was obvious from the way he rubbed his fists on the arms of his chair. But it did not prevent him from issuing another warning. ''Well, mind you don't show your face in the wrong quarter.''

Nick made an impatient movement. ''I assure you, sir, Mrs Hesket is as much opposed to a projected union between myself and her daughter as are you.''

''Damn her impudence!'' burst out his lordship. ''Not that I care for her wishes. What matters, my boy, is whether this pernicious pair can be kept from causing more talk.''

What mattered in his own view, Nick thought bitterly, was that without Friday's friendship even the prospect of seeing Hermione could not enchant him. Particularly if she meant to treat him to another fit of hysterics! If the truth was to be faced, he had lost *both* of them. For Hermione had made it clear that she would not marry him. Anything else was repugnant to him. Even if it did not mean Friday's betrayal he *could* not violate another man's rights. God, could he tolerate it himself? A female who was his must be his alone. As he would be hers—given that he loved her.

Friday was walking, in a place of secret enchantment. It did not seem to her unfamiliar, despite the misty outlines on the frosted trees. The turf under-

neath her feet was springy so that the bursting of ex-
uberance in her breast was enhanced, and she threw
herself into the air. Nick caught her as she fell again,
and they tumbled together to the soft ground, rolling
and laughing.

When they stilled, she was beneath him, his form
pinning her to the ground, his countenance above her
own alight with a radiance echoed in her own heart.

''Do you know how much I love you?'' he asked
softly.

She smiled up at him, somehow free of the loath-
some spectacles, somehow beautiful—the freckles
gone, the poor features transformed into a pleasing
whole that was worthy of the handsome ones mirrored
in her eyes.

''No, tell me,'' she begged.

''This much,'' said Nick, and his lips came down
to claim her own in a kiss so inflaming that she felt
it the length of her body.

The heat was so intense that she erupted into wake-
fulness, and threshed a little under the sheets, blinking
into the darkness. Realisation hit.

''Oh, heaven help me, not *again*,'' she groaned
aloud.

Or thought she did. But she could not be sure, for
sleep claimed her once more and there he was—sitting across the table, supping on a syllabub, his eyes
teasing her over the spoon, wicked in the candlelight.

''Do you know what I would like to do to you?''

Friday glanced quickly round for the servants, but
there seemed to be none. They were quite alone.
There was the four-poster at the other end of the ballroom. It did not seem at all odd that they should be

consuming their meal together in one little corner of this huge place.

"Show me," Friday said, and watched him rise from his chair.

How they arrived there she did not know, but the very next instant they were lying together in the bed. An enormous bed that might comfortably have accommodated ten people. Except for the fact that anyone else would have found themselves pushed out by the frantic activity of the principal couple.

Friday sighed and moaned under the feel of Nick's hands ranging over her limbs. Nick's lips were seeking out her own, and some nameless unknown force deep inside her hidden depths was pounding blood into her heart.

She awoke with a start, dragging herself bolt upright, eyes wide and staring at the enveloping blackness of her own curtained bed. The palpitating wound within began to ache as her pulse echoed the dream, hitting at her breath so that she panted in bewildered panic.

Then she remembered. A half-sob escaped her. In silent anguish, she wept despairingly, drawing up her knees and covering her head as it dropped down.

Every night. *Every night* it was the same. The days were manageable. She could force her unruly mind into safer channels. Walk the crochets out of her system. Read her favourite classics, study the Latin in which she was not nearly as proficient as Greek. *Anything* somehow to distract herself. But oh, these nights! She had begun to dread their coming—with a vengeance. For, out of her own control, her treacherous thoughts revealed themselves in these insidious *living* dreams.

Her breath caught on the sobs as the memory sent a knife-thrust into her bosom. Dear lord, those dreams! Sweet, secret, aching dreams. Impossible, fatuous dreams in which Nicolas loved her as dearly, as passionately as she loved him. Dreams for which she *cursed* those classics that had given her so much knowledge. Too much! For the passions of the gods were so familiar to her that she could readily arouse them in herself. Passions of which, as an unmarried female, she ought to know nothing.

Oh, but she knew! She knew how it would feel to have his arms about her. How his lips would caress her own. Too well she knew it. For she had felt them so strongly in that last, desperate kiss. A kiss she regretted in every respect. She must have given herself away so thoroughly. Her unruly heart leapt at the thought, but her eyes shed saltier tears for the shame she felt.

If that were but all! Before, her dreams had never led her to *this*. Now she was trapped, caught up in the throes of her own imagination, for she had sipped at the wine and found it sweet. The taste lingered, filling her with longings that could never be fulfilled. Oh, Nick! Why had she ended it? At least if she had married him these unnatural yearnings might have been stilled.

Common sense dictated that this was absurd reasoning. Would slaked desire make up for a lifetime of unrequited emotion? No, it would not. But common sense did not dwell in the small night hours, when Friday's truth came haunting her out of her rebellious heart. She loved Nicolas Weare, and to live without him was *anguish*.

Dropping back to her pillows, Friday curled up into

a protective ball, dragging the back of her hand across the dampness of her cheeks, and staring into the darkness, afraid to fall asleep again.

Morning brought relief, of a sort. She had little idea of her wan looks for it was seldom she glanced into a mirror, and then only with her eyeglasses on her nose so that the worst ravages of her disturbed nights were hidden. In the library after breakfast, she worked at her Latin, struggling through a political tome that could add not the tiniest iota to her troubled sleep. Not for her now those favourite tales of love and passion penned by the Greeks to worsen the relentless visions that plagued her. Beside her, Bruno dozed, apparently peacefully. Friday could only envy him.

Her thoughts strayed from the discussion under her hand, in which wise men debated the desirability or otherwise of having a Caesar. She seemed to have been dwelling in this unsatisfactory state for months, although it could only have been a matter of weeks in reality. Nick, she knew from Caro, was in London. She was happy to think that Lord Weare had refrained from carrying out his threat—and deeply hurt, if the truth were told, that it had been made at all to wreck her peace if he had not *meant* it. It seemed to make the whole episode worthless, and her present state of mind an unnecessary infliction that she might have been spared.

She did not hear her father enter the library, not even alerted by Bruno's raised head. She did not realise that she was sitting gazing unseeingly at bookshelves against the wall opposite the desk at which she worked, her spectacles held lightly in her hands, and the path of an unregarded tear tracing down her cheek.

Mr Edborough was in front of her before she noticed him. "What are you doing, Friday?"

She blinked. "Studying Latin, Papa."

"No, you are not," he uttered sternly. "You are moping!"

Friday looked down, fiddling with her spectacles. "Why—why should you think so?"

"Do you think I'm blind?" snapped her father. Then his tone softened. "Come, child, don't try to hide it from me, I beg of you."

Tears sprang to Friday's eyes again. Dropping her spectacles, she covered her face with her hands. "Oh, Papa, I am so *wretched*."

In a moment, her father had come around the desk and was drawing her up and into a close embrace. She cried a little into his chest, made use of his handkerchief, and soon found herself sitting on her favourite window-seat with her father's arm still about her, and his kind voice pleading with her to talk to him.

"It—it is just the nights, you see," she told him lamely. "I cannot—sleep very well."

"Fretting into your pillows, I dare say."

"Yes, and—dreaming." A hesitant, hushed confession.

Mr Edborough nodded sympathetically. "Nightmares, eh? I've suffered from them myself in bad times."

"If only they were!" Friday uttered unguardedly.

Her papa glanced down into her face. "What do you mean?"

Friday bit her lip, and then sighed. How could she explain? One could scarcely reveal the contents of such dreams! "Oh, it is just that—that in the past, you see, I could readily daydream about…him."

"Go on." There was a grimness in Edborough's voice at the mention of Nick, but he refrained from repeating the adverse comments that had poured out of him when he had heard from his daughter of the broken engagement and the reasons for her decision.

Friday caught the note, and, without quite knowing that she did so, seized his hand and clutched it, looking up at him. "Papa, don't blame Nick. It is not his fault that I feel as I do."

Edborough sighed heavily. "I should never have done it. I ought to have talked to you first."

"Don't distress yourself, Papa. You could not have known."

Indeed, she reflected, she had been ignorant herself. As little as Papa had she recognised the depths of her own emotions. Until she had glimpsed the promised land, unleashing a furnace within herself that she was now quite unable to control, she had been damping down an unsuspected fire. That was why she'd had to prevent Nick from thinking that they might readily take up where they had left off before all this began. For she knew that the torture of seeing him now—as *only* the friend he had been—must be unendurable. She struggled to put this into words that her father might understand—without actually saying it.

"There was never any *hope,* you see. That's the difficulty now. When it was just a dream that I never expected to see come true, I could bear it. But now— to have been offered the *chance,* even for the briefest time that I believed in the possibility, and to have it snatched away again—"

Her voice broke, and Mr Edboroughs's arm

squeezed tighter about her. In a voice of bitter self-reproach, he said, "I wish I had not done it, Friday. I thought it would make you happy. I thought you cared for the boy."

"Oh, I do!" she uttered huskily. "Only it wasn't *real* then. Now it is too much so to dream on…" Speech failed her for a moment or two, but she drew a breath to steady herself, and managed to lie valiantly. "It is n-not so *very* bad, Papa. It will pass."

"Not if it is anything like the feeling between myself and your mama," prophesied Mr Edborough gloomily. "It is the most extraordinary thing. She may irritate me beyond measure, but the strength of my passion for her just will not admit of the slightest defeat."

Friday could say nothing to this. At the present moment, she wanted to believe that her own feelings *might* pass. Not that she was herself in any way convinced!

"The oddest part of it," pursued her father, apparently gathered up into his own thoughts, "is that it happened so quickly. When we met, it was like a clap of thunder. And there we were."

"Only it was mutual," Friday observed quietly. "That is the difference."

Mr Edborough turned, as if he would say something more, but a knock at the door interrupted them. A footman entered. Glancing across, he noted the master sitting with the member of the household he was seeking.

"I beg your pardon, sir," he said apologetically, "but Mrs Cleeve is wishful to speak with Miss Friday."

Friday's heart missed a beat. Caro! That could only

mean news of Nick. Everything went out of her head. All the heartache of the dreadful nights, all the sensible decisions she had taken, all the stern admonitions she had made to herself. If there was something to know of Nick, then she *must* know it!

Hardly pausing to excuse herself to her papa, she jumped up, snatched her spectacles from where she had left them on the desk and dashed out of the library, taking in on the fringe of her consciousness the footman's hurriedly uttered, "In the morning-room, Miss Friday."

Caroline Cleeve had been pacing impatiently about this rosy setting. In the last week or so, her belly had suddenly begun to protrude under the figured muslin gown, and in the way of ladies thus encumbered she had thrust aside the warm woollen cloak she wore against the November cold, placing supportive hands in her lower back as she marched up and down. She halted as the door opened and struck an unconscious pose, her condition showing proud as she stood, her pretty features scanning eagerly for the face she sought.

"Friday, you will never guess!" she exclaimed almost before her hostess had entered the room and shut the door behind her. "I have been *itching* to tell you ever since I heard it."

From Caroline's expression, Friday could not tell whether the news was good or bad. It mattered little. Her heart had leapt into her throat, choking her. Wild half-thoughts chased one another around her brain, visions that she could not have identified if she had wanted to—except that they had Nicolas centred indelibly in them all.

"What?" she uttered hoarsely. *"What?"*

Caroline released her hold on her own back and threw her hands out for emphasis. "Hermione Hesket is engaged to be married!"

The blow hit hard. Friday stood dead still, blankness in her head. She felt as if she had been struck in the chest with a bullet. She knew, in some vague recess, that she was still alive, because she was breathing. But her eyes did not see and her ears did not hear.

Awareness returned little by little. A buzzing irritation invaded both sight and sound. As it resolved, she recognised Caro's pretty face and high-pitched voice, but the words she was uttering made no impression at first. When they did, it seemed incredible to her that what had just taken place inside her had apparently not even registered.

"Of course I could scarcely *believe* it, as you may suppose," Caroline was saying, "but there it was in black and white, irrefutably. I declare, I was so shocked that even Dicky was obliged to take notice—which he *never* does, let me tell you, for he says I chatter about nothing and he will *not* bear it at breakfast."

"Was it in the *Gazette?*" To Friday's own surprise, her voice was quite steady, although she spoke automatically, still possessed by a light-headed sensation, as if she were not really there.

"Yes, did I not say so? I was reading over the notices, for I always do. Especially at *this* time of year, when the season is ending and there are *bound* to be some interesting announcements."

Interesting! Was that how she saw it? Friday could have laughed, if the necessary apparatus had been operational, which it was not. Nothing was so in the odd state in which she found herself. She could not think beyond the immediate necessity for speech.

"When is the wedding?" she asked. And immediately wished she had not. She did not want to know the answer to that.

"Before Christmas, so it was stated," Caro replied. "*That* does not surprise me. Of course, Aymestrey is bound to want to have it as quickly as possible, for if his old mother should get wind of *Mrs* Hesket's origins she might well come out of retirement and try to put a stop to it."

Friday blinked. Caro's conversation no longer made sense. Struggling with the still present fragmentation of her attention, she forced herself to concentrate.

"What do you mean, Caro?"

Caroline waved impatient hands. "But I have told you! I am talking of the Dowager Lady Aymestrey, you know. Oh, of course you *don't* know. I keep forgetting how little acquainted you are with the world, Friday. Well, take it from me that she would *not* approve, be it never so much his second marriage. Though he has an heir already. In fact, I believe there are *two* boys, for his first wife died in childbed and I *think* that was a male."

Friday thought she was going to scream. Either Caro had gone mad or she, Friday, was dreaming again! A nightmare this time, for nothing that she was saying made any sense at all.

"Caro, *what* are you talking about?" she demanded despairingly.

Caroline gaped at her. "Have you not been listening to me, Friday? I am talking of Hermione Hesket's engagement, of course."

A great light dawned on Friday suddenly. ''You mean she is engaged to this Lord Aymestrey?''

''*Yes*. Have I not been telling you so forever?''

Relief poured over Friday in a wave, making her dizzy. She clutched at air for support, and found her fingers seized in Caro's hands.

''Not *again*,'' wailed Caroline.

Next moment, Friday had been thrust into the sofa, where she sat, half laughing, clutching at her palpitating heart with both hands. Seated beside her, Mrs Cleeve anxiously demanded to be told what in the world was the matter with her.

''I th-thought you meant she was engaged to N-Nick!'' Friday managed on a sobbing note. She was laughing and crying together, the dreadful blankness of mind beginning to recede.

''Engaged to *Nick!*'' echoed Caroline on a shriek. ''Have you taken leave of your senses? Do you think I would have been chattering on like this had that been the case? I should have posted straight off to London to remonstrate with him! Oh, Friday, you *idiot*. Here I had come in *such* delight, to tell you that the dratted female was out of our path at last, and what do you do? All but fall down in a faint!''

''I beg your p-pardon, Caro,'' Friday said, catching her breath at last, ''but if you *knew* what I have been through.''

As if she was seeing Friday for the first time, Mrs Cleeve took in the altered state of her countenance. She frowned direfully, seizing her friend by the shoulders and pulling her round to face her.

''Friday, take off those horrid eyeglasses and let me look at you!'' Suiting the action to the word, her fingers plucked the offending spectacles away and she glared into Friday's face. "What in the *world* have you been doing to yourself? You look *dreadful*."

"Do I?" Friday tried to turn her face away. "I—I have not been sleeping too well."

"I can see that! And you have been *weeping* your heart out. I declare, Friday, you are the most *frustrating* person to deal with that I have ever met! Why did you send him off if you want him so much? Not that I blamed you, in the circumstances. But for heaven's sake let bygones be bygones! Call him back and tell him that you have changed your mind. Especially *now*."

"But I have *not* changed my mind," Friday burst out, pulling away and rising quickly to her feet. "*Especially* now."

Caro remained seated, watching her friend begin to pace the morning-room, much as she herself had done earlier. "Why not? *Why* not? You are quite obviously *dreadfully* unhappy, and—"

"Yes, I am unhappy," Friday confessed, turning on her fiercely, "but do you think Nick is any the less so? If I am feeling this way because I have lost him, how do you imagine he is feeling having lost Hermione?"

"Relieved, I should think," Caro stated baldly. "Men *hate* the sort of riot and rumpus she kicked up. I dare say he is thanking his stars for his deliverance."

Friday shook her head. "No. He might have been a trifle put out at the time, but he must soon have forgotten it when he saw her again in town—when he was *free*. I was in the way, Caro, don't you see?"

"I see that you are even more woodenheaded than

my nincompoop of a brother!'' declared Caroline crossly. "*Send* for him, Friday. *Ask* him.''

"Ask him what? Whether he is glad to be rid of her?''

"Yes, yes, *yes!*''

Friday stared at the fuzzy blob of Caro's face, for she had forgotten to retrieve her spectacles. She could not see her expression, but the vehemence of the near shriek on which she ended rang still in her ears. Send for Nick and ask him about Hermione Hesket? It was preposterous. It was outrageous. She *could* not do it…could she? A sigh escaped her, and she dropped back down into the sofa.

"Oh, Caro, why must you come here with your insistent illogic and undermine everything I have sorted out in my mind? If not for you and your persuasions, I would never have become embroiled in all this, for I would have ended the matter days before that female came anywhere near the place.''

"It is too late to think of that now,'' Caro said practically. "The point is *she* is now to be married. Which means that—''

"No!'' Friday said sharply. "No, Caro.''

As she turned to the other woman, she saw the familiar shape of her eyeglasses resting in Caroline's lap and reached out for them, firmly jamming them back into position on her face. They gave her confidence, for she at once felt more like herself.

"You are trying to say that the field is clear now for my marrying Nick, I understand that. That is why you came with this news.''

"Of course it is, and—''

"Caro, listen to me! The betrothal was a mistake from start to finish. Whether Nick is in love with Hermione Hesket or if he is only infatuated is not really the issue. He is *not* in love with me.''

''But *you* are in love with him,'' asserted Caroline.

Friday nodded. ''Yes, that is just why I cannot marry him. Had my feelings been equal with his—a fondness for a friend—then we might have been happy together. Many successful marriages are based on such a foundation.''

''Well, then.''

''Caro, *think*. You are married to Dick. You are *daily* in his company. It is well-known that you are one of the fondest couples in the neighbourhood.'' She smiled a little as Caroline blushed, and reached out to take her hand and squeeze it. ''Think but a little. I don't *know* how you conduct yourselves when you are alone together, but I may perhaps guess. What if you could *not* be natural with him, for fear of importuning him with unwanted attentions? What if you must put a curb on every word, every look, every little natural observance that your love dictated to you? Shame alone would keep you silent and guarded, if not fear that he might become angry to find you hanging on his sleeve.''

Caro Cleeve was silent, dismay writ large in her countenance. ''I never thought of it like that.''

''No, because you had no reason to,'' Friday pointed out. ''But I have long years of concealment behind me, Caro. I could do it *then,* for I had no thought of any possible future with Nick. I had assumed he would marry some day, and had steeled myself to bear it. I *could* have borne it. But to be day by day in his presence and hide my heart—no, a thousand times!''

"Then what is to be done?" demanded Caroline, pouting.

"Nothing," Friday said wearily.

"You will not even see him?"

Friday shook her head. "I *cannot*."

"No, because you are afraid you will give in to what you really want," Caro guessed shrewdly.

"And if I am, is it to be wondered at?"

Caroline eyed her, thinking deeply for a moment. Then she stood up in a determined way. "Very well, then. If you will not send for him, I shall."

At once the pulse began to throb in Friday's veins. Quickly she too rose and faced her friend. "Caro, I beg of you, don't put me through this. I know you. You say you will send for him, and the next thing will be that you will send him to see me."

"It would be very odd indeed," Caroline said in an airy way, "if Nicky did *not* visit you while he was in the neighbourhood."

"Caro!"

"No, Friday. You will not fob me off, I promise you. At the very least it will lessen the constraint between you if you *do* see him."

Friday began to feel sick. "Caro, I warn you, I shall not be at home to him."

"You will not know when he is coming," retorted Caroline. She relented a little, taking Friday's hands and holding them in a warm clasp. "Don't put yourself about, Friday! I see what it is. You have worked yourself up into such a nonsensical state over this whole business that Nicky has become a *monster* to terrify you. And all for *nothing*. It is only Nick, after all. You have known him forever. I declare, anyone would think he was some sort of god in your eyes!"

"Why do I trouble myself to explain to you?" uttered Friday in exasperation. "Pray, Caro, *heed* me this once!"

But Caroline was adamant. "You will see that I am right, Friday. If nothing else, it will give you an opportunity to discover for yourself the true state of his mind. Is not *that* worth going through just a little inconvenience of feeling?"

Inconvenience? How little Caro knew or understood! But she knew nothing of the dreams at night. Could not then realise the embarrassment the very sight of Nick must cause. Had no inkling of the waves of fluctuating emotions that must attack her in the preceding time before he should come. And what if he did not *wish* to come? Caro had not thought of that. And she, Friday, waiting despite herself, for she knew Caro's determination. Waiting, and dying every day. A slow, painful death with the sting of apprehension mingled with the unquenchable thrill of anticipation.

In the event, Friday was not called upon to suffer the dreadful tortures of her imaginings for long, for within a week Caroline sent a note round to state that Nicolas had gone up to their father at the close of the season and was not expected in Hurley until after Christmas.

To her own annoyance, relief was not the emotion uppermost in her breast. Despite all, she longed to see Nicolas. An admission that caused her to slam shut her tome of Latin and bang it on the table. Making fists of her curled hands, she hammered out a frustrated rhythm on the desk, letting out a stream of ancient Greek oaths.

"This will not do, Friday Edborough!" she told herself angrily, and got up with determination.

Bruno rose, eyeing her in a puzzled way—as he was wont to do these days, never quite knowing what to expect from a mistress who had until lately been happily predictable. He shifted to and fro uncertainly until Friday noticed him.

"Yes, Bruno, we are going out," she told him firmly.

A glance through the window confirmed that yesterday's fall of sleet had not renewed itself this morning. But it would be colder today. Indeed, she had been obliged to call the footman to make up the fire more strongly in here. However, her heavy pelisse and a stout pair of boots would serve.

The icy ground crunched underfoot as she went, and she took a perverse pleasure in the destructive force of her passage that left a trail of heavy prints, with the marks of Bruno's lighter tread alongside. Her cheeks stung with the bite of a December wind, and the tip of her nose protested. The ubiquitous spectacles, while they kept the worst of the wind from her eyes, were prone to mist a trifle as her warm breath sent clouds of vapour upwards.

More than once, Friday wiped impatient gloved fingers across the glass, and would have removed the things had she not been heading through the forest towards her hilltop retreat. In winter the bare trees, with their glimmering white coating of frost, seemed unfamiliar, and she was afraid of missing her way. The last thing she wanted was to end up at Delamere Place instead! Especially after the last occasion. Although Lady Delamere had been less distressed by the outcome of Friday's abortive betrothal than angered by the fact that the rumours had emanated from her own home.

The cracking pace that Friday had set herself very soon brought her out into the clear area that she felt to be her personal domain. She headed for the peak, and halted, panting with effort. With the trees empty of leaves, the view on this winter's day was breathtaking. A measure of peace settled into her heart, and she sighed.

"Look at it, Bruno!" she called aloud to the dog, her gaze wandering over the rolling countryside that stretched away into the distance, punctuated here and there by little clustering houses. "Is it not magnificent? I defy anyone to be sad in the face of such a sight!"

For the first time in a long while, she thought perhaps she might recover her erstwhile tranquillity. After all, what was she, set against this panorama of many lives? What right had she to hide her head and weep, and bewail her lot?

Flinging out her hands, and throwing back her head, she took a deep breath of the freezing air, and began to cough a little. At that precise moment, Bruno broke out in a frenzy of barking.

Turning, Friday saw him moving back towards the frost-ridden forest, and her glance swept along its rim. She became aware, under Bruno's noise, of the scrunch of heavily booted feet coming towards them. Hardly had she time to speculate on a possible intruder when a hatted and greatcoated figure came into sight, stepping smartly through the trees.

Friday tensed automatically, watching the man's long strides, the skirts of his greatcoat swirling about his booted legs. He was coming towards her. Her heart turned a double somersault, and she began to tremble.

It did not need the raising of his hat to reveal the fair locks of Nicolas Weare as he came out of the forest and on to her hilltop retreat. Friday's quivering senses already knew that it was he.

Chapter Seven

Nick's smile was tentative as he came up, as if he was unsure of his welcome. He gestured towards the forest. "I followed your footprints."

Friday drew a breath against the unruly pulsing of her heart. All she could think was how beautiful he looked. Not at all haggard as was she. No evidence of any distress of spirit. The visions of the night hours came whirling into her mind, and she felt herself grow hot. A shadow seemed to cross his face as she continued silent.

"Do you—object to my coming?" he asked hesitantly. "Shall I go?"

"No!" came at once, unbidden, from her lips. She tried to control their quivering, and faltered, "I th-thought—Caro said you had g-gone to your home."

Nick nodded. "I am on my way there. At least, I was." He looked away. "I turned around and came back."

"To see *me?*" Friday asked incredulously before she could stop herself.

A half-laugh escaped him. "Is it so odd? I have wanted to see you. Only I didn't know if—" He broke off, snatching off his hat and dashing it impatiently against his side. "Dash it all, Friday, this is absurd!"

She bit her lip, unaware that she was tightly clasping her fingers together. "Is it?"

"Yes! No one would imagine that we had been friends for years and years. I feel as if everything I say to you is *suspect*."

Friday could not look at him. "I told you it would not work."

"It should work, Friday. It *should*," he uttered vehemently. He took a step towards her, but Friday drew quickly back. Nick's face changed. Bitterly, he demanded, "That bad, is it?"

She swallowed. "Worse."

There was the most dreadful silence. An eerie silence, out here in the still winter day, the enveloping white frost hushing the world. Such a constriction attacked Friday about the chest that she thought her lungs must explode. How could she have spoken in so hurtful a way? Why did he not say something? What was he thinking? At length she dared to lift her gaze to his face. Through the spectacles, she saw that his eyes glistened and wondered at it.

At her glance, he turned instantly away, shoving the hat back on his head, and she saw him raise a hand briefly to his cheek. All at once she understood. Her heart melted.

"*Nick*," she cried, and reached out her hands to him.

Next instant, he had turned back to her, catching at her gloved hands. Then he released them, and she found herself dragged against his chest, his arms tight about her—just as they had been in her dreams.

Only it was not like her dreams. There was no sensuality about this fierce embrace that muffled her face into the folds of the many capes that adorned his greatcoat. There was instead a desperation, a panic, as of a small child whose mother had been thought lost to him. The impression was strengthened by the words that jerked hoarsely from his throat.

"I *need* you, Friday! Don't turn against me! I cannot *bear* your enmity!"

Friday could not speak herself for the emotion that instantly choked her. He did not love her, no. But there was balm in such words. She *was* important to him. She meant *something*.

A nagging sharp pain made her realise that her spectacles were jammed so tightly against her face that they were digging into her skin. She struggled a little, and felt the tight hold release. All at once she was speaking, quite naturally, in laughing protest.

"Only look what you've done to my eyeglasses!"

Nick's face cracked in a grin as he saw that they sat lopsidedly on her face, almost falling off her nose. "They are all misted over, too. Here, let me!"

Quickly stripping off one of his leather gloves, he delved into his greatcoat pocket for a handkerchief and deftly performed the operation of cleaning the lenses for her. Then he set them carefully back in place, still smiling.

"There, that's better. You looked more than usually demented."

"Thank you very much, Nicolas Weare!"

He grinned. "I always think of you as looking like a mad owl, as a matter of fact. Have I never said so?"

"On pain of death, I doubt it," Friday said severely.

Nick laughed. "On pain of expulsion, more like."
This was so apposite to the current situation that his
grin faded. He frowned and cursed under his breath.
Then he said hurriedly, "Yes, I begin to see what you
were at. Is *nothing* possible to be said without a double meaning?"

Friday did not answer this. The resumption of constraint hurt her, together with the implications inherent in his understanding. For it must mean parting—
again. They could *not* be friends. She shivered, and
at once put it to use.

"It's cold. Let's walk a little."

They turned together and began to stroll up and
down, as if by mutual consent not setting foot in the
forest. For both were reluctant to put an end to this
meeting, however painful it was proving to be. Why
had he come? Friday thought heavily. This put her in
mind of Caroline's tottyheaded advice, and she immediately resolved not to ask Nicolas about Hermione
Hesket. The decision left her tongue-tied, for naturally
once she thought of the girl no other subject presented
itself for discussion.

In a moment it became clear that Nick's own
thoughts were running in the same direction, for he
cleared his throat and began, "I dare say Caro may
have told you—about Miss Hesket."

Friday stopped dead in her tracks. From whence it
came she could not have said, but she was suddenly
conscious of annoyance. Inevitable that he thought of
her, but why in the world must he bring it up now?
Was *that* why he had said he needed her? Because he
wanted to talk about Miss Hesket? Yet she could not
bring herself to repulse him, to tell him that she
wanted to hear nothing at all about the matter.

"What is Lord Aymestrey like?" she asked, finding, as she thought, the least provocative question.

Nick snorted. "He is more than twice her age! The whole affair is nothing short of farce. I tell you, Friday, I have been *sickened* by this business."

"Indeed?" she said, biting down the natural retort she wanted to make. *He* was sickened? How did he imagine *she* had felt when Hermione had accosted her that day?

"It was of a piece with everything else, however," he went on, apparently at ease enough to talk of it. "Like a betrayal of everything I believed in. How I could have been so *blind* I do not know."

Friday turned to look at him, frowning. "I do not think I understand you."

Nick flung up his hands. "Why should you? I don't understand myself! Can you imagine what it is like to be so thoroughly disillusioned with someone, to discover that you had been wrong in your judgement about them in every particular? It is no pleasant thing, Friday, I assure you. For I am forced to concede my own stupidity, and recognise that I was wrong and everyone else was right."

"How?" Friday found herself asking. "*How* were they right?" It seemed to her to be overwhelmingly important to know just what it was he had recognised.

"In warning me against her," Nick said without hesitation. "She has proved herself to be as mercenary—as *wanton*, damn her to hell!—as her mother."

The violence of his language, for which he made no apology—why should he? She was only Friday, before whom he was not accustomed to mind his speech!—convinced her that a veritable volcano of emotion was seething inside him. It argued so strong a feeling *for* the female—else he had not cared so *deeply*—that Friday was compelled to test it further.

"I dare say you feel betrayed by her betrothal?" she offered.

"By that—and everything else," Nick grated, recalling the way Hermione had propositioned him when he was still engaged to Friday.

That had been bad enough. But he had been ready to forgive and forget when he had returned to London. Because he had kept his promise to meet her, only with the intention of saying a final farewell. But Hermione's attitude to the broken engagement had disgusted him. She had not only displayed intense satisfaction, and a callous unconcern about his distress over the loss of a valued friendship, but she'd had the temerity to renew her persuasions—in far less veiled terms that had brought a blush even to *his* cheek— that they should become lovers when once she was safely married. When he'd discovered that her sights were set on a widower of middle years, Nicolas had made bold to protest.

"But why, Nick?" Hermione had demanded in the most innocent-seeming way. "He is very wealthy, you know. My ma is convinced that we may between us bring him up to scratch." She tinkled with the laughter which had before seemed so delicious to Nick, but now set his teeth on edge. "Ma knows *exactly* how to do. He is mad for me, see, and she has taught me how to lead him on to suppose he may succeed, and then, just as he thinks that I am about to succumb, I simply *deny* him, and demand a ring on my finger. *And,* let me tell you, it is already beginning to work!"

Her smug satisfaction had set the seal on Nick's

disillusionment. To play such a whore's trick was bad enough—profiting from some poor fellow's desires. But to boast of it to the man she knew to be in love with her! It had disgusted him so much that, with scarcely a word of farewell, he had left her flat.

Unfortunately, Miss Hesket's persistence would not permit him to forget her. She seemed determined to regain his favour. She sent him pleading notes, put herself in his way to flutter those falsely dampened eyelashes at him, and in general behaved in so ill-bred a manner that by the time her betrothal was announced he was heartily sick of the sight of her. But his bitterest anger was directed at himself, that he had allowed something so worthwhile to be destroyed by someone so worthless.

Haunted by that last interview with Friday, he had wrought with himself daily. Much as he wanted to see her, to try if he might to mend the rift that had been brought about, he felt so badly regarding the outcome that it seemed he *must* respect her wishes. She did not *want* him to try and renew their friendship. When Caro had attempted to persuade him to visit Friday before he left for the family estates at Morton, he had been adamant. Indeed he had stood over her while she'd written that note and himself directed the servant to carry it to Finchamstod.

But when he'd left for Morton a day or so later, he had been suddenly seized by a desire so urgent, so all-consuming to see Friday that he had turned his phaeton and driven directly to her home. When he'd discovered that she was not in the library, he had instantly come this way, spurred on by the sight of those two sets of prints that told him, in his intimate knowledge of her habits, where she would be.

He had longed for her smile, for the warmth of her voice. Inevitably, the reception he met with from her at once distanced him. Resentment against Hermione—the unwitting instrument of this hideous estrangement—flared up in him, and thus he found himself pouring out all the bitterness he felt to the one person before whom he should rather have held his peace.

"Do you wish," said Friday a trifle wistfully, "that it were not Lord Aymestrey, but *you?*"

"My God, no!" exclaimed Nicolas, turning a glare upon her.

In his mind, the glare was directed at Hermione, but Friday did not know that. She shifted, moving a little away from him. How desperate he must be! How unhappy! Why had he come here, when the sight of her own plain features must provoke so stark a contrast to what he had lost? Without thinking, she followed up this thought aloud.

"She is so very beautiful. I see that you must envy Aymestrey."

"Envy him? Nothing of the sort!" declared Nick, revolted. "Oh, yes, she is beautiful. She bowled me over with that lovely face and that enticing voice. I freely admit that. But there is nothing under her beauty but selfishness and the soul of a gold-digging courtesan. Aymestrey is welcome to her!"

Bitterness was rife in his voice. His hurt ran very deep, Friday thought. So deep that he could not keep from speaking his mind, no matter that his words were addressed to her. He did not know, did not realise, what she had suffered. But he *should* have done so, whispered a tiny voice in her head. If not that kiss—which she had so regretted, but which seemed now to have screamed the state of her heart aloud to him!—her tears must have told him. He did not hesitate to pour out his feelings, quite regardless of how his words might affect her. Regardless indeed of what her own emotions might be. Had he no thought for anyone but himself?

Just then Nick turned to her, speaking rapidly, his voice low. "Friday, I must say this now, or I will never say it. If nothing else, this affair has taught me how much I value you. You have said that we cannot be friends and I believe you are right. We have gone beyond friendship. I know I did not think it at the time, but there *is* merit in a union between us. Don't you feel that we would do well to marry after all?"

Friday stared at him. Something sparked within her, igniting a spurting flame of anger which caught and burned. Her ears had not deceived her, had they? What, was she entitled to as little consideration as a *dog?* Had he actually *dared* to come to her with a mouthful of complaints about another woman, and then throw her a bone? Was this how little he thought of her? Marry "after all". "Merit" in a union? Was she the balm to take the edge off his bitterness? Heaven help her, but had he to insult her a *second* time?

The fires erupted, flaring through her in a path of screaming heat that threatened to tear her apart. The emotion was alien, yet all too familiar, mirroring in its passion the strength of the agonies that had been haunting her for so many painful weeks.

A tremble began within her, seeming to overtake her very bones. His face blurred as hot tears misted over her eyeglasses, but the rage was so great that she did not even think to lift her fingers to remove them.

"Oh, no, Nick," she uttered in a guttural voice that shook with emotion. "Oh, no! I know your Trojan horse for what it is."

She could only just see the change that swept across his face. She recognised bewilderment and it only increased the power of her own emotions.

"What in the world—?" he began.

But Friday did not even hear him, for her tongue was loosened now, and she *must* let it out. "You came like the treacherous Greeks to a naked foe. You offered me a gift of *paradise*. And I accepted it. *I accepted it.* But it was no gift." Her voice began to fail, her breath catching pitifully. "It was a h-hollow *sham*—that dealt out pain...desecration...and heart-break!"

"Friday, what are you saying? I don't understand!" he uttered, and started forward as Friday began to gasp painfully on rising sobs. *"Friday!"*

Friday saw his hands come at her and dashed them away. "Don't *touch* me!"

She ran from him, back towards the forest, hardly aware of Bruno barking madly beside her, of the heavy thud of footsteps behind.

"Friday, wait! Friday, don't run from me! What is the matter? What have I said?"

She felt him seize her and, turning, beat at him with her fists, croaking out, "Get away from me! Go away! *Go away.* I never want to *see* you again!"

Stumblingly, she flung herself forward. She saw the shadow loom up and threw out her arms. The impact was severe, depriving her momentarily of breath and knocking the spectacles from her nose. By instinct rather than reason, she realised that she had floundered into a tree. Her arms closed about it, and she hung there as her shuddering breaths began to drive air back into her lungs.

"Friday, Friday, have you run mad?" came Nick's voice, anxiety rampant in its tone. "Are you hurt? Let me help you!"

Friday's head jerked in protest as if she would fling off the touch on her shoulder. But her cry was a plea now, the flame of anger quenched by a deluge of the grief she had been controlling all this while.

"Go away, Nick! *Pray.* G-go, *go!* I cannot *b-bear* any more."

Nicolas hesitated, standing off a little, his expression compound of puzzlement and concern. His gloved fingers fiddled with the spectacles he had retrieved, and he absent-mindedly pushed with his leg at the hound, who was nudging him between wheezy grunts and whines of protest.

Like Bruno, he knew he was at fault, yet he knew not *what* he had done. He had never seen Friday like this! He felt terrible, his heart wrung with compassion at the rasping sobs, but he dared not touch her for fear of provoking her into another appalling outburst.

"Friday?" he uttered tentatively, when she seemed to quieten a little.

Her eyes opened. They were red and swollen, her features ravaged, but she looked him full in the face, the words ragged on her breath.

"Don't...come...again."

Then her cheek closed into the tree-trunk once more, its icy surface blessedly cool for the moment. One hand waved Nick away, and then she was still, her heaving chest the only evidence of the recent explosion.

There was nothing for Nick to do but to take himself off. Carefully, he slipped the eyeglasses into the curve of the fingers that had waved, and were now lying loosely against the tree. He did not think Friday even noticed, for her eyes were closed and she did not move at all. He hated to leave her like this, but what could he do? He would not have known how to comfort her, even had he stayed as he wanted to. Retrieving his hat, which had fallen off in the recent battle with the tree as he'd tried to help, he started to go.

Yet his steps lagged, and he looked back several times. The last time, when Friday still had not moved, he turned fully round and gazed at her now distant figure. She was only just visible through the bare trunks, a small huddle against her tree, the dog sitting on his haunches as if he guarded her, his glance still on the retreating enemy.

Nick felt as if he had just lived through a nightmare, but that final picture remained in his mind, a constant reproach for an unknown sin, and a fresh spur to the nagging ache that accompanied him everywhere.

Leaning close to the mirror, Friday examined the results of the dour abigail's ministrations. The hair, she had to concede, was certainly a success. How Murdishaw had managed it she did not know, but the fluffy halo that usually puffed out around her face had been tamed into clusters of little curls that crept on to her forehead. A high topknot, banded about with a ribbon, ended in more ringleted little curls bunched at the crown.

Somehow, she had found a way to reduce the impact of the freckles, Friday saw, peering in surprise.

But naturally there was little the maid could do about the rest of her nondescript features. And *nothing* she could do about the gaunt look about her cheeks, the deep shadows under her eyes!

Friday sighed deeply. Was it really only a matter of three short months since that dreadful day? It felt like a lifetime. An aeon of doubts and agonies, during which she had all but been torn in two by unprecedented emotions.

How long she had remained clutching that tree she had no notion. She knew only that there had come a moment when cold had obtruded itself upon her consciousness. The sleeves of her pelisse had been soaked from the ice, as also had the body of the long garment, right down to its hem. Her arms had been stiff and numbed with cold, and her legs had dragged her weight like the trunks of the leafless trees through which she had made her weary way homeward.

She'd changed, and slept a long while, dreamlessly for once. But it was the waking nightmare that had tortured her the more. When she'd realised what she had done, how she had conducted herself towards Nick—oh, the shame of it! Yet a bubble of rage tumbled about her still, and she could not shake it. She longed one moment only to see Nick that she might excuse herself and ask for his pardon. The next she wanted to claw his handsome face with vengeful nails, baying for his blood.

She heard within herself the shrieking madness of the Furies, Athene's call to arms. But yet the tender warmth of Aphrodite soothed her heart towards him. Worse, like Phaedra, her loins still echoed the yearning of her bosom, seeking after the unattainable. But the dreaming had stopped. There was no sweetness left, even in the recesses of her soul, to taunt her with *those* aching tortures. No. Instead hot tears of fury and frustration soaked her pillows when she should have been sleeping.

These emotions could not last, of course. Not at the same intensity. They dulled in time, leaving Friday with an overwhelming lack of purpose that made even the everyday acts of life seem like a burden. Christmas had come and gone in a haze of nothingness, even the necessity to appear cheerful for the sake of her parents seeming to require a superhuman effort. Afterwards, she retired day after day with Bruno to her refuge in the library. But not to study. She sat sighing over her Latin tomes, reading dully without taking in the content of what passed before her bespectacled eyes.

By the time Caroline visited her in the early weeks of January, she had no other thought in her head, no other desire in her otherwise numb heart but to *forget* Nicolas Weare.

Caroline had last seen her only a few days after Nick's disastrous visit when Friday had been ablaze with all sorts of passions. Now she expressed herself as being shocked by Friday's altered appearance, and said that she could see her proposition was coming not a moment too soon.

"What proposition?" Friday asked listlessly.

"Has not Lady Delamere told you?"

"I have not seen Lady Delamere."

"You have not? I declare, I thought she *must* have told you by this! But if she has not, it makes no matter." Mrs Cleeve seized Friday's hand and dragged her down to sit in the sofa of the morning-room. "Now, Friday, attend to me! You will achieve *noth-*

ing by moping here. I am very glad I had this notion because it is obvious to me that I have hit upon the very thing to bring you *out* of this dreadful slough of despondency into which you have allowed yourself to sink.''

Friday's hand lay slackly in the one that gripped it, but she fetched a sigh at this and tried to pull away. "Pray leave me be, Caro."

Her fingers were gripped more firmly. "That I most certainly will *not* do. I have the whole matter planned. Lady Delamere is to sponsor you, for naturally I *cannot* manage it in my condition—" casting a glance down at the protuberance that had vastly increased in size so that there was now no mistaking its import "—although naturally I should not *dream* of absenting myself. So you need not feel I shall not be there to support you."

Friday's senses were not so dulled that she could not understand the drift of Caroline's conversation. Tiredness washed over her. It seemed all of a piece with the rest of her burdensome life that Caro should come and try to drive her into an activity for which she was known to have little taste.

"This is for the season, I take it?" she uttered in an unmoved tone.

"Just so," agreed Mrs Cleeve excitedly. "Now, Friday, I know you are going to say no, but only think! You cannot continue in this way, and what in the world else is there for you to do to encompass a *change?*"

"Why should I need a change?"

"Why, because there is *nothing* so efficacious, I do assure you. You are as blue as megrim, don't tell me! And I utterly *refuse* to let you remain so."

"Oh, Caro, pray *don't*," Friday begged. "To be dragged to town, and have to face all those people. I *could* not."

"Yes, you could, and you shall!"

Friday groaned. If Caroline had made up her mind, she could visualise a whole vista of weary argument ahead of her. A sensation of impending exhaustion caused her to lean back in the sofa, dragging her mind into gear to summon all the defences she would need. And then Caro touched on the subject of her young brother.

"For my part, I believe that nothing could better serve to bring Nicky to his senses."

Something stirred in Friday's hitherto frozen emotions. Bring Nick to his senses? What in the world was Caro talking about? What had *she* to do with Nick now, in any event? What was more, if Caro imagined that she had any desire even to *see* Nick after the hateful manner of their last parting, she was the more mistaken.

The apathy that had possessed her seemed to vanish abruptly. She sat up, and out poured a tirade that burst from the fury she had supposed she had buried, and erupted from her mouth without any prior warning or thought.

"I don't wish to talk of Nick, I thank you, Caro. I don't wish to talk of him, or think of him, or *hear* of him. He may be your brother, but pray don't mention his name to me again! All I want to do is to *forget* Nick. Do you understand?"

Caroline stared at her for a moment, brows raised. To Friday's utter astonishment, she said only, "Certainly, Friday. I shall not mention his name again. But that does not mean that I shall abandon my purpose.

You are coming to town. On *that* you may depend, for I am quite determined.''

Mrs Cleeve had proved true to both promises. She had visited Friday again in a day or two. And yet again until Friday finally yielded. She had *not* mentioned Nick's name, but she had contrived nevertheless to bring him into the conversation, Friday remembered indignantly. *And* Caroline had prevailed, for here she was! Installed in Lady Delamere's house in Berkeley Square, at the mercy of the ministrations of that lady's very own highly experienced abigail—who might have been a governess, so strict was she!—and about to make her début at a party at the house of Lady Holt.

Friday pulled back from the mirror with another sigh. She did not wish to look at her gaunt face. Thank goodness she could not see more than a white blur at even this little distance from the glass! The gown, however, was another matter. Without thinking, she replaced the spectacles so that she might examine the high-waisted creation in wispy yellow muslin. It was quite plain with only a border of straw-coloured ribbon to match the one in her hair.

Yes, it was pretty. Her only objection was that she felt she must undoubtedly freeze to death tonight! Even with the fire in the grate of the bedchamber she was using in the elegant Delamere town house, she was conscious of the chill of February. Murdishaw had permitted—one felt that she *permitted*, she was so superior a female!—the use of a thin shawl, but as it was narrow and designed to lie across the arms at elbow level it was, in Friday's view, less than useless. In any event, if she did not die of cold, she might well do so from sheer nerves!

Why in the world had she allowed Caro to talk her into coming to town? Except that she knew the answer to that. She *had* to get over Nicolas Weare if she was going to regain any peace of mind at all. And this was the only way of doing so that had as yet presented itself. She was certainly not going to do so at Finchamstod, where every haunt of hers was walked by the ghosts of the past. Ghosts that had cut up her peace, invaded her dreams, and wrecked her future.

What future? was the question that had driven her in the end to succumb to Caroline's persuasions. Though *that* particular persuasion, the one that Caro had tried to hold out as a lure, had *nothing* to do with her decision, she told herself—as she had done a thousand times since.

"What you need, Friday, is a change of image," Caro had stated positively on one occasion. "I have been telling you forever that your wardrobe will not do. Now perhaps you will *attend* to me. For let me tell you, my love, there is nothing does so much *good* for a female as a casting off of the old— I am speaking of *dress,* you understand. I cannot tell you the number of times I have found myself become a new woman, all because of a new hairstyle or a new gown. And the impact on the male sex, my dear, can only be termed *devastating.*"

"I frankly doubt my ability to devastate anyone at all," Friday had said candidly, "let alone—"

She had bitten her tongue on the name that almost escaped her lips. No. *No.* To suppose that Nick might be induced to fall in love with her merely because she had altered her appearance was an absurdity she was far too intelligent to allow to weigh with her. Or she hoped she was. No, she *knew* she was. Just because Caro's words had operated powerfully upon her, it did not mean that she was foolish enough to allow herself to be swayed by them.

"You are not precisely an *antidote*," Caro had uttered, laughing. "I am sure there will be any number of gentlemen who will fall at your feet. And *that*," she'd added with a meaning look, "will be all to the good. *Jealousy,* my love. I believe I have mentioned the efficacy of jealousy before."

"Caro, don't think I do not know what you are at, because I am not stupid!" Friday had said crossly. "I have *ceased* hankering after your abominable brother."

"Stuff! I have no notion of your *hankering* after him. Indeed, I should be *livid* with you if you did. There is no question of anything of the sort. You, Friday, are to display the utmost indifference towards him. Nothing could be better."

Friday groaned. "Caro, I am not falling in with this stupid plot of yours. If—I repeat, *if* I go to London, I shall do so only so that I may be aided by it into *forgetting* Nick. Gracious, but there *must* be other males in whom I could develop an interest! And I have to suppose," she'd added cynically, "that the settlements that go with me are *bound* to attract a suitor or two."

"They will be baying after you like bloodhounds," Caroline had promised comfortably. "I will see to that."

Papa had been delighted with the whole proposal, enthusiastically encouraging his daughter to accept Lady Delamere's invitation *this* time. His wistfully expressed hope that the project might alleviate the

distress caused by his error of judgement had caused
Friday to waver. Even Mama had added a word of
encouragement, observing with the utmost candour
that Frideswid could as well be miserable in London
as at Finchamstod, if she chose. Perhaps it was
Mama's *other* sapient observation that had weighed
with her. For Sophia Edborough had pointed out that
if even the prospect had done so much to animate her
daughter she thought Caroline Cleeve's notion might
well achieve a greater victory at restoring her to her
normal self.

Friday had been obliged to realise that her spirits
had lifted, if only for the sake of arguing with Caro!
In any event, she had at length given in, although *not*,
she'd insisted to herself rather frantically, to Caro's
subtleties.

But now that she was here, and the dreadful day
of her appearance in society had arrived, she began
to feel sick with dread. She hated parties. She was so
stupid in a great company. No one was going to talk
to her. Worst of all, everyone who met her would
immediately remember the abortive betrothal and the
scandalous involvement of the Heskets, and start to
whisper about her behind their fans. Her dread naturally had nothing to do with the *vague* possibility of
meeting Nicolas Weare. She was *not* going to be dis-
commoded by *that* thought.

Courage, Friday! she told herself. There was nothing for it but to draw a deep breath and turn to thank
Lady Delamere's abigail for her invaluable assistance.
Miss Murdishaw's grim acceptance persuaded her
that even this genius felt she had failed with so poor
a subject. Until she arrived downstairs to find Caroline waiting for her with Lady Delamere, and was left

in no doubt about the real reason for the abigail's evident disapproval.

"Friday!" shrieked Caro after one glance at her face. "I knew it! You are wearing those *dreadful* eyeglasses. I declare, I am astonished that Murdishaw allowed you out of your chamber! The wonder is that she did not snatch them off your face!"

She came up to Friday and made a grab at the spectacles herself. But Friday put up her hands and held the things firmly in place.

"Caro, I cannot *see* without them. I shall be useless in company."

"That, Caroline, is perfectly true," adjudged Lady Delamere. "It is no use if the poor girl cannot identify a soul."

Caroline waved impatient hands, and dived for the cloak that she had discarded over a chair. "I have thought of all that, never fear." Rummaging, she drew something out of her cloak pocket and waved her trophy in the air, exclaiming triumphantly, "You see?"

Both Lady Delamere and Friday moved closer to look at what Caroline was holding up. It was a single eyeglass on a handle, strung upon a long ribbon. She held it out.

"There, now. You may wear it about your neck and use the glass as you need it. It will make you look like a quiz, I dare say, but *anything* is better than those atrocious spectacles."

Lady Delamere was surprisingly enthusiastic. She was a handsome creature, her dark hair untouched by grey, not tall, but with a strong personality that matched the jut of her nose—a feature she had not bequeathed to her son. As Friday now realised, she owed in some degree her extremely fashionable appearance to the expertise of her abigail, but her own taste in dress, which she put at the disposal of her young charge, was excellent.

Yielding to two strong wills, Friday allowed herself to be persuaded into giving up her eyeglasses, which her hostess laid on the mantel for the moment, and trying out the beribboned single one. It was odd indeed to peer through one lens and Friday was at first inclined to shut the other eye.

"You *do* look like a quiz," Caroline said despairingly. "Oh, dear, what is to be done?"

"No, no, Caroline," uttered Lady Delamere soothingly. "I believe it will answer. It is so rare to see a *young* female using one that I dare say it will draw a great deal of attention. There is nothing people like better than to have an oddity to gape at."

"I thank you, Lady Delamere," said Friday drily. "But in that case, why can I not be odd in my eyeglasses?"

"Because spectacles are for elderly females, Frideswid," pronounced her ladyship firmly. "*This* will be something quite out of the common way."

"Yes, and I will be *seeing* quite out of the common way," Friday protested. "It is not at all satisfactory, you know."

"My dear Friday," Caroline told her firmly, "in the world of fashion, *sacrifices* are a necessity. Besides, although I had not thought of it before, I believe Lady Delamere is right. People *do* love an oddity. It might well *make* you."

Friday was no match for the determination of her two kindly benefactresses, and in a way it was a relief that she would largely be unable to see anyone's face.

Particular faces might then go unnoticed by her. She was sure that if she must lift the wretched glass to her eye every time she wanted to have proper vision she would soon tire of using it.

This proved to be the case at Lady Holt's rout certainly, for at the house in Grosvenor Square they walked into such a press of persons that she was surrounded by a veritable sea of blurry faces, and the introductions came so fast that she quickly abandoned any attempt to put names to them.

Titles floated by her ears, and here and there a name she had heard of caught her attention. But she rapidly became more concerned with keeping her balance as she was jostled to and fro, than with remembering the people to whom she was presented. It was also extremely hot and she understood now the wisdom of Murdishaw's choice of gown. She had never been so uncomfortable, and it was with intense relief that she recognised the voice of her oldest friend.

"All settled in, then, Friday?" asked Delamere.

"Charles!" Friday cried, groping for the eyeglass and lifting it to peer at him. "Her ladyship told me she did not expect you back from Leicestershire until tomorrow."

"Arrived just after you left for the party. Changed my togs at Berkeley Square and came on as fast as I could."

Friday smiled. "That was kind in you. Your mama and Caro are looking after me very well, however."

"It's not that," Charles said, dropping his voice and leaning close. "Thought I ought to warn you. Came down together, you see, with—"

"With myself," interrupted a new voice acidly. "I

thank you, Delamere. It might have been kinder in you to give *me* the warning.''

Friday's guts went hollow. Nick! Through an eye grotesquely enlarged by the ridiculous single glass, she saw his countenance—unsmiling, the green eyes accusing as they met her own.

Chapter Eight

The eyeglass fell from Friday's nerveless fingers, and the features before her thankfully blurred. Breathless from the horrid gyrations of her pulse, she managed only a murmured rejoinder. An inane one at that.

"How do you do, Nick?"

He did not answer. Unable to see the tautening of the muscles in his face, Friday yet felt the impact of his hostility. The memory of their last meeting came sweeping back, and she swallowed on a dry throat. She heard Charles cough, and turned her gaze on his fuzzy features.

"Don't concern yourself," she uttered in an attempt to relieve his embarrassment. "It was bound to happen sooner or later."

"No doubt you'd have preferred it to be later," came Nick's cold tones. "Have no fear! I will remove my unwelcome presence immediately."

He turned sharply and walked away, hardly aware of the persons who stood in his path. Still reeling with shock, he murmured automatic excuses, making his way through the throng in an effort to get as far away as he might from the object of his thoughts.

Friday *here?* Why had she come? What did it mean? Why had no one thought to *tell* him? Caro! How *could* she? How could she leave him to find out like this? She must have known. Known? Dear God, was he mad? She must have been *instrumental* in this. It was impossible that Friday had herself decided— out of the blue, in this extraordinary way!—to come to London for the season.

Damn it to hell, what was his sister playing at? After what had passed between them at Christmas, too! Had he not *told* her his concern over Friday's welfare? Yes, he had. But Caro, of course, had sided with Friday against him, he remembered. Even though she must have recognised his own intense distress. She *had* recognised it. She had even spoken of it, hinting that their father had mentioned the matter to her over the short holiday that she and Richard had spent at Morton.

Nicolas knew that his father had delighted in a visit that had given him a rare sight of his first grandchild. He was himself aware—as he could scarcely not have been, for his brother Tony had not hesitated to mention it on every possible occasion!—that his own lack of spirits had thrown a damper over the company. He had done his best to be of good cheer, but it was very difficult when his mind was so full of recent happenings.

The arrival of Caro and her husband, however, had offered a grain of hope that he'd waited for an opportunity to satisfy. But at first it had proved almost impossible to catch Caro alone. At dinner on the day after Christmas, his patience was exhausted. After a single glass of port, he'd excused himself to the gentlemen, and had gone after his sister.

Caroline was found to be resting, with her feet up, on the *chaise-longue* in the little-used "family" saloon, a rather shabby apartment, with faded brocade hangings, and stained and scuffed, rather ugly old-fashioned furniture that had none of the elegance that prevailed elsewhere. Bearing the marks of youthful ill-use, it yet felt home-like and comfortable, and the children of the house invariably drifted back there when they came home.

With her relaxed hands encircling the bulge at her front, Caro had looked quite matronly, and Nick had said so, by way of opening the conversation.

"I *feel* matronly," Caroline returned airily, but Nicolas thought her bright eyes were watchful. Had his father spoken to her of his low spirits? He hesitated. How should he broach the subject? He fiddled with one of a cluster of antiquated ornaments on the mantel, until his sister begged him acidly not to screen her from the warmth of the fire.

"I beg your pardon," Nick uttered absently, and went to sit in a chair opposite her sofa. He still could not think how to begin. But if he did not hurry, Richard and his brother would shortly join them and the moment would be lost. There was only one thing for it. Go directly to the core of the matter. He drew a breath.

"Caro, have you seen Friday recently?"

Caroline's eyes widened. "Why?"

Nick frowned. Must she ask that? "I just want to know how she is."

"Why?" repeated his sister, her tone sharpening.

Frustration exploded out of him. "Damn it, Caro! What sort of a question is that?"

"The last time I saw you," Caroline stated, sounding like someone repeating his misdeeds to a child, "you refused even to go and see Friday when I urged you to do so."

"I know that," Nick uttered impatiently. "But now—"

"*Now,* all at once, you want to know how she is. Why don't you visit her and find out for yourself?"

After the last time? Good God, no! He looked away, uttering gruffly, "I can't."

"Oh, indeed?"

There was an edge to Caroline's voice, and Nick's eyes came back to her, a frown in them. What did *that* mean? Dear God, she was baiting him! She already *knew*.

"You *have* seen her, haven't you?" he accused.

His sister evaded the question. "I certainly did not expect to hear you asking after her. After all, you have made it abundantly clear that *you* don't want to see her—"

"The boot, Caro, is on the other leg," he interrupted, recalling Friday's hurtful words.

"*Is* it? How did you find that out, since you have not set eyes on her since I don't know when? And you cannot have *written,* for you would not be asking me—"

"Very well, I *did* go and see her!" Nick snapped, jerking to his feet. Trust Caro to force it out of him! He paced away. "Are you satisfied?"

"No, I am *not* satisfied," Caroline said crossly, "and I wonder you should dare to ask me if I am, after the *dreadful* manner in which you treated poor Friday."

Nick swung round. "But I *didn't*. We were talking perfectly pleasantly, and then suddenly she went off like a keg of gunpowder!'' He stiffened, staring at her. "She told you what happened?''

"Heavens, Nicky, you must know Friday better than that! I had positively to *drag* it out of her, and even then I could make neither head nor tail of it.''

"What did she tell you?''

"Not a great deal,'' Caroline told him, and he was conscious of some vestige of relief. It was short-lived, for she went on, "Only that you had been to see her, and that she had found she was mistaken in your character, and that the discovery had upset her very much so that she lost her temper with you. For which she stupidly apologised, but I very soon set her right on *that* count.''

"I'll go bail you did!'' Nick uttered in sudden anger. How *could* Friday say such a thing of him? "Mistaken in my character? I thank her! Merely because I offered for her a second time.''

"Oh, is *that* all?'' Caro uttered in a voice that reeked of sarcasm to Nick's sensitive ears. "To my understanding, you gave her the impression that you had as well marry her as not.''

"I said nothing of the sort!'' objected Nicolas indignantly. Then, remembering the terms in which he had uttered his proposal, and the emotions under which he had been labouring at the time, he flushed darkly. "At least—well, I never *meant*—I suppose it might have sounded as though— Oh, my God!''

Dropping back into the chair, he sank his head in his hands, running disarranging fingers through his pale gold locks. What had he *done*? Of *course* Friday had rejected him. He had hardly made it sound as if he *wanted* to marry her!

Caroline's bracing tones interrupted his thoughts.

"Nicky! For heaven's sake, do not fall into despair again! What in the world is the matter with you? *Don't* tell me all this has to do with your quarrel with Friday?"

"There was no quarrel," Nick groaned from under his hands. "I wanted only to mend matters, and I have put myself in a situation where I cannot even *approach* her."

"Nicky, listen to me," Caro urged in a kinder tone that made him look up at her, dropping his hands from his face. She was sitting up and leaning towards him, the sisterly care back in her face for the first time in this interview, he thought. "You really must start thinking about Friday, you know."

Nick stared. His frustrations came pounding to the surface. "Think about her? What do you imagine I've been doing these many weeks? I cannot think about anything else! If it is not that *hideous* memory of the way she was when—" He broke off with a heavy sigh at the picture instantly in his mind of Friday clutching that tree, and then started painfully up again. "If not *that,* then it is some stupid remembrance of the things she has said to me to make me laugh. She had always a ready wit." There was a constriction in his chest as a little laugh escaped him now—mirthless, however.

"When I am engaged in conversation, I catch myself out thinking of the things that Friday would probably say. Silly things, about the gods and the ancient Greek heroes." Memory hit again, darkening his thoughts. "She even used *that* analogy against me. *My* Trojan Horse! As if I had *planned* to distress her for some hateful purpose of my own."

He had almost forgotten Caroline's presence. When

she spoke, it took him quite by surprise. And her words were positively inane!

"Well, Nicky, it is my opinion that it is time and past that you examined your own *feelings*."

What in the world was she at? As if he had not done so times out of mind! He could scarcely ignore his feelings, they burgeoned so strongly. He got up abruptly.

"I don't know of what you are talking, Caro. And I doubt if you do either! I have no need to examine my feelings. I know my feelings. I have lost a very dear friend. Is not that enough?"

Caroline's brows rose. "You did not seem to know your feelings over Hermione Hesket."

"That was different," Nick protested instantly.

"Altogether different," agreed Caro in a meaning way.

She was mad! What possessed her to bring that up? And what the devil was he supposed to make of that knowing look? He headed for the door.

"I can't stand this! I wish I had not opened my mouth!"

Which was true enough. He had not spoken of the matter to his sister again. In fact, he had done his best to avoid any confrontation of the kind. Evidently he had said quite enough to put one of her idiotic notions into her head—though what precisely it might have been he had not the remotest guess!—for he had no doubt whatsoever that it was she who had persuaded Friday to come here to London for the season. And if there was not some purpose behind her refusing to apprise him of the fact, he did not know his own sister!

He discovered that he had wandered, almost un-

knowingly, into an alcove where he might hover unnoticed. His eyes, as he turned to the room again,
distractedly searched the throng. He was conscious of
feeling rather stupid. There was no need for him to
have rushed off like that. He would have done better
to have stayed. After all, Friday must have been
forced to speak to him with civility in company such
as this.

His features darkened in a flush as he realised that
any incivility had been entirely on his side. She had
greeted him politely enough, and what had he done
in return? Snapped at her, and walked away. God,
how could he have behaved so? Where was she?
There was such a press of persons here that he might
never get a sight of her again tonight.

All at once he did see her. She was in Caroline's
company—had he not *known* his wretch of a sister
was in on this?—making a purposeful way through
the crowds. It was Caro in the lead, was it not? Of
course it was. His gaze wandered, and he caught sight
of his brother standing to one side of the large saloon
with a young lady. Griselda Apperley. So that was it!
Caro was hell-bent on *another* of her infernal inter-
ferences. Dragging Friday in, too.

His eyes remained on Friday, however, and he lost
interest in his sister's intentions. Only now did he
perceive how very different she looked in all her fin-
ery and that rather becoming hairstyle. Not at all like
the Friday he knew. It was a realisation that deprived
him momentarily of all power of thought.

Friday, meanwhile, was moving in Caroline's wake
with the steps of an automaton, with as little attention,
did she but know it, on what she was doing as Nick
was experiencing. Her initial reaction had been a re-

surgence of that dreadful sick feeling that seemed always to attack her now in Nick's presence. His appearance was just what she had been dreading, and it was quite as bad as she had foreseen.

"Better go after him," had muttered Delamere worriedly. "No saying what he might do, such a devilish humour as he's been in these many weeks. See you later, Friday."

Friday had been left alone for a moment, her treacherous heart seizing instantly on the possibilities inherent in Nick's "devilish humour". What did it mean? Don't be silly! she'd answered herself. What should it mean, but that he was still pining miserably for Hermione Hesket? If she could not ignore the instant stab of pain that accompanied this thought, she was able at least to curse it. She would *not* give in to such emotions again.

Fortunately, perhaps, Caroline Cleeve had chosen this moment to accost her. But her first words had done little to ease Friday's unquiet mind.

"Was that Nick I saw with you a moment past? What did he have to say for himself?"

"Nothing at all," Friday responded truthfully.

"Good!" uttered Caroline, inexplicably pleased. But she did not pursue the subject. "Now, Friday, I must beg you to do me a very great kindness, if you please."

"Certainly, if I can, Caro," Friday said at once, although she hoped that it might not entail too much concentration. Her mind would not readily relinquish the image of Nick's accusing eyes that she had come upon so suddenly through the single eyeglass, and she was hard put to it to formulate any other thought. But she was, she reminded herself, indebted to Caroline in many ways, even if the methods she employed were not always to Friday's taste.

"I have got to get Griselda Apperley away from Tony, and bring Julia into his company again," whispered Mrs Cleeve into her ear. "If you, Friday, will keep him talking, I can make the switch."

Friday sighed. She was at it again! "Have you learned *nothing* from your experiences with Nick and myself?"

"Hush!" begged Caroline, adding aloud, "I declare, Friday, anyone would think you were unacquainted with my *other* brother. I dare say people are unaware that we have *all* been friends—the three of us, together with you and Charles Delamere, I mean—for years and years."

Looking quickly about, Friday recalled that she had not her spectacles on, and groped at her breast for that irritating eyeglass on a ribbon. Was this Caro's manner of quieting public interest? Did that mean that people *were* talking? It must! For Caroline would not bother to express herself in such terms, deliberately to be overheard, if there were no reason to do so. She hoped very much that Nick was out of earshot. Perhaps, she thought with a sinking heart, he had already left the party, too angered to stay.

By the time she had raised the eyeglass to her face, any interested features had already been turned away, she guessed. For she could find no searching glances in her immediate vicinity. No Nick either. Instead, she found herself face to face with the Honourable Anthony Weare, whom she had not seen for a very long time.

His resemblance to his young brother was slight, for it was rather himself and his sister Caroline who looked alike. His was a good-humoured countenance, with a ready smile and a pair of friendly eyes under sandy hair like his sire's, but shorn to a Bedford crop. Friday liked him very well—one could not do otherwise with such a friendly personality—but just at this moment she felt a little wary. Tony could not always be depended on for tact!

"Friday, you here?" he uttered pleasantly, without a trace of consciousness about prior events.

"For heaven's sake, Tony!" uttered Caroline impatiently, for, unlike the bulk of his acquaintance, his sister found his insouciance exasperating. "I *told* you she was coming."

"So you did, so you did," responded her brother, quite unperturbed. "I forgot." He turned to his companion, a pretty girl with a shy smile. "Grissy, this is Friday Edborough, if you haven't been presented before. Old friend of ours, you know. She was engaged to Nick for a space."

"Tony, be quiet!" snapped Caroline crossly, slapping his arm.

"Eh?" demanded her brother, startled.

She had known it! Friday thought. Though if it had not been for that dreadful encounter with Nick a few moments past she might have been more amused than embarrassed. As it was, she glanced involuntarily around, half afraid that Nicolas might be lurking close by, ready to snap at her again.

The young girl at Tony's side put out a hand to Friday, saying in a soft voice, "Don't heed him, pray! I *had* heard of it. I am so very sorry. How do you do? I am Griselda Apperley, you know." She gave a little laugh, throwing a glance up at Mr Weare that was unmistakable in its message. "Forgive me, but it is no use waiting for Tony to give you my name."

"I beg your pardon, Grissy," uttered the culprit guiltily. "I forgot!"

Warming to the kindness in both face and voice, Friday disregarded her own discomfort and took the hand held out to her. "It makes no matter. I am very happy to meet you—"

"Griselda!" interrupted Caroline firmly. "*Do* come with me a moment. I simply *must* tell you something *terribly* interesting."

Friday noted a quick exchange of looks between Griselda Apperley and Tony Weare. A raised eyebrow from the girl, which Friday could have sworn betokened amusement, and a brief casting of Tony's eyes to heaven demonstrated clearly that both were quite aware of the purpose of Caroline's tactics. It was evident that Mrs Cleeve was wasting her time. With a pang, Friday recognised that these two people were very much in love with one another. It was equally obvious that they felt it prudent for the moment to humour the gentleman's guardian sister, for Griselda at once moved forward.

"Certainly, Caroline," she said quietly, and cast a quizzical glance back at Friday. "I dare say you will not object to keeping Tony company for a space? Until *other* company appears."

The words, uttered in a pleasant tone that argued innocence, were nevertheless barbed enough for Friday's intelligence. Did she mean Nick? Surely not. Of course not. It must be that other female that Caro had mentioned as her own choice for her brother.

"We'll have Julia Kilmartin here in a moment,"

Tony remarked once his sister was out of earshot, confirming Friday's guess.

She looked up at him. "Why do you let Caro continue in this way if you mean to marry Griselda in any event?"

Tony laughed, apparently not at all put out by a discussion of his personal affairs. "She won't listen to me. Stubborn as a mule, is Caro. I'm only waiting for a propitious moment to put the notion to my father."

"And you have been delayed by this dreadful business with Nick and me, no doubt," Friday said sapiently, a little shiver attacking her as she gave another involuntary glance around—quite uselessly, for she could see nothing beyond a foot away. But she was conscious of an eerie conviction that Nicolas was keeping her under observation.

"Just so," agreed Tony, grinning. "It's not the moment to spring it on him. Grissy and I discussed the matter, and decided it was better to wait."

"So you have already asked her to marry you," Friday observed, trying to ignore the prickle at the back of her neck.

Tony laughed out. "I didn't have to. We both knew the thing was a certainty about five minutes after we met! Haven't looked at anyone else since, either of us."

Such a shaft of anguish shot through Friday that she was obliged to close her eyes for a moment. And Nick was so *close*. Heaven help her, but she could almost feel him! She had been mad to come to town. How she wished she had not given in to Caro's persuasions, to lay herself open once more to such *pain*. Papa had said just that of himself and Mama. Had

Tony and Griselda Apperley any notion of how *fortunate* they both were? No secret yearnings. No aching dreams. Just a simple realisation, and instant agreement.

"You all right, Friday?" came Anthony Weare's concerned tones above her. "You look a bit done in."

Friday pulled herself together, forcing a smile. "I am perfectly well, I thank you, Tony."

"Uh-oh!" he uttered suddenly. "Here comes the enemy!"

Instant apprehension rushed through Friday, and she quickly lifted up the eyeglass. But it was not Nick, as she had immediately feared. Caroline was on her way back, with a tall, graceful female in tow.

"Lady Julia Kilmartin," whispered Tony. "Nice-looking girl. But she hasn't a tithe of Grissy's cosiness."

This was sufficiently distracting to bring Friday's attention to bear on the approaching female. Turning, she lifted the eyeglass and peered through it.

Some feet away, Nick let out a snort of disgust.

"What's to do?" demanded his friend's voice.

Nick looked round briefly, taking in that Delamere had materialised at his side without comment, for annoyance had once more attacked him.

"What in Hades does she think she looks like with that thing stuck at her eye? I've never seen anything so ridiculous!"

"What, the eyeglass? More fashionable than spectacles, though," observed Charles in the tone of the worldly-wise. "Dare say your sister recommended it. Or my mama."

"Caro! Of course it was she," uttered Nick snappily. "She had the effrontery to tell Friday to smarten herself up when we were betrothed."

"Yes, but she was right. Must admit that, looking at the girl now. Much more the thing."

"Not with that idiotic eyeglass!" insisted Nick angrily, his frustration unaccountably increased by the sight of it. "And now look! If that is the way Caro means to allow her to conduct herself, I don't know what will be the end of it."

Delamere gazed at him in open astonishment. "What's eating you, old fellow? Only talking to your brother and Lady Julia. Nothing wrong with that."

"Are you blind? She is surrounded by the most inveterate mischief-makers in town!"

His friend needed no further elucidation. There was only one trio who fitted that description. His eyes snapped back to their slightly obscured view of Friday, and he tutted at once, shaking his head, as he saw who had approached her.

"The Three Witches, no less."

"Yes. And Tony is taking the opportunity to slope off, curse him!"

Friday hardly noticed the departure of the Honourable Anthony Weare. She had failed to find anything in Lady Julia Kilmartin's conversation—for Tony could not be said to have participated in the desultory chat—to keep her mind off Nick's possible whereabouts. But she was instantly diverted when she was accosted by a female of middle years, accompanied by two gentleman of her own age.

"Forgive me, Julia, my dear," uttered the lady, "but this, so I am told, is Sophia Edborough's daughter. *Such* an amazing female, Sophia. I simply *must* meet her daughter. Present me!"

It was a command, and Lady Julia rather grudgingly performed the necessary introductions. The newcomer, a Lady Dalmeny, was very fashionably dressed, Friday saw as she lifted the eyeglass the better to inspect her. A half-robe of blue sarcenet, trimmed with gold lace, was worn over a round gown of white muslin. A turban confined most of her dark hair over a strong-featured face with a prominent nose that must, Friday felt, intimidate her acquaintance.

"My dear Miss Edborough," she began sweetly, "I am delighted to make your acquaintance. It is so rare in these days to discover a female with *anything* in her head other than cotton wool. But you, I understand, are quite a scholar."

"Hardly," Friday answered, with a flash of her friendly smile. "My Latin is abominable. I am rather better at Greek."

"As who could not be?" remarked one of her companions. He bowed as Friday turned to him. "Victor St Abbs, ma'am. So crass, the Romans. So cultured, the Greeks. There can be no comparison." He gave a thin-lipped smile that did not reach his eyes. "I am sure you agree, Miss Edborough."

An odd undercurrent ran through his voice, and Friday felt a little menaced. But before she could answer the third party intervened.

"So *romantic*, the Greeks, more like," he corrected, and bowed in his turn. "I am Percival Luss, Miss Edborough. I cannot think that such a young lady was led to the Greeks by culture."

Friday hesitated briefly, uncertain how to respond to such banter. She supposed it *was* banter? She was still holding up the glass, and, unconscious of the way her eye was thus magnified, she studied them both.

They were equally fashionably dressed, both in silk suits of one colour, with high stand-fall collars to their coats and bright steel buttons. St Abbs was slim and sharp-featured with snapping black eyes, while Luss was portly, with eyebrows that appeared to be permanently raised in an expression of surprise over amused bright eyes.

"As a matter of fact," she said slowly, allowing the glass to fall, "it was the myths of the gods that attracted me, and they were as prevalent in Rome. I think Greek is more lyrical a language, perhaps."

"There now!" exclaimed Lady Dalmeny, giving out a squealing laugh that was unsuitably girlish. "That has put *both* of you in your places. Well done, Miss Edborough!"

"I shall come about," promised Luss, grinning.

"Not if you mean to place this female of *superior* wit on a par with others of her age," remarked the other man cuttingly.

"Be quiet, Stabbs!" ordered the lady gaily. She turned apologetically to Friday. "We call him that, you know, for he goes among us with an all-too-ready knife."

"That will do, Lavinia," said his victim. Moving forward to take Friday's hand, he raised it momentarily to his lips. Friday felt that the gesture was performed ironically, as were the words that accompanied it. "I delight in superior females."

"Oh, ho, ho! Stabbs the gallant!" mocked Percival Luss. He grinned at Friday. "For my part, it is the *eyeglass* that delights. I *love* it, ma'am. And you use it *so* well. An excellent touch!"

Friday was obliged to laugh. "Indeed? I cannot say

it delights *me*. And Caroline Cleeve tells me it makes me look like a quiz."

"It does," Mr Luss assured her. "But then we are very fond of quizzes."

A brief sigh escaped Friday. "To tell you the truth, I had far rather have worn my spectacles."

Mr St Abbs pursed his lips. "You mean it is not an affectation?"

"Gracious, no! I cannot see a thing without it," Friday said frankly.

All three burst into laughter, and Lady Dalmeny laid a hand briefly on Friday's wrist. "We are quite confounded, my dear. Here we had thought ourselves outclassed—"

"Outgeneralled," added Mr Luss with a lift of his brows.

"*Outwitted,*" put in St Abbs pointedly.

"And instead," went on Lady Dalmeny, without explaining these interruptions, "we discover you to be *genuine*. It is a great deal too bad!"

Friday blinked. "I have not a notion what you mean."

"We know," said St Abbs with a smirk of satisfaction. "That is what makes the whole affair particularly enjoyable."

Somewhat bewildered, Friday looked to Tony Weare for enlightenment, only to discover his absence. Lady Julia had likewise escaped, and she felt quite suddenly adrift in an alien world. Who were these people? What did they want with her? And what in the world did they mean by all this nonsense about the eyeglass? She could not believe that there really were people who wore such things just for show. The thing was so very uncomfortable to use, and virtually useless unless one held it in place all the time.

Despite her lack of clarity of vision, she noticed the man St Abbs lean towards Lady Dalmeny and whisper in her ear. By instinct, she raised the eyeglass once more, and was just in time to intercept a conspiratorial glance among the trio, who were looking away from her at some object at too great a distance for her to be able to identify it. Before she could make anything of this, Lady Dalmeny closed in to her side and cradled her arm.

"Don't you feel hot, Miss Edborough? Why do we not move out of this dreadful press of persons?"

Friday would have like to move, certainly. Away from these people! Instead she found herself pushed with them and in a moment came face to face with Charles Delamere.

"Ah, Friday!" he uttered, jostling his way between St Abbs and Luss who had been leading. "Been hunting for you all over."

"Oh! Why?" asked Friday, assailed all of a sudden by the memory of Nick's face. Was he near? Charles had said he was going after him.

"My mother wants you," said Delamere fluently, and firmly took her arm, ousting Lady Dalmeny.

As he shifted his position, Friday saw a little way behind him the familiar outline of Nick's features. Her heart skipped a beat. Oh, God, but she had known it! He *was* there. She had no time to say or do anything, however, for Charles was on the move. She went with him, perforce, forgetting in the instant shock of her senses at seeing Nick again even to excuse herself to the trio with whom she had been conversing.

"You don't want to get mixed up with those three," Delamere muttered in her ear as soon as they were out of earshot.

Friday glanced quickly round at him, catching his expression of concern as she peered into his face. Involuntarily, she uttered her instant thought. "Since when have you been concerned for my welfare, Charles?"

"Not me," he told her frankly. "Nick bade me get you away from them."

"What?" uttered Friday, a spurt of irritation flaring up. "What business is it of Nick's whom I talk to?"

"Don't get up on your high ropes," recommended Charles. "You ought to be grateful to him. Lethal, they are. Dashed if the Dalmeny ain't the worst of the lot!"

Curiosity superseded her annoyance with Nick's apparent interference. "What do you mean? I admit I did not feel quite comfortable in their company, but—"

"Shouldn't think anyone would. Everyone calls 'em the Three Witches. After that play by the Tudor fellow—what's his name?"

"Shakespeare. You mean *Macbeth?*"

"That's the one. Poison is what they are, and that's a fact. And what with all the talk over your betrothal—"

"Oh, I see," Friday said flatly. "Nick is only afraid there will be more scandal, is that it? For a moment I was stupid enough to imagine he had *my* interests at heart."

"Don't you go all sour on me, Friday, for I can't bear it!" warned Delamere. "Enough on my hands with Nick and his black moods, I thank you."

Friday's treacherous heart instantly mellowed into tenderness again. And—which was far worse—*hope*. She longed to ask more about these "black moods". What had caused them? If Charles *knew,* which she dared not suppose was the case. Besides, she did not wish to hear what she was already sure of—that Hermione was the cause of his depression. How could it be otherwise?

Yet she had not bargained for the effect on herself of meeting with him again. Just seeing him—for she could not be said to have spoken with him—had brought everything back. So strongly that she felt as if she had progressed not one iota towards her goal. Her awareness of him was intense—for after what Charles had said there could be no doubt that he *had* been watching her—even though she could not see him. And if her memory of that brief glimpse of him through the eyeglass was to be trusted, he had looked so drawn, she realised now. He was as beautiful as ever. Nothing could change that. But the strain she had herself lived through was mirrored in his face. Her feeling for him was too acute to allow her to be unaware of it. As she suffered, so did he. Worse, in fact. For Nick's grief must be compounded by the disillusionment he had experienced in the woman he loved so dearly. Why, oh, why had they both to love where their love was unrequited? Why could they not have been like Tony and Griselda—so sure, so clear, so much *together?*

Fool! She was baying for the moon again. Things were as they were, and *nothing* could change them. The best she could hope for, as long as she remained in town, was that Nicolas would avoid her.

She was glad to be restored to Lady Delamere's

care, and even happier when Caroline declared that the curfew imposed by her husband was up. The three of them travelled home in the Delamere town carriage, dropping Caro off at her own town house around the corner in Bruton Street on the way. But Friday slept badly.

She joined Lady Delamere after breakfast in the blue saloon—furnished with the same exquisite taste that characterised Delamere Place, with here the graceful stamp of Sheraton throughout—having been summoned thither in the expectation of morning callers, who might, as her ladyship insisted, prove useful in furthering Friday's prospects. The first caller was, unsurprisingly, Caroline Cleeve, who came to confer with Lady Delamere about which invitations she proposed to accept on Friday's behalf. She seemed, for once, not to notice that Friday had reverted to her spectacles this morning. Much to Friday's relief, for she thought her eyes might be suspiciously puffy. She did not wish to have to explain *that*.

"I do trust you will take her to balls, Lady Delamere," Caroline said agitatedly from her seat near the fire, "for Dicky is insistent that I may *not* go to anything more strenuous than a soirée. I have *promised* him that I will rest every afternoon, but he is *adamant*. And you know Dicky! He will fetch me home himself if I *dare* to go against his wishes."

"So I should hope!" stated her ladyship severely. "You are a great deal too careless, Caroline. When I was confined, I remained home throughout."

"Yes, but only think, Lady Delamere. Dicky's family has *endless* babies, and if I should find myself confined year after year I should never come to town at all!"

Lady Delamere snorted. "Rubbish! I have no patience with these men who will keep their wives permanently in a condition of expectancy. It is quite unnecessary and very selfish indeed! And so I shall inform Richard when next I see him. Let me tell you, I have very strictly instructed Delamere in such matters, when it comes to his turn. He would do better to get himself a mistress than trouble his wife into an early grave!"

Caroline exclaimed against the implied suggestion that her husband ought to do likewise, begging the elder lady not to encourage him in any such fashion. For her part, Friday dissolved into uncontrollable giggles, amused in spite of her heavy heart by Lady Delamere's outspoken views. She was still hiccuping on her laughter—indignantly berated by Caroline—when the butler entered to announce another visitor.

"The Honourable Anthony Weare, ma'am," he said.

Tony came dashing in, half panting with effort. "I came at once. I thought you'd wish to know, Friday. Nick's on his way."

"Nicky is coming *here?*" shrieked Caroline.

"That's what he said. He's been grumbling all through breakfast that no one told him she was coming to town."

"Of course we did not tell him," said Lady Delamere sharply. "That would have ruined everything!"

Friday glanced across at her. Under the unruly beating of her pulse, she experienced, for the first time, the feeling that she was being deliberately manipulated. She and Nicolas both! Looking over at Caroline, she was just in time to see the quick shake of her head directed at Lady Delamere. Heaven help her, but they were in this together! Oh, why could they not let it *alone?* Nick did not *want* her. When would they realise that?

She could scarcely voice her feelings with Tony in the room, but before she could say anything at all they heard a knocking at the front door below. Within a very few moments, the butler announced Nick, who marched into the room, saw his brother, and came to a dead stop.

"What in Hades are you doing here?" he demanded suspiciously.

"Why shouldn't I be here?" countered his brother.

"Good day, Nicolas!" uttered Lady Delamere in a voice of cold reproof.

Nick turned quickly. "I beg your pardon, Lady Delamere." He bowed briefly. "How do you do?" His glance travelled to his sister and he nodded. "Caroline." Then he found Friday's face and glared at her. "How do you do, Miss Edborough?"

"Oh, don't be so *stupid,* Nicky!" exclaimed Caroline crossly. "If that is the way you mean to conduct yourself, you had better go away again at once."

Lady Delamere rose from the scroll-ended sofa. "Do, pray, remember your manners, Nicolas! I do not scruple to speak to you so, for I have known you from your earliest years and I have long thought of myself in the light of an aunt towards you." She glanced at Caroline as Tony stepped forward to open the door for her. "I will return shortly, Caroline. Try if you can hint your brother into a proper mode of conduct, if you please."

Nick flushed scarlet as her ladyship stalked out of the blue saloon, and Friday, having taken umbrage at his formal manner, instantly felt herself growing compassionate towards him. They need not treat him like a child! After all, he was labouring under strong emotions. Though why he was being so horrid to her she could not imagine.

"Nick," she uttered a trifle breathlessly for all her determination to remain calm.

He turned towards her, but he did not speak. His lips were compressed, his eyes sombre, but the flush was dying down. God knew, he had not *meant* to behave so badly! But the very sight of Friday looking so—so *tonnish,* damn it!—threw him instantly on the defensive, for some reason even he could not fathom.

"Nick," Friday began again, "let us at least be civilised."

"Civilised?" he echoed, the hurt once more making itself felt. "Was it civilised of everyone to keep me in ignorance of your presence in town? You have no idea what a shock it was to me to see you at Lady Holt's last night."

Unexpectedly, it was his brother who answered this. "Yes, but why should anyone tell you, Nick? It's not as if you have any claim."

"I know that," Nick snapped. "But after—I mean, Caro *knew*— Damn it, I've a *right* to know!"

"Language, my boy, language," Tony admonished him.

"Don't, Tony!" begged Friday. "It does not matter to me."

"There is no need to tell us that," Nick interpolated in a bitter tone before he could stop himself.

Friday's brows snapped together. Through the spectacles, her eyes flashed at him. "What is that supposed to mean?"

"I should have thought that was obvious," Nick said stiffly.

"Should you, indeed? Well, since you are *obviously* mistaken, perhaps you would like to explain yourself."

"Don't be sarcastic, Friday! It doesn't suit you."

"What do you care what suits me?"

"Hey! Hey!" cried Tony, breaking in between them. "There's no need for this sort of thing."

"It was Nicky who started it," Caroline said crossly. "I have never known you to be so horrid, Nicky! What in the world is the matter with you?"

Nicolas turned on her. It was, after all, *her* fault. "I have told you, Caro. I think it utterly thoughtless of you to neglect to inform me that Friday had the intention of coming to town. I might understand that she would not wish to tell me herself, but *you*. How could you leave me to find out that way?"

Tony eyed him frowningly. "It sounds to me, old fellow, as if you object to poor Friday's coming to town."

"Of course I don't object to it. Why should I? What I object to is that no one saw fit to tell me of it."

"Well, you know now," Caroline told him flatly.

There was a silence. Friday, ashamed of her own conduct, determined not to say another word. She was still too irritated by Nick's attitude to trust herself not to carp at him again. It was as if he took her arrival without notice as a personal affront to himself!

The door opened, and into the uncomfortable pause walked Charles Delamere. Catching sight of Nick, he stared at him open-mouthed. Nicolas instantly took umbrage again.

"Don't you start!"

But Delamere at once asked the obvious question. "What are you doing here, old fellow?"

"I came to see Friday!" Nicolas announced. His glare encompassed the company. "There. Are you all satisfied?"

"No!" said Friday crossly, resentment flaring again. "I am not in the least satisfied, if you wish to know, Nicolas Weare. You have not come to *see* me, but to snarl at me, just as you did last night."

"I did not 'snarl,'" objected Nick irately. "Merely because I was shocked—"

"Shocked! Oh, yes, and I dare say you were 'shocked' by seeing me in company with Lady Dalmeny and her friends—"

"What?" shrieked Caroline.

"—since you took it upon yourself to send Charles to drag me away," ended Friday, unheeding.

"Friday, you never said a *word* of this!" uttered Caro, aghast.

"I had no need to, since Nick saw fit to intervene."

"You ought to be thanking me for that!"

"Yes, truly you ought, Friday," said Mrs Cleeve earnestly. "You have no idea how *dreadful*—"

"I have, for Charles told me so, but I am not a *baby*, Caro." She glared at Nick. "I have *some* intelligence, let me tell you. I could very well see for myself what sort of creatures they were."

"Then I am astonished you had not the wit to remove yourself from their vicinity!" Nick sneered.

"Well, I certainly have enough to remove myself from *yours*," retorted Friday, sweeping towards the door.

"Stop it, the both of you!" called out Delamere

before Nick could respond to this. His hand stopped Friday in her tracks. "Someone's coming!"

"Callers!" uttered Caroline despairingly. Her eyes, darting from the door back to Friday, widened suddenly, and she hissed frantically, "Friday, your spectacles!"

Still seething, Friday snatched them off without thinking as she marched away from the door and, turning, held them in her hand behind her. Blinking, she saw the outline of the door open, and the blurry form of the butler.

He entered on a scene of utter silence, with five questioning faces turned towards him. He bowed calmly. "Lady Dalmeny, Mr St Abbs, and Mr Luss."

The Three Witches strolled into the saloon.

Chapter Nine

For a moment or two, the entire company was frozen with embarrassment. Without her spectacles, Friday was hard put to it to recognise the faces of probably the least welcome visitors in the world, but she recalled the names easily enough.

Caroline, always at home in Society, was the first to recover. Gushing a spurious welcome, as if she herself were the hostess, she moved forward. Charles, recognising his cue—for it was his house, after all—followed suit.

As greetings were exchanged all round, Friday felt that she, the least experienced at this sort of thing, was probably the last to regain her self-possession. Although no one could possibly walk in here without feeling the almost tangible tension. She could not think what had come over her, to be drawn into a stupid battle with Nicolas. Over *nothing*. Heaven help her, but this was the man she loved! What was the matter with her that she must bicker and snap at his every utterance?

In a moment Lady Dalmeny was upon her, forcing her out of these thoughts and into some semblance of courteous response as she was told that the lady had come to invite her to a party at her house the following evening.

"I trust you will forgive the short notice, but I could not have invited you before, now, could I?" said Lady Dalmeny on that girlish laugh, dragging Friday down to sit with her on the sofa recently vacated by the lady of the house.

"It is very kind in you, ma'am," said Friday politely, "but I must consult with Lady Delamere first."

"But Lydia is promised already," said the other gaily, keeping hold of Friday's hand. "Where is she? I made sure she would be here and I might persuade her to bring you."

"I think she has gone out," Friday lied, hiding her spectacles to one side with her free hand. She was thankful that Lady Delamere had chosen to leave the room, and hoped very much that these people would have departed before she came back. She might then have a hope of rejecting an invitation she had no wish to accept.

"It makes no matter. I can always persuade Mrs Cleeve to bring you in her stead," uttered Lady Dalmeny, throwing Friday into relief.

She could not believe, after Caroline's outburst, that she would agree to this. As Lady Dalmeny chattered on, Friday's blurry gaze travelled anxiously across the room to find Caro, and saw that she had drawn what must be St Abbs into conversation. Hoping, Friday supposed, to keep him away from herself. And was that Luss talking to Charles? Tony, she recognised, was hovering by the door, all too obviously awaiting his moment to remove himself. Standing between Caroline and Delamere, Nick was paying attention to neither. Friday felt his eyes on her and glanced briefly in his direction. She might not be able to see, but she knew he was watching her.

"Nicolas!" uttered Lady Dalmeny, apparently having noted the direction of Friday's gaze. She released the hand she held and Friday thankfully shifted slightly away. "Come and tell me how your father does."

"He is as well as can be expected," Nick said shortly, moving a few paces towards the sofa.

It was the standard response to all such enquiries, for the Weare children knew well that most people only asked out of politeness and would not relish a catalogue recital of Lord Weare's sufferings. He was, however, hardly paying attention to what he said. The reappearance of the Three Witches, hard on the heels of their capture of Friday last night, did not augur well for their intentions. If the Dalmeny thought to try her tricks on Friday, she and her infernal associates would have him to reckon with!

But Lady Dalmeny was all sweetness. "Dear boy, do give Weare my best when you see him next. We all miss him terribly still." She turned to Friday. "Do you know that this boy is the *image* of his mother?"

"So I have been told," Friday agreed, her eyes straying over Nick's enchanting features. They were not entirely in focus, but she knew them so well that her imagination made up for the deficiencies of her sight.

"An exceptionally beautiful woman, your mother," went on the lady gently.

"Yes, she must have been," said Friday almost absently, for Nick's glance, as he stepped even closer, had caught hers, and somehow she could not look away.

Nicolas hardly heard the woman. Instinct took him to Friday's side. Then she had looked up into his face and those naked eyes—so rarely seen, but so *mesmerising*—met his own. All thought went out of his head. He was conscious only of a spreading warmth in his chest and a feeling of intense *need*.

"I remember thinking last season," came Lady Dalmeny's purring tones, "that the sight of you and the little Hesket girl standing together simply took one's breath away!"

Nick's head snapped round. "I beg your pardon?"

Lady Dalmeny's eyebrows lifted delicately. "Didn't you *know*? Why, everyone was in raptures over the two of you! One felt that Botticelli ought to rise from the grave and paint you both."

Friday's betraying heart went cold on her. She could not see the woman's face clearly, but she saw enough to know that Lady Dalmeny's eyes were on her and that a smile was playing about her mouth. Heaven help her, but that was intentional! What sort of female was this, to inflict such torture merely for sport? She vaguely heard Lady Dalmeny's voice continue, and saw the woman rise and move away.

"Stabbs, dearest! We positively *must* go. I have Miss Edborough's promise to come tomorrow night, and so we may safely retire."

The figures became a blur at the other end of the room, with Caroline apparently ushering the party out. Then Nick was speaking close to her ear, and his reassuring voice was for once the most welcome sound in the world.

"Don't heed it, Friday, I beg of you! She is nothing but a malicious cat."

Friday turned to find that he had sat down beside her. She gave a little laugh. "Yes, but she only spoke the truth." Her breath caught as her own memory of the picture of Nick and the girl Hermione standing together flashed into her mind. She scarcely knew that she spoke aloud the thought that instantly followed. "It was far more Paris and Helen than you and I could ever have been."

"Friday, don't *do* that!" came Nick's anguished tones. "I cannot *bear* it."

"No, I'm sorry," Friday said in quick remorse. "It must be painful for you to speak of it."

"It is painful for me to hear you make such idiotic comparisons!" Nick retorted forcefully. "Besides, I have no wish to remember Hermione. You must believe me when I tell you that all that is *over*."

Without conscious intention, Friday brought up her spectacles and put them on, the better to examine his face. He looked so sincere, she almost did believe him.

"Is it?" she asked quietly.

"The whole episode is dead and gone," he insisted.

Easy to say! She might have said the same—she *had* done so, trying to convince both herself and Caroline. And if it was the truth, what then? What did he want? That she marry him "after all"? God knew she had been over *that* impossibility a hundred times! She managed to smile.

"Perhaps. But you see, it does not make any difference."

His face changed, stiffening. The green eyes narrowed to chips of marble, hard and cold. "I see."

The transition hurt Friday so much that she cried out involuntarily, "No, you *don't*. How *can* you see? You are blinder than I am!"

"Oh, I'm blind? Is it any wonder, since you insist on keeping me at such a distance?" He jumped to his feet. "Well, have no fear, *ma'am*. In future, I shall refrain from coming anywhere near you!"

Ignoring Caroline's open-mouthed astonishment, he strode to the door, Delamere and Tony giving way as he reached it, neither having the slightest notion how to handle this emotionally charged scene. Friday's voice stopped him as he laid his fingers on the door-handle.

"Wait, Nick!"

Nicolas turned, the light of battle in his eyes still as they went directly to Friday's face. She had risen, and he took in that her fingers were curled with tension, her funny little face taut. Instantly he was reminded of the stressful sight she had presented on the hilltop that day. God, what was it that made him speak to her in such a way? She was so vulnerable! His heart softened. So indomitable she was as she stood there now, the owl-like spectacles her shield against the world.

"It is quite r-ridiculous for us to continue in this way," Friday said in an attempt at a matter-of-fact tone that did not fool Nick in the very least. He knew that tremor! "We are b-bound to meet, after all."

"Yes," Nick managed to say, aware that his voice was constricted.

Friday hardly knew how to continue. She had thought she wanted to forget him. But when it came to the point, when it looked as if the silly bickering had driven him to distraction, she'd *had* to stop him from walking out of her life. Fighting to control the threatening tears, she sought Caroline's face.

"Caro!" she uttered helplessly.

Mrs Cleeve did not fail her. "Yes, indeed, Friday. I *quite* agree. You cannot possibly avoid each other. You will only make yourselves a laughing-stock, and incite *more* gossip."

"That's true enough," put in Delamere. "Ain't as if everybody doesn't already know the full sum of it."

"You mean they are talking again?" asked Nick quickly.

"What do you think?" returned Charles witheringly. "Now that the Dalmeny has got her claws into Friday—"

"Oh, Caro, what in the world shall I do?" Friday broke in suddenly, the urgency of her thought killing all desire to weep. "I told Lady Dalmeny that I must consult with Lady Delamere before I could accept her invitation. But she says that Lady Delamere is promised."

"Stuff! Lady Delamere would not set foot in her house."

"I can vouch for *that*," agreed Charles. "My mother can't bear the woman."

"Very few females of distinction can," put in Tony. "But her parties are always amusing."

"That is quite beside the point," Caroline stated. "We are not concerned with amusement, but with Friday's position. If she does *not* go, then Lady Dalmeny will have triumphed."

"I don't see how," objected Nick, suddenly enter-

ing the lists. "Why in Hades should Friday go anywhere near the place, since we already know that
woman is targeting her?"

"Just *because* of that, of course," said his sister.
"So as not to give those *wicked* creatures the satisfaction of knowing that they have successfully intim-
idated Friday. Really, Nicky, you have no *notion* how
to launch a counter-attack."

"Loath as I am to agree with Nick—" Friday began, and was interrupted by Tony Weare.

"Don't start that all over again!"

"But I have no *wish* to launch a counter-attack."

"You have no choice, Friday," Caroline said
firmly, sinking down into her chair by the fire. "You
have been singled out, and you must demonstrate that
you are not *afraid* of what they may do. You must
be seen everywhere. You and Nick both."

"What, *together?*" demanded Nick.

"At times, yes. But not in *particular,* you understand."

"Thank God for that!"

"Your sentiments are entirely echoed," Friday uttered snappily.

"Well, you can count me out," said Delamere. "I
ain't going to the Dalmeny's, for one thing. And if
you think I can bear listening to these two nag at each
other, you can think again."

"But Charles," pleaded Caroline, "if we are to
confound those hideous witches, we must all stand
together."

"That's the way," said Tony encouragingly, moving to his sister's chair, as if to pledge his support.
"If Nick and Friday are at least seen to be on—" he
hesitated over the word "friendly" and substituted

something less dangerous "—*normal* terms from now on, I don't see the tabbies getting their teeth into it again."

Nicolas drew a breath. He would not look at Friday, but he was aware of the futility of the way in which they had both been behaving. He was hurt, yes. But that was no excuse for ill manners.

"I don't know if even 'normal' is possible. But I am willing to do whatever—whatever Friday wants, if it will allay any further scandal."

"It is not merely what Friday wants," objected Caroline. "This affects *all* of us. There is nothing for it. We must all five appear as friendly as possible. Just as if nothing had ever happened between you two."

"*That* is not possible," Friday uttered involuntarily.

"Well, if you want to stay in town, you must make it so," said Nick, snapping again.

"For God's sake!" exclaimed Charles, exasperated.

Tony cast up his eyes. "It ain't going to work, Caro. Just listen to the two of them!"

Both Friday and Nicolas ignored him, but Caroline groaned as the sparks began to fly again between them.

"Are you suggesting that I should leave town again?" demanded Friday.

"I never said anything of the kind. However, I don't wish to be exposed to further scandal, if you do."

"Then why don't *you* leave town?"

"Why in Hades should I, just because you can't even bring yourself to speak to me?"

"What am I doing now, I should like to know?"

"Will the two of you be *quiet?*" screamed Caroline, topping them both.

As one, Nick and Friday swung away from each other, Nick moving to glare into the fire in the grate, while Friday threw herself into an elegant Sheraton chair at the other end of the room.

Caroline cast a glance of despair at Tony, who merely shrugged and grimaced. But Delamere frowned direfully, and cleared his throat, moving so that he could keep both parties to the debate under observation.

"Bound to say Caro's in the right of it. All very well for you two to snap each other's noses off every five minutes, but it ain't very comfortable for the rest of us."

"I beg your pardon, Charles," Friday uttered in a contrite tone, without looking up.

"Accept my apologies," Nick said stiffly, not to be outdone.

"No use to *me,*" uttered Charles, exasperated. "What you ought to do is apologise to each other, and be done with it."

Neither of the principals had anything to say to this. Nick threw a frowning glance Friday's way, but she pointedly turned her face in the other direction. Delamere sighed.

"Did my best, Caro."

Caroline shook her head. "It is of no use, Charles. I declare, I begin to wish I had never thought of this scheme!"

"You are not alone in that!" Friday said roundly.

Nick swung round. "I knew it! It had to be all your idea, did it not, Caro? Why must everyone *interfere?*"

"Because if they did not you would have been married to that idiotic female—" began Caroline crossly.

"Instead of which, I am blessedly single still! I thank you, Caro. I had not realised for how much I had to thank you and my father."

Friday was on her feet. "There is no necessity to be insulting—yet again! Have you not said *enough* on that score?"

Nick took a pace or two towards her, such *hurt* in his eyes as pierced straight to her heart.

"If I have insulted you, Friday, then count yourself wonderfully revenged in your treatment of me. Whatever I have done, I have never been deliberately *cruel*."

Lady Dalmeny's rooms appeared woefully thin of company. Which was not, in view of the sentiments expressed by Lady Delamere—"I am sorry, Frideswid, but wild horses would not drag me across That Woman's threshold!"—very surprising to either of the two young ladies as they negotiated the long stairway to where their hostess awaited them.

Caroline had prophesied that this would be the case, for none but the "scaff and raff" of London were generally in attendance at the Curzon Street house. Friday, however, having been urged into accompanying her friend, had little interest in the identity of the guests and even less in their possible quality.

She was in uncertain mood. Ever since Nick's abrupt departure the previous morning—for after he had said that *dreadful* thing he had marched straight out of the saloon!—she had been attacked by violent and wholly opposing emotions. At one instant fury would be uppermost. The next she was cast down by remorse. The very word haunted her—"cruel".

How could he *dare* to call her that? If she was cruel, what then was he? Had she committed one tithe of the acts against him that he had done against her? She had tried to be fair. To be kind. To be understanding. But there was only so much one could *endure*. He seemed incapable of recognising her pain, and yet *she* was cruel!

But no. That was not strictly just. He *had* seen— just a little. There had been moments of tenderness during that abortive betrothal that she had welcomed, even if they had not meant what her heart yearned for them to mean. Perhaps she had been selfish. What was her love worth, if she could not offer him *something?* Something, that was, other than the snarling ill-temper she had so far demonstrated. Oh, he was right! She had been singularly unkind—if not *quite* "cruel".

She was at a loss at first to understand *why* he had flung the word at her like that. Until she recalled the change that had come over his face when she had told him—just *what* was it she had said? Yes, that it made no difference that all was over, as he had stated, between himself and Hermione. But that had been nothing but the *truth*. It *did* make no difference. Was it "cruel" to say so? If it was, then she had been so *unintentionally*.

But indeed, what had *he* been except marvellously ill-tempered since the moment of seeing her in town? Oh, heaven help her, but *what* was she to feel? Except that she could not dictate her feelings—any more than poor Nick could dictate his own. But he must be made to understand, somehow, that there could be no turning back the clock. What was done was done. They must both of them learn to live with a *new* kind of relationship. If that was possible. He had no claim on her, nor she on him. Neither of friendship, nor of love. She had accepted that. Nick must also learn to do so. And he would *not* so learn by flinging emotive words like "cruel" at her!

The less they met, the better for them both, she felt. Yet the instant that she stepped into one of Lady Dalmeny's drawing-rooms, which had been thrown open all around the gallery to accommodate the guests, the ubiquitous single eyeglass was brought to bear, scanning the company for a sight of Nick's features.

He was not there. Disappointment washed over her in a wave and she dropped the eyeglass, glad of her inability to see the faces. She was vaguely conscious of greetings made to her by St Abbs and Luss, and did not even remember the dangers of their possible incursion into her private affairs. She was forced, however, to give her attention to Caroline, whose high-pitched tones were buzzing in her ear.

"What did you say, Caro?"

"Only look at these people!" Caroline muttered in a low tone of censure. "I declare, I should be astonished to learn that there was more than a smattering of even the *lesser* gentry, let alone anyone of the highest *ton*."

"Well, you would come," Friday said unsympathetically. "I will say one thing for it, however. At least one can *move*."

"And thank heaven for it! To be jostled by a parcel of *tradesmen*." She shuddered eloquently. "Not that I would care to find *my* rooms so dreadfully empty."

Friday lifted her eyeglass and looked about her with faint interest. "Are they tradespeople?"

"I should not be at all surprised," Caro said. Then she uttered a muted shriek. "*Heavens,* would you believe it? Tony is here."

Glancing vainly around, for the eyeglass gave her a sort of tunnel of vision that fuzzed at the edges, Friday protested, "But you told him to come, Caro."

"Yes, but not with Griselda! I dare say he hoped I would not *notice* in this motley collection of so-called guests. *And* that the impropriety of escorting her without a duenna would pass without comment. Friday, I shall *have* to leave you for a space."

She was off on the words, darting away to where Friday could just make out through her eyeglass the Honourable Anthony Weare standing over by a door to one of the several upper saloons leading off the gallery that had been thrown open. At his side was a female form that must be Griselda, decided Friday. As she watched, she saw him start, grab the girl, and vanish through the doorway. Her laughter was interrupted.

"Miss Edborough, is it not? How do you do?" said a pleasant voice.

Looking round, Friday focused the glass on an unknown male face, lined a trifle with dissipation rather than years, for his complexion was pasty. She murmured a polite greeting, sighing inwardly at the necessity to make conversation. But the gentleman caught her interest at once.

"I could not help but overhear Mrs Cleeve a moment since. Allow me to put you straight, Miss Edborough. We are not *all* of us here engaged in trade."

"Oh?" Friday said, dropping her eyeglass.

"No, no. One does not think of lawyers and doctors—even the theatricals among us—as being in trade. These are *professions,* ma'am. Something that even certain of our high-born gentry have no alternative but to engage in."

"That is true," agreed Friday, recalling with a sensation of guilt the political profession Nick hated so much, from which she'd had the power to save him. Pushing the thought away, she asked, "Have you a profession, Mr—I do not know you name?"

"Mashbury," said the gentleman, bowing. "Whether you would call it a profession precisely I am unsure. Some might."

"Well, then what is it that you do?" Friday demanded, rather intrigued.

"I gamble, Miss Edborough," he confessed frankly.

She could hear the laugh in the voice, and wondered if she was being teased. "Not for your living, I imagine?"

"Alas, yes!" sighed Mr Mashbury. "And thus I instantly forfeit your esteem."

"No such thing!" Friday rejoined indignantly. "I am not so judgemental, I assure you." She smiled a little. "I am something of a classical scholar, you must know, and thus perhaps more liberally inclined than your average young lady."

"Ah, a ready acquaintance with vice. How happy for me!"

"Hardly *that,*" she uttered, shocked.

"I meant, I need hardly say, in *mind,* not in deed."

All of a sudden, Friday felt her elbow gripped hard. She turned her head, expecting Caroline. Instead, she encountered Nick's blurry features.

"Your servant, Mashbury," he said curtly, and added in a stern undervoice to Friday, "I must speak with you!"

Friday had no time even to bid the gentleman a polite farewell, for she found herself whirled about, and marched rapidly away towards some unknown destination.

"What do you think you are doing, Nick?" she demanded wrathfully.

"I might ask the same question," he rejoined in a heated way. "Mashbury, of all people!"

Friday found herself in some small recess, away from the main body of the party, in which her flicking gaze recognised under the usual blur a bow-shaped set of drapes. At the back of her mind she took in that Nicolas had brought her to a window alcove, but she was far too angry to pay much attention to her surroundings.

"How *dare* you drag me off like that? What right have you to interrupt my conversation? And what do you mean, 'Mashbury, of all people'?"

"I will tell you what I mean," he uttered in an irate tone. "The man belongs to the worst of company. He is an inveterate gambler, and—"

"Yes, so he informed me. What has that to say to anything?"

Nick's voice sharpened. "Did he also inform you that he is a confirmed fortune-hunter? Perhaps he neglected to mention *that*."

Friday was silenced. She stared up into his face, frustrated all at once by her inability to see him clearly. Forgetting the eyeglass on a ribbon around her neck, she thrust closer so that he came into clearer focus. The storm in his face did nothing to assuage her irritation. Rather it fanned it to a flame.

"And if he is," she almost spat at him, "what is it to you, Nicolas Weare?"

"Do you imagine I will stand by and allow you to consort with fellows of that kind?" he demanded furiously.

"*Allow* me? How dare you?"

"There is no question of daring. *Any* gentleman worthy of the name would feel it incumbent upon him to steer an innocent female clear of such importunities. I cannot think what Caro is about, to leave you alone at such a party!"

"Oh, indeed?" retorted Friday. "Yet I don't recall you announcing your intention of escorting us. No doubt, like Charles, you consulted only your own pleasure."

"Do you think it is any pleasure to me to be here? The only reason I set foot in the place was to keep an eye on you, if you must know."

Friday's jaw dropped. Outraged, she simply stared at him for an instant. *"What?"* she croaked at length, unconsciously groping for her eyeglass. She brought it up to her face and, through it, saw Nick's jaw tighten.

"That," he said acidly, "is quite the most *stupid* thing I have ever seen! Where in Hades are your spectacles? Or do you leave them off precisely because you *wish* to attract the likes of Mashbury?"

The eyeglass dropped. Friday's hand flashed up, striking him on the cheek. Nick flinched, but his own fingers seized her wrist, gripping it so hard that she winced.

"Let go!" she ordered in a guttural tone.

Nick did nothing of the kind. He was breathing heavily, conscious of a wish to hurt her back—*somehow*. But as he stood there it suddenly came home to him what he had said. How *could* he have spoken to her so? Good God, what was the matter with him? He could barely *see* her without experiencing the most crippling emotions that seemed to be driving him insane!

"Friday!" he uttered, anguished. "Friday, what are we doing?"

"We!" she said in a withering tone. "What is it you *want* from me, Nick?"

Nicolas released her wrist abruptly, and instead his hands grasped her shoulders. "Friday, I don't understand what is happening. To you. To me. This isn't *right*."

"*What* isn't right? I don't understand *you*. Why can't you leave me alone?"

He shook her a little. "*Listen* to me, Friday! We cannot continue in this way."

"*Exactly* what I have been trying to tell you all along."

"No. No, it isn't. You're trying to deny your past. *Our* past. We had so much!"

Friday's anger dropped right out. *Had,* yes. That was the truth of it. "Pray release me, Nick," she said wearily. "It's no use. We can't go back, don't you see?"

Slowly his grip relaxed, and his hands dropped. "That is what you were trying to say the other day. You mean you believe that there is nothing left for us."

Friday lowered her eyes so that he would not see

the instant rush of tears that pricked at them. Her voice was husky. "Nothing."

For a moment Nick did not answer. He did not, however, attempt to touch her again. Did she imagine he could not see her distress? That in itself showed him that his senses did not deceive him. She was lying! At length he spoke, trying for a calm manner that he was far from feeling, but unable to keep a throb of passion out of his voice.

"I don't believe you, Friday. We had something precious together, you and I. It's still there! I *feel* it. And so do you. However much you deny it, it cannot be destroyed." He paused, and took a painful breath, adding deliberately, "Unless you yourself destroy it."

At that her head came up. "And you, Nick? Have you no share in that destruction?"

"I *will* have," he grated, giving in suddenly to the unaccountable churning in his breast, "if I catch you *flirting* with so worthless a creature again!"

"Oh, this is intolerable!" cried Friday. "Go away, Nick, for goodness' sake! I *hate* you."

"It needed only that!" Nick declared roundly, and, turning abruptly, he marched purposefully towards the main door.

Friday was left looking after him, torn between natural fury and the immediate onrush of frustrated despair. What in the world was the *matter* with the man? How *dared* he take it upon himself to censure her company? And to suggest that she had been "flirting"! She did not even know *how* to flirt. He should know that.

She remained unaware, because of her ineffectual sight, how people were staring first at her, then at Nick's retreating figure. That there were only a very few persons in this particular saloon made no difference at all, for wagging tongues travelled with ease. And at considerable speed.

Friday found a chair in the alcove and sank down into it, glad of the opportunity for a little quiet reflection. Not that her brain was in the least quiet as thoughts jostled one another to the accompaniment of the uneven pulsing of the blood through her veins.

It was as if Nick had decided to take out all of his own unhappiness on her, she decided. Perhaps he blamed *her* for the sad betrayal of his love for Hermione Hesket? For she had, all unwitting, been in some sort responsible for the breakdown of their relationship. It seemed incredible that only yesterday he had tried to convince her that nothing remained with him of that affair, and yet today he was exhibiting precisely those emotions that argued *against* his words. Heaven help her, was she not herself subject to these unyielding and difficult passions on account of her feeling for him? What did that betoken, then, if not that *his* conduct proved that he felt still very much thwarted in love?

So absorbed was she in her own thoughts—a residue perhaps from that ability in herself to become totally divorced from the world whenever she read—that she did not even hear the approach of rustling gowns. Only when a vaguely familiar stentorian voice boomed in her immediate vicinity did she come to a sense of her surroundings.

"Ah, so you *have* shown your face, have you? And not before time, if you ask me!"

Friday jumped, glancing up in shock. A female of gargantuan proportions stood before her, and it did not need the assistance of the eyeglass hanging around her neck to enable her to identify the monstrous creature.

"Mrs Hesket!" she uttered faintly, quite unable to think how or why in the world she was being thus accosted.

"That it is," corroborated the woman, "and mighty glad I am to see you, young Monday."

"Friday," corrected the purring voice of Mr St Abbs. "Frideswid, you know."

"Very well, Friday, then," conceded Mrs Hesket impatiently. "I knew it was something outlandish."

Squealing laughter made itself heard and Friday groped for the eyeglass, becoming conscious that she was being rapidly surrounded by a group that included Lady Dalmeny. Through her mind flitted the logical conclusion, confirmed as she recognised St Abbs. *They* had brought her the Hesket woman. Probably *invited* her for this express purpose, if she only knew.

"My dear child," said Lady Dalmeny, all sweetness, "hardly had Nancy here stepped into the house when young Nicolas came rushing past us both."

"Folks are saying as you slapped his face for him," said Mrs Hesket, breaking in.

"What?" gasped Friday, suddenly and painfully aware of the dreadfully public nature of her confrontation with Nick. Her fingers began to tremble, and the eyeglass dropped, mercifully relieving her of the sight of the smirks on the faces that formed a circle about her. What should she do? Where in the world was Caro?

"Not that I blame you for it," went on the woman in her over-loud voice. "I've wanted to do it myself, I don't mind telling you. But it won't do, ma'am, and that's a fact. The last thing I need is *him* coming chasing after my girl again. And if you're of a mind to send him packing, that's exactly what he will do, mark my words!''

The titters that greeted this prophesy made Friday thank God for her bad sight. Inwardly shrinking, she was obliged to summon all her courage not to jump up and run ignominiously away. If she did that, Lady Dalmeny would have won. Drawing a steadying breath, she prepared herself to respond with a cool rationality she was far from feeling.

''*Such* a pity, dear Nancy,'' came from her ladyship, getting in before Friday had a chance to open her mouth, ''that your enchanting daughter chose to marry Aymestrey, after all. I was only saying to Weare yesterday—''

''No, it ain't!'' interrupted Mrs Hesket forcefully. ''What would have been the use of her marrying Weare, I should like to know? What has he to offer beside his handsome face? I'll tell you, my lady. *Nothing,* that's what.''

''But think what a deprivation for us lovers of the aesthetic,'' put in St Abbs on a mournful note.

''I don't know anything about that,'' admitted Mrs Hesket. ''But 'lovers' I do know about, and I won't have—''

''Nancy, Nancy!'' intervened Lady Dalmeny in mock-remonstrance. ''Such a suggestion! In front of Miss Edborough, too.''

''Don't you worry about *her*. She ain't missish. Didn't turn a hair when I confronted young Weare with having tumbled my innocent girl—covering up his intentions with this shamming betrothal, too!''

Friday got up swiftly, a blaze of sudden anger making her brave. "No, I am *not* missish, Mrs Hesket. And as long as you mean to make the world a present of Nick's affairs, kindly adhere to the truth—that he did *not* seduce your daughter while he was betrothed to me."

"Yes, but he *ain't* betrothed to you now," argued Mrs Hesket, not in the least abashed. "That's just what I complain of. And if you mean to treat him the way you did tonight, it's as sure as eggs is eggs that he *won't* be betrothed to you. And *then* what am I to expect?"

Friday hardly heard the muffled laughter that came from all about her. She did not know that her features registered the contempt she felt. "How should I know, Mrs Hesket? The matter has nothing whatsoever to do with me. Frankly, in your place, I would be addressing myself to the *lady* in the case. She is *married,* after all. Are you *expecting* her to betray her vows?"

"Bravo!" called a voice from somewhere behind the circle. "Bravo, Friday!"

Friday glanced quickly about, crying out, "Tony! Oh, thank God! Pray get me *out* of here!"

Whereupon the Honourable Anthony Weare muscled through and seized Friday's arm, dragging her unceremoniously to safety to a chorus of laughter and clapping.

"Quickly, Miss Edborough!" uttered the soft voice of Griselda Apperley, and Friday found herself closely protected between the two of them as they hurried out of the fatal saloon. As the trio exited, they ran straight into Caroline.

"Friday!" she uttered in agitated tones. "I have

been hunting for you all over! What in the world has been happening? I have been told the horridest tale!''

"Leave her be, Caro!" instructed her elder brother, keeping on the move and making directly for the long stairway. "Had the most shocking time of it, poor girl. She don't need you in shrieking hysterics as well!"

"How dare you, Tony?" uttered Mrs Cleeve aggrievedly, rushing along to keep pace beside the three. "I wish you will *stop* for a moment!"

"Do wait, Tony!" begged Griselda urgently. "It is quite unnecessary for us to dash out like a collection of mad things. Poor Miss Edborough will be quite out of breath!"

Thus urged, Tony came to a halt at the top of the stairs, looking anxiously down into Friday's face. "All right, Friday?"

A trifle bewildered by the rapid turn of events, Friday blinked up at him, nodding. "Yes. Thank you both so much!"

"But what has *happened?*" demanded Caroline imploringly. "*Tell* me, one of you!"

"Those wretched creatures are at their tricks again, that is all," explained Miss Apperley calmly. "They brought Mrs Hesket to Friday—"

"Oh, Friday, no!" wailed Caroline. "And you had but just had the stupidity to *hit* Nicky in public. Now it will be all over town!"

Of this there could be no doubt whatsoever. Even as the three rescuers hurried Friday down the stairway to await the coming of Mr Cleeve's town carriage to take her and Caroline home, the pointing and whispering could be seen all around the gallery above. The future looked decidedly black.

* * *

That night the dreams came back. In full flood. Friday woke in the early hours, threshing and turning, filled with such yearning that she wanted to die. Why now? Why must she dream like this *now?* Her relationship with Nick was at a point lower than any they had experienced. Heaven help her, she had said that she *hated* him.

But only in the heat of the moment, pleaded her heart. Hate him? If only she *could*. And now, with those imagined whispers still wreathing the visions of the dream that lingered in her mind, she knew that she would not. *Never.* For when the dreamed image had murmured that he loved her, his lips covering hers in a kiss whose sweetness ached still in the hidden recesses that encompassed her longing, her heart had answered with all the fire that she had been desperately damping down these many weeks.

And he knew! He had said he did not believe her. He knew, he *knew*. She felt suddenly as if her whole heart had been exposed to him all this while, try as she might to conceal it. Oh, Lord in heaven, how could she face him again?

Chapter Ten

An unusual entertainment had been devised by Mrs Apperley, the first that Friday felt she could truly enjoy. The guests drove out to her big house at Richmond in the morning, where they were provided with a substantial collation of delicacies laid out in the dining-room to which they could return as and when hunger drove them thither. Anyone who fancied themselves a Garrick or Siddons was invited to join those getting up a game of charades upstairs, where masks and costumes had been provided in two of the bedchambers.

Every room in the house seemed to have been thrown open, including the ballroom where the charade-players were to perform later in the afternoon. For those who had no theatrical ambitions, there was a room set aside for the inveterate card players, a music-room with both a pianoforte and a harp, the library, or the drawing-rooms where people might gather in idle chat. The grounds, for those brave enough to venture forth into a windy March day, were extensive with beautifully laid out gardens, a small stream and a maze which afforded the younger guests a great deal of amusement.

It was generally agreed that Mrs Apperley had hit upon the perfect solution to the intolerable sameness that the nightly prowls of Society had already begun to take on, even this early in the season. Friday, relieved to find herself in a situation where it was all too easy to escape from the eyes of the curious—for even with *her* poor sight she was able to make out the lifted fans, the heads that nodded in her direction—left Lady Delamere to her cronies, and Caroline to keep her eagle eye on her brother Tony's traffickings with Griselda, and sought out the library.

This proved to be a much more sumptuous apartment than her own haunt at home in Finchamstod, if less well stocked with the sort of books that she favoured. There were two desks, a number of window-seats and several chairs dotted tastefully about. Apart from one elderly lady, nodding over an open volume in an easy-chair near the window, Friday was mercifully alone. Putting on the spectacles that, abandoning the single eyeglass, she had once more taken to carrying—concealed from Caro's sharp glance in the pocket of her gown!—she wandered slowly along the shelves which lined the walls in between the windows and doors that threw light and air into the large room. Mrs Apperley seemed to have purchased every novel ever written! From the wit of Henry Fielding, the satire of Jonathan Swift, to Fanny Burney's latest romance, they were all there.

She had just taken down the first volume of Laurence Sterne's *Tristram Shandy*—for she recalled that Papa had assured her she would enjoy its amusing classical allusions—when movement on the periphery of her vision made her turn towards the smaller door at the window side of her room.

Her heart leapt. Then it began to thud violently. Nicolas was standing there. Friday had not seen him for several days. Not since that dreadful quarrel at Lady Dalmeny's. But she had *dreamed* of him every night. Shame flooded her, and she could not speak.

Nick glanced across at the elderly dame. Friday followed his gaze and saw, with relief, that the lady appeared to be sleeping peacefully. Then Nick was coming towards her, a finger to his lips to hold her silent. As if she could utter a word, in any event!

"I knew I should find you here," he said in a low tone as he came up. A smile flickered on his lips. "Just the place for an owl!"

She did not speak. The book in her hands was crushed against her chest, as if its hardness might still the frenzy of her bosom.

Nick's smile died and his eyes grew sombre. "You haven't forgiven me, have you? For the other night, I mean."

"Yes." It came out automatically. Without the benefit of thought or decision.

The frown on Nick's face deepened. "What is it, Friday? Are you afraid of the gossip? Caro told me we are being watched. And I heard from Tony all about that Gorgon's attack upon you."

Friday drew in a ragged breath. This would not do. She must pull herself together. He could not, after all, see into her thoughts and find himself mirrored in the memory of her dreams. She was glad that she had on her spectacles. They gave her confidence—and hid her eyes!

"You...should not have come in here, Nick. We ought not to be seen together."

"To the devil with that!" he answered in a suddenly fierce whisper. "Do you think I care what people may say? I won't be coerced into giving up my friendships. All this trouble between us came about only because I allowed myself to be manipulated—like a marionette. Well, I will not do so any more. And I won't have you kowtow to the busybodies either."

"But it is all so unnecessary," Friday protested. "What are you trying to prove, Nick?"

"Nothing." He shook his head. "I don't know. I've had the most devilish time of it, Friday. And I'm not sure these last few days have not been the worst of all!"

"Because we are the subject of talk, I dare say."

"Because I have been *away* from you. Because you hate me—or said you did."

"I don't," Friday said in a small voice.

"I so *hope* that may be true. If not, I know you have reason enough."

"Perhaps you have reason to hate me. You said I was cruel."

Nick shook his head. "I wanted to hurt you. You were so much against me. I don't even know what I am supposed to have done! All I do know is," he said hesitantly, low-toned, "that I want you back."

Friday turned away from him. "It is not *me* you want, Nick. I am just some symbol for you—of something you have lost."

"You're *wrong*," he uttered vehemently. Taking hold of her arm, he drew her back to face him. There was real contrition in his eyes. "Friday, I am so *sorry* for everything that has happened. For the pain I've caused you. Oh, yes, I am aware of it! The things I have said—I didn't *mean* them."

A smile wavered on Friday's lips. "Nor I. We have both been victims, perhaps, of the manoeuvrings of others, as you have said." She felt the grief welling again, and her voice began to shake. "You say you want me back, but something has gone, Nick. There was an *innocence* about our—our friendship, don't you, see? Now it is no longer—I *cannot* any longer…"

Her voice failed, and she shifted a little, as if she might escape him. But Nicolas was more or less hemming her in before the bookcase, and any move she made to get away must tell him her state of mind.

"Friday, be *still*," Nick said gently.

One hand caught her shoulder while the other removed her spectacles, exposing the luminosity of her gaze. The hand left her shoulder and cradled her cheek, and there was a tenderness in his face that Friday did not recognise.

"You don't know what it does to me to see you weep," he murmured in little above a whisper. "All I want to do is to take you in my arms and…"

His expression altered. Astonishment swept across it, as though a thought of stirring proportions had entered his head.

"Friday!" he exclaimed in the oddest voice she had ever heard him use. "My God, Friday!"

His finger pushed up her chin and his face came down towards hers. He was going to kiss her! Blank shock held her frozen. Then all at once she became aware of the sound of voices approaching outside the open double doors that led through to the hall.

"Someone is coming!" she uttered, pulling away. Snatching the spectacles from his hand, she jammed them instinctively on to her nose.

Nick let her go and whirled about. Next instant, a clutch of people were flocking about the doorway, in the centre of which was the face that Friday thought of as Helen of Troy. Hermione Hesket! Or rather, as Victor St Abbs reminded her the very next instant, Hermione, Lady Aymestrey.

"There now, Lady Aymestrey," purred the gentleman in a satisfied tone. "What did I tell you?"

"Nick!" uttered the breathy voice joyfully.

"Oh, my God!" groaned Nick.

As Hermione advanced towards him, he beat a hasty retreat, dashing back to the door through which he had entered and slamming it behind him, so that the old lady in the easy-chair awoke with a start, dropping her book.

Hermione, Lady Aymestrey halted, her great blue eyes coming round to where Friday stood, rooted to the spot, gazing in dismay at the vision of loveliness. She did not notice that Nick had gone, nor for the moment identified the escort that accompanied the girl. Her whole mind was intent on simply taking in her presence.

"You need no introduction, I believe," came Lady Dalmeny's silken tones.

"Oh, no. We have already been presented," said Hermione, smiling with false brightness at Friday.

"In Reading, wasn't it?" asked Mr Percival Luss, coming to her side and taking her arm as she moved towards Friday.

Waking up to the fact that the Three Witches were responsible for this, Friday glanced from one to the other of them and back to Hermione. She was shaking inwardly, but Nick was right. She must not kowtow to the machinations of these truly evil people. As always, she drew unconscious strength from her ability to see properly.

"In Reading, and again at Delamere Place," she uttered flatly, taking the wind out of their sails. "And yes, it was due to that latter meeting that I broke off my betrothal to Nick. There. Now you need not rack your brains to recall every last detail and fling it in my face!"

"She has fight, you must give her that," laughed Percival Luss.

"Unlike the fellow in the business," said St Abbs nastily. "Tut-tut! Who would have suspected he would turn tail and run, leaving the ladies to fight it out between them?"

To his astonishment, it was Lady Aymestrey who turned to him, almost spitting flame. "Be silent, you! How dare you speak about Nick like that? Get out of here, all of you! Go on. You will not get the better of *me*, I promise you."

"Well, well!" commented Lady Dalmeny. "The creature is showing her origins."

In utter astonishment, Friday saw Hermione raise a fist to threaten the older lady. Laughing, the Three Witches retreated out of the door, promising to pass on the glad tidings of a burgeoning cat fight in the library.

"I'll show them cat fight!" threatened Lady Aymestrey.

A scuttling figure rushing out after the rest showed the old lady who had been dozing here to have taken fright.

"Good riddance!" said Hermione, and, shutting the doors behind them all, she turned to confront Friday. "Now then, Miss Edborough, we'll have this out alone."

Friday's confidence had grown, and she faced the girl boldly. "There is nothing to have out, Lady Aymestrey. At least not between you and me."

"Oh, yes, there is," argued Hermione. "From what my ma says, I've reason enough to worry. What's going on between you and Nick? Tell me at once!"

Before today, Friday would have answered that nothing was going on. But the memory of Nick's extraordinary conduct came sweeping back and she felt herself blushing. Had he really been about to kiss her? Or was it her imagination playing her tricks again? As for this female, she would not give her the satisfaction of believing that she even understood her.

"I beg your pardon?" she uttered in a blank tone.

"You heard me," said the girl belligerently. "What are you up to? Trying to get him back?"

"I might ask the same question," Friday returned icily. This was hardly the pathetic, woebegone creature she had seen at Delamere Place! Had it all been an act, then? Was *this* the real Hermione? Unthinkingly, she spoke the thought in her mind. "I begin to wonder whether he is not to be congratulated after all."

"Don't come the fine lady with me, for it won't work," snapped the other.

"I am no fine lady, ma'am, but I am not stupid," Friday said with an edge to her voice. "Why are you not disporting yourself with the would-be actors upstairs? I am sure you would find yourself mightily at home."

Lady Aymestrey uttered her tinkling laugh. "You don't think I'm going to waste my efforts on you, do you?"

"You will certainly be *wasting* them if you try them on Nick," Friday told her flatly. "He said he had been disillusioned, and now I believe him."

"What in the world do you mean?" asked the girl, wide-eyed.

Friday stared at her. "Heaven help me, but you have not the smallest notion how you have hurt him, have you? Is it *nothing* to you that he should suffer so?"

Hermione smiled, and Friday thought she could almost hear her purring. "Did he suffer indeed? That is *excellent* news. It will make everything so much easier."

Something stabbed in Friday's chest. Under the spectacles, her eyes darkened with distress. "You mean to draw him in again. Oh, poor Nick!"

"I never meant to let him go," said Lady Aymestrey airily. Her tone changed suddenly, and the blue eyes sparked a warning. "And *you* are not going to stand in my way, see!"

With which, she strode across to the door by which Nick had left and, wrenching it open, marched through, leaving it wide behind her. At almost the same moment, the double doors burst open, and both Charles Delamere and Tony Weare hurtled into the room.

"Friday! Are you all right?"

"Nick said that wretched female was in here!"

"Sent us to rescue you," said Charles, coming up to her. "Thought it better he made himself scarce, considering all the talk."

"Where is he?" Friday asked them quickly. "She has just gone after him through there."

"She won't find him," Delamere said confidently. "And if she does, she'll get short shrift, I can tell you that!"

"Where are the Three Witches?" demanded Tony. "Nick said they brought the Hesket—no, she's Aymestrey now, ain't she?"

"Oh, Tony, she is the most *dreadful* girl!" uttered Friday shakily. "She thinks—she thinks I am trying to take Nick from her, and she is positively *glad* that he has suffered over her defection."

Charles nodded. "Hermione all over, that is. Should have been a play-actress."

"That is just what I thought," Friday agreed. "It seems as if she had been *acting* all the time to gain Nick's favour."

"Nothing but a harpy," commented Tony disgustedly. "Sold herself to Aymestrey for advantage, but won't let go of the fellow she wanted."

"She's barking up the wrong tree," Charles put in. "Won't get anywhere with Nick. He can't *bear* her now."

Friday gazed at him blankly. Her breath caught, and she felt the rhythm of her pulse distort. "You must be mistaken, Charles."

"No, I ain't," he argued frowningly.

"But he is conducting himself precisely as if he has been crossed in love!"

"I didn't say he wasn't crossed in love."

As if she sought enlightenment, Friday glanced at Tony, and surprised a grin on his face. "What in the world is so funny?"

The Honourable Anthony Weare laughed at her.

"You are, Friday." He put an arm about her and gave
her a quick hug. "Never mind it. If you are all right,
I'm off to perform another gallant rescue. The last
time I saw Grissy, Caro was guarding her like a dog
with a bone. Poor girl is going to be driven out of
her senses if I don't get my sister away."

"Oh, yes, please go," Friday said quickly. "I am
perfectly all right."

She would have been glad of a period alone to
gather her thoughts, and wished very much that
Charles—who had set her unruly mind into *stupid*
thoughts and visions with his cryptic remarks!—
would follow Tony's example. But Delamere suggested a little refreshment.

"Come on, it'll do you good. You look as if you
need feeding!"

The last thing Friday wanted at this present was
food, but as they ran into Caroline on the way she
was quickly induced to give in to Delamere's suggestion. For Tony had cunningly diverted his sister's
attention from Griselda by telling her about Friday's
encounter with Lady Aymestrey. Thus Friday was
obliged to endure a catechism on what had been said,
which culminated most oddly in an inconsequent
complaint about her spectacles.

"Don't say you have been *seen* wearing those
things," uttered Mrs Cleeve despairingly. "It is all of
a piece, Friday! You do *not* make my task any easier."

"Well, I did not ask to come to town," Friday
pointed out, removing the offending eyeglasses and
stuffing them in her pocket. "You would insist upon
it. To tell you the truth, I should be very happy to go
home tomorrow."

"What, and leave the field to that *creature?* You will do no such thing!" declared Caroline.

"Then pray don't carp at me, Caro," Friday begged. Really, even eating would be preferable to this! She glanced at Delamere. "Besides, Charles wants to fatten me up. Why do you not join us for some refreshment?"

But it appeared that Caro had already eaten and was about to take her obligatory nap. To Friday's relief, she left them to go and find Mrs Apperley, and they continued on their way to the dining-parlour, which was beginning to fill up with hungry guests in search of sustenance.

Friday toyed in a desultory way with some of the delicacies, but soon, while Charles was engaged with acquaintances, found an opportunity to slip away unseen. She headed for the front parlour, in which a pair of French windows stood open to the gardens for the convenience of the assembled merry-makers.

It was not all that cold, she insisted to herself, stepping outside and slipping her eyeglasses back on so that she might see her way. Although she shivered a little in her muslin gown, she comforted herself with a reminder of its long sleeves and the overgown of pale green—which might also help her lose herself in the foliage! There must be a spot, perhaps around the side of the house, where she might be quite alone for a little.

The encounter with the girl Hermione had overset her, and she wanted—more than anything else in the world!—to think through those cryptic remarks made by Charles and Tony that had set her thoughts wandering along such a *dangerous* path. Particularly now that she thought Nick had been going to *kiss* her in that moment in the library just before that creature came in.

The idea that she might have been mistaken in Nick's sentiments could not but obtrude itself upon her mind. She had hardly dared to imagine what those different sentiments might be! Supposing—supposing he was *not* as heartbroken over that girl as she had thought? What then did his excessively *emotional* conduct denote? And towards herself! It could not be, could it, that he thought of her as *more* than a friend? As—*dared* she even think it?—someone he might… *love?*

The very word in such a connection caused her heart to contract with the desperation of her hope. So that was it! She *had* been hoping. All this time, when she had been assuring herself of her determination to *forget* him, what had been the truth of it? Fool! Hopelessly, *stupidly* dreaming of the impossible. Still!

She crossed the front of the house, and, passing the front door, she threw back her head in frustration at the thought of her own helplessness, enmeshed in the invisible chains of her love for Nicolas. Her head turned, and an image beyond the French windows of another little parlour caught her eye. Abruptly she halted, taking in the identities of the occupants in a flash. Nick and Hermione—locked in each other's arms!

Having made an instant decision to avoid a public scene—for he knew Hermione's capabilities in that direction!—Nick had left the library quickly. But almost at once he was assailed by fears for Friday, left alone to manage without him. Swiftly locating his brother and Charles, he dispatched them to Friday's rescue and breathed a sigh of relief. Then he sought for some private spot where he might contemplate in peace the bombshell that had exploded in his brain.

Across the wide hall from the parlour that led to the gardens, he located a similar little room which was, for the present moment, unoccupied. Slipping in, he took a chair that faced the gardens and thought deeply—about Friday.

Everything made sense at last. So much so that he could not imagine how the truth had managed to escape him for so long. He must be quite as foolish as his father had always claimed! The odd thing about it was that everything else had dimmed in importance. There could be nothing—*nothing*—as vital as this.

He began to think over the past weeks, picking up all those signposts, now clearly to be seen, that he had missed—or ignored!—along the way. For there were many. So many, indeed, that a prickle of apprehension began to eat at his new-found confidence, all but destroying it. He was sure he was right about those signals. He *was* right. But—might it not be too late? Had he, by his tardiness, his dunderheaded inability to recognise something so *obvious,* forfeited his chance?

The thought was so unpalatable that he jumped up from the chair and began to pace, hunting down the latest signals in his mind. Searching, somewhat feverishly, for the reassurance he desperately needed. For if he had lost his opportunity—if it *was* beyond mending—oh, God, but that could not be endured! Not now. What in Hades would he do then?

The thought obsessed him for some little time, so that he became wholly unconscious of his surroundings. When the click of the latch penetrated as an alien sound, he had no idea how much time had passed. Turning, he became aware that a female was standing in front of the now closed door.

His first thought was one of irritation at being disturbed. His second, as he made to leave simply to get away from any sort of company, was that his way was barred. Then he saw who it was who had entered.

"Hermione!"

She smiled in a winning way, and her voice was warm. "Nick, I have been looking for you all over! I am so *glad* to have discovered you at last."

Nicolas was not paying attention. He had no need to ask himself what she wanted with him, for that he knew already. But her presence here might be turned to advantage. It was private enough just now, and this could be exactly the opportunity he needed to settle with this importunate female once and for all.

As he made the decision, she came a little away from the door. "Oh, Nick! I have *missed* you so."

Good God, let him nip that sort of talk in the bud at once! He adopted a formal tone. "How do you do, Hermione?"

Her eyes widened, but she rallied her forces, increasing the seduction in her voice. "Me? Oh, I am well enough. But you! Oh, Nick, I have been hearing the most *dreadful* things about you."

"Have you?" he asked automatically. He was finding it difficult to concentrate on what she said, for he had made a surprising discovery.

She was still breathtakingly lovely. Only he did not find himself in the least deprived of breath. He was not aware of any stirring whatsoever within his breast. Or anywhere else, for the matter of that! It was as if the thought of her beauty came to him in a detached way, as he might have felt about some object of artistic merit.

"I never, never meant for you to suffer, Nick," she was saying in that breathy way that used to affect him. Now he could not imagine why, for it was so patently false!

As her eyes passed over his face—in a considering way, he thought, as if she tried to fathom his mind— the smile remained on her lips. The blue orbs, however, held a calculating look. Nick almost laughed out. Good God, the wench was weighing her chances!

"It is of no use, Hermione," he said quite calmly, even with a hint of amusement in his tone.

A frown came into her eyes, and she pouted prettily. "Oh, Nick! You do not mean that."

"Indeed I do."

"You *cannot* mean it," she protested, stepping closer. "Why, I have been *utterly* true to you—in mind. You must not blame me for the *deed*. I could not help that."

Nick moved a little away. "Really, Hermione, I have no interest in the matter."

She tinkled with laughter. "I see what it is! You are so jealous that you cannot now bring yourself to forgive me." Gliding to him, she reached her hands up to his shoulders. "*Dearest* Nick. You know well you are the one I *truly* care for. But we *agreed*. I had to marry Aymestrey to secure my position. But it is just as I foretold! *Now* there is nothing to prevent us enjoying each other."

All Nick was conscious of was a faint feeling of distaste. He did not even attempt to release himself from the clutch of her hands, nor to interrupt her with protests. He was wondering how it could be that nothing she did or said had the power to move him—in any way at all. He was simply disinterested.

Hermione must have seen something of it in his face, for she drew back a little, a spark of anger in her eyes. "Why do you look at me like that?"

"I don't know how I look," Nick told her flatly. "But if you are expecting to discover the sort of reaction you excited in me in the past, I must warn you that you will look for it in vain."

She all but glared at him. "You *cannot* have changed towards me. You are trying to punish me!"

"Punish you? Don't be ridiculous!"

"You are! You are!" she cried vehemently. She released him, and made a play with a handkerchief that she whisked from its place of concealment in her sleeve, fluttering her lashes over her brimming eyes. "Oh, Nick! How can you be so *horrid?*"

Not one iota of the sensations that had attacked him when Friday had wept assailed him now. He was instead fascinated by the ease with which she called forth the necessary tears, and watched with reluctant admiration her pantomime with the wisp of handkerchief dabbing at the corners of her lovely eyes.

"That's very good, Hermione," he uttered without thinking. "If Aymestrey should ever throw you out for infidelity, you can certainly make a living on the boards!"

Arrested in full flight, her practised act gave way to a look compounded of astonishment and dawning fury. "How—how *dare* you?" she sputtered. "You—you—you *beast!*"

She came at him with claws raised, and Nick was obliged to catch at her wrists to save his face from assault. Hermione spat obscenities that showed him—

for the first time—her gutter origins, and as he fought her off he thanked God for those well-meaning persons about him who had steered his course otherwhere.

"Calm down, Hermione, for God's sake!" he begged, only now showing any sort of reaction.

He ought to have known better! Hermione in a fury was as unstoppable as she had been in hysterics, and Nick found himself obliged to pull her arms behind her and struggle with her chest to chest.

He did not notice, in his fight to subdue her fury, the shadowy figure outside the closed French windows who looked a moment in frozen shock, and then turned and ran away.

For the figure could not wait for the outcome. The vision she had seen was all too clear in its essentials, and she simply ran and ran until she could run no more.

The palpitations of her heart were inexpressibly painful. Friday did not herself know whether they were due more to the mad dash she had made—away from that *agonising* sight—or to the return of that wrenching pain that she had known that dreadful day when Nick had accosted her at her snowbound retreat. Her labouring breaths bore witness to the speed with which she had absented herself from the fatal windows, chasing down the lawns towards the clump of trees.

Trees, she thought inconsequently, seemed always to be her salvation. For this sturdy trunk held her secure against the tremor that had invaded her limbs as soon as she halted. She had not known where she was running. But as she glanced around she saw that she had crossed the lawns, leaving the house and the hateful picture in that window well behind. She drew a sobbing breath.

Heaven help her, but until this moment she had not known how *much* she still cared! Nothing—not the quarrels, the upsets, the tensions, even the *dreams*—had prepared her for this resurgence of emotions she had begun to believe might be dulling at last.

If she *could* laugh, she must have done so at the foolish manner of those thoughts which had driven her outside in the first place. For there she found the refutation of her idiotic wish to believe that Charles had meant that Nick's feelings had animated towards her. Her own *futile* feelings had betrayed her yet again!

The anguish lessened at length, and she realised that she must not stand there, clutching at a tree like the pathetic fool she was. *Anyone* might see. And now, more than ever, she must hide her inner feelings from prying eyes. If people had talked before Hermione, Lady Aymestrey made her reappearance in town, how much more would they do so now? Let her at least retain the little dignity that remained to her! Let her not wear her all too fragile heart on her sleeve.

Glancing about, she noticed a little bridge over the stream. It appeared to be bathed in sunlight, and she looked up in surprise. An unexpected parting of the clouds had eased the cold, and the wind had dropped. She had not noticed in her preoccupied state. Preoccupied! Almost she laughed aloud, mocking herself.

But these were dangerous thoughts and she was obliged to draw steadying gulps of the cool air. After a while, as always, nature had its solacing effect on her and the tremors quieted a little. Perhaps she could move now.

Making her way to the bridge, Friday dropped down to sit on it, drawing up her knees in the fashion she favoured on her window-seat at home. She could almost fancy herself back there, for, just as the sun warmed her in her private corner, so did it do so here, sending its rays to cocoon her in comfort. She removed her spectacles and pocketed them, closing her eyes and lifting her face to catch the unexpected warmth on her cheeks.

Her thoughts—commanded into obedience which long practice enabled her to effect—drifted, avoiding the untoward. The pain was there still. How could it not be? But, like toothache, it had dulled away, leaving in its wake a state of semi-consciousness in which the patient did not probe at the sore place for fear of the pain flaring up again. That characteristic capacity to become totally absorbed stood her in good stead.

Thus she did not take account of the passage of time, and did not notice that the guests of Mrs Apperley were choosing to take advantage, as she was doing, of the sudden sunshine and moving into the gardens.

Vaguely, somewhere in the recesses of her consciousness, Friday was aware of chattering and laughter floating somewhere in the distance. But it was only when a shriek rang out, all too close, that her eyes flew open. Glancing round, she caught sight of Hermione, Lady Aymestrey advancing towards her, and realised that the chatter was a great deal nearer at hand than she had supposed.

"You—you—you *jezebel!*" screamed out Hermione.

Too dazed to do more than gaze at her, Friday sat watching her striding up to the bridge.

"I'll teach you to queer my pitch, you—you ugly *frog!*" shouted the girl.

And before Friday had a chance to do anything to save herself, Hermione rushed on to the bridge and, leaning down, thrust at her victim with an almighty shove. Friday was flung from the bridge, her body splashing into the water.

The only sensation at first was the gasping shock of the icy cold that drenched her limbs. Instant reaction made her thrust upwards so that she sat in the mercifully shallow stream, blinking and shaking her hands as she struggled to catch her breath.

In the far reaches of her consciousness she heard sounds of protest and alarm. Then footsteps pounded on to the bridge, and a familiar voice yelled in a tone loud enough to penetrate her numbed mind.

"You spiteful little cat! Take that!"

There was a piercing shriek, then a loud splash, and a burst of mirth and shouting that deafened Friday so that her flailing hands came up to stop her ears against it. All she could see was a surging mass of fuzzy humanity lining the stream. But someone was calling her insistently, and instinctively she responded, looking about for the source of that too well-known voice that made itself heard despite the cacophony about her.

"Friday! Friday, give me your hands!"

Nick's face came into blurry focus above her. He was kneeling on the bridge, leaning over, his hands reaching down to her.

"Give me your hands! Hurry, Friday!"

Friday obeyed, and felt herself pulled up so that

she was standing in the water. Inconsequently, she remembered that it was his voice that had abused her as a "spiteful little cat". As Nick's hands slipped under her shoulders, and his strong arms heaved her up, his face focused properly and she entered her protest at once, her teeth chattering with cold.

"I'm n-not a s-spiteful little c-cat!"

Nick grinned as he set her on her feet. "Not you, my precious idiot!"

Friday blinked, uncertain that she had heard aright. "Wh-what?"

"Come on!" Nick ordered briskly, beginning to bundle her across the bridge. "You'll catch your death!"

As she was hurried away, Friday caught a glimpse of some billowing object in the water on the other side, and became aware that the shrieks of dismay and fury that she could now make out over the buzzing of the crowd were emanating from there. She would have halted to investigate, but she was given no opportunity to do so.

"I'll take her in, Nick!" uttered Griselda Apperley's soft voice. "Mama! Mama! Pray find Lady Delamere!"

"I'm coming with her to the house," Nick said firmly, his arm locked about Friday as he bustled her along.

Other known voices came in now. An older female one that she did not recognise. "Do you take care of it, Griselda. I have my hands full here!"

"Oh, dear, she is struggling with Lady Aymestrey," said Griselda. "Tony, pray go and find Lady Delamere for me."

"In a moment, Grissy. There is something to do

here first.'' He added in an undervoice, "Nick, take care!''

Friday began to realise that her enforced movement was accompanied by all her friends, as though they had gathered about her in defence against the roars and laughter of the crowds that rang still in her ears. But what was the odd tone of warning that was creeping in here?

"Think you'd better stay out here, Nick,'' came urgently from Charles.

"Delamere's in the right of it, old fellow,'' murmured Tony. "Here comes trouble!''

Then another voice—unknown to Friday—made itself heard. A voice hoarse with rage. "Weare! Stand, I tell you! *Stand*. You'll answer to me for what you did to my wife!''

"Confound it!'' muttered Nick, pausing briefly.

Friday glanced up at his face and found a frown there. Who was this? What had happened? Whose *wife?*

"Let Grissy take Friday out of this!'' muttered Tony Weare. "Get her inside, Grissy, for God's sake!''

"Listen to your brother, man!'' said Charles insistently. "Nothing you can do for her. Needs a female's ministrations, not yours.''

Puzzled, Friday glanced round at the unformed features about her. There was nothing for her to see, nothing to tell her what the difficulty was. But she could hear the concern and she could feel the tension. She tugged at Nick's hand.

"Nick, wh-what is the m-matter?''

His fingers closed over hers, quieting them. "Nothing you need concern yourself about, Friday. Go into the house!''

She felt his arm grow tighter about her briefly, and then he released her into Griselda Apperley's care, with a stream of insistent instructions. ''Make sure she changes her clothes, Griselda! And see she *rests*. Something hot to drink. And blankets—plenty of them!''

''Yes, yes, Nick! I will see to it. You deal with Aymestrey, for heaven's sake! Come, Friday!''

Friday dragged back a little, peering to try and see where Nick had gone. The other two gentlemen had drifted out of her periphery of vision, together with the unknown man who had launched his verbal attack upon Nick. But he was not unknown. The most dreadful premonition came to her. Aymestrey! Hermione's husband. And it had been Hermione who had pushed her off the bridge. What had Griselda said about her mama? That she was in some sort of difficulty with Lady Aymestrey. Heaven help her, but what had Nick done?

There was no time to indulge this question, however, for as they entered through the French windows Caroline's high-pitched shriek suddenly broke into her agitated thoughts.

''Friday! Heavens, what has happened? Was that *you* screaming out there? I declare, you are drenched to the bone! What in the world has *happened?*''

''I f-fell into the s-stream,'' Friday uttered.

''Fell nothing!'' Griselda uttered scornfully, propelling her charge before her as she kept on the move. ''She was *pushed*. By that horrid creature Hermione Hesket.''

''What?'' screamed Caroline. ''Oh, *no,* Friday!

Don't say you have publicly quarrelled with the
wretch!''

"Get out of the way, Caro!'' snapped Griselda in
a quite unaccustomed manner, pushing Mrs Cleeve
away from the stairs and forcing Friday up them. "Of
course Friday did nothing of the kind. She was sitting
on the bridge—not that I know why, for I don't—and
Hermione rushed up and shoved her off! Scores of us
saw her do it, too.''

Following them upstairs, Caroline launched into a
speech compounded of dismay and agitation, in which
expressions of disgust jostled with declarations of pre-
cognition. Caro had known just how it would be the
moment that Aymestrey creature returned to town.
She was appalled that no one had seen fit to snatch
her from her afternoon nap to put a stop to these
stirring events, and she had every confidence that
Nick would make bad worse if left to himself.

"Both Tony and Charles are with Nick,'' Griselda
answered, guiding Friday into her own bedchamber,
"so you need have no worries on that score.''

"Tony and Charles? I declare, Griselda, if you
mean that for a recommendation, I do not think much
of it! They are as bad as one another.''

"But do not forget that my father is also there. Not
to mention a great many other gentlemen of good
sense. I am sure nothing untoward will be permitted
to occur.''

By now Friday was shivering so badly with cold
that both her companions lost interest in Nick's possible activities. For once the two young ladies were
in sympathy as they fussed over their charge, Griselda
rummaging among her clothes for something suitable

for Friday to wear, and Caroline bullying her out of the wet clothes she had on.

Friday's mind was torn between the need to recover her spectacles from her gown before Caro should crush them in her haste to rid her of the offending garment, and the dreadful apprehension which had seized upon it. Was Nick in danger? Would Tony and Charles be able to help him? It sounded very much as if a quarrel was brewing! But *why?* Had Aymestrey caught him kissing Hermione?

The thought caused her an echoing pang of the original agony that had attacked her at the sight, but it was forced away—as were her thoughts—by the sudden onslaught of two pairs of determined hands rubbing vigorously at her limbs with towels. And by Caro's voice, demanding to know why Hermione had done it.

"Heaven knows!" answered Griselda, holding up a chemise ready for Friday to put on. A giggle escaped her. "But Nick, if not heaven, had his revenge."

Friday froze with the chemise half on. So too did Caro, who was assisting her, demanding, "What *can* you mean, Griselda?"

A smile flickered over the other girl's lips. "Nick threw her into the stream."

"What?" uttered Caro and Friday together.

Friday saw that Griselda was biting her lip against threatening laughter. For herself, she could scarcely believe her ears. She felt dazed. "Nick threw *Hermione* into the water?"

"You are making it up!" snapped Caroline, jerking at the chemise to pull it properly over Friday.

"I swear I am not," said Griselda insistently, making ready one of her own muslin gowns. "That is why Aymestrey was so furious. Nick saw Hermione push you in, Friday. Well, we all did. I have never seen anything like it! He uttered a roar of rage, and went dashing off before anyone could stop him. I thought he was just going to get you out, Friday, but *no*. The next thing we knew, he had grabbed the wretch, called her a cat, and given her a taste of her own medicine."

Friday stood stunned as the inevitable commentary broke from Caroline's lips. Friday hardly heard it. Nor did she join in the gales of laughter in which her two companions were indulging as they flung the gown over her head, laced her up and prinked at its folds, and then pushed her to sit on the bed so that they might tidy her hair.

So *that* was the thing that billowed in the water! That was why Mrs Apperley had her hands full. *Hermione* had been pushed in the water, too! And by *Nick*.

Friday still could not believe it. How was it possible that at one moment Nick could be embracing the female with fervour and at the next throwing her into the stream? It did not make sense. Small wonder that Aymestrey had shouted that Nick would answer to him! After all, Hermione had answered to Nick for what *she* had done.

Her heart seemed to swell in her bosom. Nick had punished Hermione for *her* sake! Did that mean— *could* it mean that he—? *No*, Friday, you fool! She was at it again. Setting too much store by what Nick had done. For, while he might have thrown Hermione in the stream, he had not *kissed* Friday.

She became aware that the gales of laughter had

given way to silence. She could just make out that both Griselda and Caro were facing the door. Quickly she put on the spectacles she had been so desperately clutching. As the room came into focus, she found that she was staring straight at someone in the doorway. Hermione, Lady Aymestrey herself, looking somewhat the worse for wear.

Chapter Eleven

Only the soiled hem of Hermione's muslin gown was visible, clinging damply to her ankles under a voluminous heavy brocade cloth that had been thrown over her, evidently appropriated from the wardrobe of the would-be thespians. But her golden curls hung bedraggled from the remnants of a feathered head-dress, and there was mud on her cheek.

The silence was broken by the lady herself.

"So!" she uttered, borrowing from both her mother's stance—putting her arms akimbo to reveal more of the sorry damage to her hitherto spotless gown—and that redoubtable lady's manner and vocabulary. "You find it funny, do you?"

Friday slowly shook her head. She did not find *anything* in this situation in the least bit funny. She heard Griselda stifle a giggle, and saw Lady Aymestrey's dagger glance flick over to her and back.

"Go away, if you please, Lady Aymestrey," began Caroline in a high-handed way, moving towards the door.

"I'll go when I'm ready!" menaced Hermione belligerently, striding into the room. "I've a thing or two to say to *her* first."

At once, Friday's champions stepped into the fray.

"Oh, no, you don't!"

"Out, I said!"

"Wait!" Friday called urgently.

Both Caroline and Griselda turned to stare at her in astonishment. "But, Friday—"

"One moment, Griselda," she begged, rising to face the woman. "Tell me, pray. *Why* did you do it? I—I don't understand."

Hermione's lovely features reddened with fury, coarsening her skin. "Don't come the innocent with me, *madam*. You know well indeed how you've been *luring* him."

"Luring?" repeated Friday, amazed. "But—"

"Don't trouble yourself to deny it!" snapped the girl. "I've heard all about it, and I *know* those tactics. Blow first hot, then cold, until the poor fellow don't know whether he's on his head or his heels. Well, let me tell you, Madam Jezebel, I won't have it, see?"

"She's mad!" stated Griselda with conviction.

"You *stupid* creature!" uttered Caroline scornfully. "Friday wouldn't know a tactic if it was presented to her on a silver salver."

"Oh, wouldn't she?" uttered the female, her tone raucous now. Her vengeful eyes did not leave Friday, whose astonishment was plain to be seen even under the concealing spectacles, for she was simply gaping. "Don't you stand there with your mouth at half-cock. I know your type and I'm up to every rig in the book, so don't think you can outjockey *me*."

Friday shook her head in mounting confusion.

"You have it quite wrong. I am not the creature you think me. I cannot conceive where you come by these extraordinary notions."

"I come by them, Madam Jezebel, because I've heard of all your doings, I have. Slapped his face for him, didn't you? *Well* do I know how *that* may arouse a man, for a start. *And* with my own eyes I saw you together in the library today. Soft and tender with him you were *then* all right. I'm not *blind,* madam."

"Blind!" echoed Caro furiously. "You're an unmitigated *idiot*."

"She cannot help it, Caro," Griselda said judiciously. "Being a schemer herself, she cannot perceive innocence when it is waved in front of her face."

"Do stop, the both of you!" begged Friday. She stepped forward, unaware of the contrast her quiet dignity made against this female's ravings. "You are quite mistaken, Lady Aymestrey. My wish has always been only for Nick's happiness. If that lay with you, then I had nothing to say about it. *Before*."

Hermione looked taken aback for a moment. Then she uttered a contemptuous laugh. "Poppycock! Do you take me for a simpleton, to believe you mean that? You always meant to have him! You've been cozening him with your devious ways."

"On the contrary. I have been trying to make him see that he and I have *no* future." Something sparked within Friday. Why *should* she argue the case with this female? Anger shuddered into life, and came out in her tongue. "I am afraid, however, that I now have a very different view. I *cannot* any longer believe that

Nick could possibly find happiness with a female such as yourself.''

"Oh, indeed? Well, let me tell you—"

"Setting aside the fact of your marriage," went on Friday, ignoring her interruption and with difficulty holding in check the passions churning in her breast, "and, setting aside any deeper relationship there might be between him and me, he is my *friend*. And from now on I will do my *utmost* to persuade him that you simply *will not do!*"

Hermione's blue eyes flashed at her in triumph. "Highty-tighty! But you don't fool *me*. I knew you were after him. Oh, but I *knew* it. I tell you now that you won't succeed. It's *me* he cares for," she asserted, adding, with a fine disregard for grammar and thumping at her breast dramatically, "and it's *me* as can give him what a man wants most of all from a woman. What you couldn't give him, for all your high and mighty ways—for you've no notion *how*. For he *knows*, see. He's *tasted* it. Yes, *and* begged for more."

The brave flourish of fury fell away. Friday went white. "You mean that you have—he has—"

"That's just what I do mean, Miss Innocence. He's *bedded* me. While he was betrothed to you and all!"

A hollow opened up inside Friday's chest where the anger had been. She did not hear Caroline and Griselda's words, although she knew that both were speaking. She discovered that her legs were too weak to stand and stepped quickly back so that she might sit again, her mind in torment with the cruel thought of what she had been told.

It could not be true! Nick *would* not—would he?

Only why would he not? Men regarded these things differently from women. And if he had already made Hermione his mistress—and since she herself had seen them embracing, why should she doubt it?— there was nothing to stop him from renewing the liaison. Only it meant that he had *lied* to her. All these weeks! He had said—only *today*, he had insisted on it!—that there had been nothing between them.

Griselda's voice penetrated, for her words were most welcome. "Mama! Thank heaven! Pray take Lady Aymestrey into another room."

"I have a gown for you, Lady Aymestrey," came Mrs Apperley's voice.

In her relief Friday heard no more, although she was aware of Griselda and Caroline muttering together. She was conscious only of her wish to be gone from this place. To be gone from London! Away from that heartless schemer who had entrapped Nick in her coils so strongly that *no one* could drag him out. Least of all herself. Even if she wanted to. Which, after what she had just been told, she most certainly did *not*. Indeed, she did not wish to face him—or indeed anyone else in London!—ever again.

She greeted the arrival, a few moments later, of Lady Delamere with unaffected enthusiasm. Tears sprang to her eyes as she leapt up.

"Oh, Lady Delamere! *Pray* take me home."

Nick faced Lord Aymestrey in the rose garden, whither they had been led by Mr Apperley. Appealed to by an anxious Lord Delamere, who had run to find him at Tony Weare's suggestion, their host had immediately hurried to where the argument was already taking place—in full view of the entire company, including the ladies!—and drawn the combatants away to this private place.

Tony and Charles, both fearful of the consequences, naturally refused to desert Nick, but, as Mr Apperley persuaded a couple of his older cronies to make sure that no one else was permitted to follow them, the curious were mercifully kept away. As well, for Aymestrey at first had been all too ready to declare his wrongs to the world.

"Private!" he had uttered furiously, when Nick had suggested that they settle the matter alone. "By what right, sir, do you dare to demand privacy? You have humiliated my wife in public and I say you shall answer to me!"

Nick had sighed. He was really quite sorry for the fellow. A man of middle years, not of particularly prepossessing appearance, who could be under no illusions as to why a beautiful young girl should blackmail him into matrimony. Not that his marriage was destined to afford him happiness. He was looking hangdog already, poor fellow, if Nick was any judge! As who would not be, wedded to Hermione? he thought, once again offering up silent thanks for his own deliverance. Well into his forties, Aymestrey had succumbed to an irresistible temptation, for which he was evidently already counting the cost. Although it was all too clear that he was still so much a victim of Hermione's wiles that he could not recognise her for what she was.

Fortunately, Mr Apperley had intervened before any further exchanges could be made, and Nick for one greeted the privacy of the rose garden with relief.

"You must be aware, my lord," he said, when Aymestrey reiterated his desire that Nick answer to him, "that a similar public humiliation had first been inflicted on Miss Edborough."

"Beside the point!" snapped the other. "It didn't give you the right to molest my wife."

Sharp gasps left the throats of both Tony and Charles, but Nick put out a hand to stay any action on their part. He himself had given an incredulous laugh. "Molest?"

"You dare to laugh, do you?" raged Aymestrey. "I'll teach you manners, you young cub!"

"Steady, Aymestrey!" cried Mr Apperley, moving between them as the elder man started forward.

Nick's eyes had narrowed. "You mean to teach me manners, do you? How, may I ask? With a cane, perhaps? Or are you intending to blow a hole through me?"

"Don't quibble, man! I've challenged you. Answer!"

There was a breathless hush. Nick was aware of his brother Tony, frowning now, shifting a little as if he would flank him. And Delamere, who took a step to the other side. Apperley, he noted, obviously saw these manoeuvres, but said nothing, only muttering under his breath. No doubt he was concerned that such an occurrence should take place at a party of pleasure at his house. As well he might be! Nothing could more surely give rise to gossip. What the devil should he do?

At length—and reluctantly, for he knew what the consequence would be—Nick shook his head. "I will not meet you, sir."

"*What?*" broke from Charles's lips.

"Hush!" uttered Tony, and Nick could feel his brother's eyes on his own profile. Tony at least understood, even if Charles did not. He thought Apperley sighed in relief, but he could not be sure. Still, Tony's clear support gave him confidence.

Aymestrey grew red in the face and his eyes widened. "You refuse to afford me satisfaction?"

"I do," Nick said staunchly.

"Nick, are you mad?" demanded Delamere, turning to stare at his friend in undisguised disapproval. It did not need Aymestrey's next words—which were exactly what he had expected—to tell Nick what Charles thought!

"Am I to call you a coward?"

Tony spun. "You dare!"

Mr Apperley intervened once more. "Keep your head, boy! Don't need any young hotheads in this situation. Leave your brother be! He's doing very well."

Tony stepped back. "Yes, he is. I beg your pardon, sir."

"Good God, Tony!" uttered Charles disgustedly. "You're as bad as Nick."

"*Apperley!*" came in irate tones from Lord Aymestrey. "Keep out of this, man!"

Mr Apperley held up his hands. "I'm not interfering, my friend. Just keeping the other *boys* out of it."

The faint stress appeared to agitate Aymestrey. He shifted his shoulders and glared at his host. "You saying I'm acting dishonourably?"

"Nothing of the sort, Aymestrey. It is, however, just a *trifle* irregular, don't you think?"

"So it may be, sir," Nick put in swiftly, "but that is not why I am refusing his challenge."

Yes, it was against all the unwritten rules for a man of Aymestrey's age to challenge a youth, Nick knew. Although the case must be regarded as borderline. He was, after all, three and twenty and very much of age. But he was well aware that his own father would heartily disapprove of Aymestrey's action, and would have advised him to refuse the challenge on that count alone. But had that been all Nick would have accepted it without an instant's hesitation!

"What do you mean, sir?" demanded Aymestrey angrily. "What other reason could you have, other than being a lily-livered scamp?"

Nick was obliged to grit his teeth on the surge of anger that bubbled up within him. Charles must have seen it, for he turned towards the older man and threw up his chin.

"You don't call him that in *my* presence!"

"Hold your tongue, Delamere!" snapped Mr Apperley.

"Be quiet, Charles, for God's sake!" begged Tony.

The little episode had an effect, however, in reminding Nick that he could not afford to give way to emotions born of pride. Something more important than his own honour was at stake here. He drew a calming breath.

"Lord Aymestrey, while it might afford you personal satisfaction to fight me, it would serve only to make us both a laughing-stock to go out over such a matter."

"So that's it!" pounced his would-be opponent. "Afraid of looking ridiculous. Well, you'll look *more* so if you refuse me, for I'll not keep silent on the matter.''

''I had rather look ridiculous,'' Nick uttered curtly, ''than subject Miss Edborough to the insult of having her name bandied about the gentlemen's clubs in connection with a dispute of this kind!''

For a moment, Aymestrey looked utterly taken aback. Then he began to bluster. ''Nonsense! Nonsense! Nothing to do with the wench. Between you and me, over my wife!''

''Even if that were the case—which it most certainly is *not*—are you so ready to lay Lady Aymestrey open to the same sort of gossip?''

Mr Apperley looked a warning, but it was too late. Aymestrey's features empurpled, and the true reason for the whole business was instantly revealed.

''We come to it! We come to it!'' he bellowed. ''*You*, sir, have been the greater cause of exposing my wife to gossip! And I won't have it, do you hear? I won't have you worming your way in—trying to resume your—your *damned* liaison! Do you hear me, sir? I *will not* tolerate it!''

''I should think the entire gathering can hear you,'' Nick told him acidly. ''And the boot, Lord Aymestrey, is very much on the other leg!''

''Weare!'' gasped Mr Apperley, quite appalled, as his lordship showed signs of wishing to leap upon his rival there and then.

But Tony and Charles were on Aymestrey in a second, grabbing his arms and holding him back.

''No, you don't!''

''Be still now, sir! Be *still*.''

"You'll answer to me for those words! You'll answer to me, I say!" roared Aymestrey, struggling.

"For God's sake, Aymestrey!" cried Apperley. "Calm down, will you? Keep hold of him, boys!"

"We will, sir, don't worry!"

"He ain't going to get away from us!"

But in the event the two young men had to tackle Aymestrey to the ground before he would surrender, Apperley dancing about in distress. Nick was caught by a reprehensible desire to burst into laughter, and wished very much that Friday might be present to share a sight that reminded him of nothing so much as the Greek stories she was always reading.

The thought of her sobered him, and he stepped forward, raising his voice to be heard above the grunts and groans of the struggling trio on the ground.

"Lord Aymestrey! Pray calm yourself, sir. I will apologise for the whole."

It was some moments before Aymestrey lost his will to fight on, but he lay still at length, gasping for breath. Nick wondered if he had any idea how utterly foolish he looked, and for his sake was glad that Apperley had insisted on bringing them away from public view.

"I beg your pardon, Aymestrey," he said, when once the man had been allowed up and Tony had obligingly brushed him off as well as himself. For all three had acquired a fair proportion of dust and debris on their garments.

"Quite right, Weare," put in Mr Apperley, anxious to keep things on an even keel. "No business saying what you did."

"None at all, sir," Nick agreed. "But, while I have no wish to fan the flames, I must add this."

"Careful, Nick," warned Tony, reaching out towards Aymestrey again.

His lordship moved away. "Let me alone! Not going to go for him again. What is it you wish to say, Weare?"

"My lord, I do not deny an earlier association with Lady Aymestrey. But I beg you to believe that there never was—nor will there *ever* be, and you may depend upon my word for that!—any liaison between us of the sort you suspect. As far as I am concerned, any connection between myself and Hermione ended when I became betrothed to Miss Edborough."

"Is that the truth?" asked Mr Apperley, apparently impelled either by curiosity or concern for Aymestrey's feelings.

"You have my word on it, sir," Nick assured him unhesitatingly.

"All very well," cut in Aymestrey grudgingly, "but you ain't betrothed to Miss Edborough."

"Not at the moment," agreed Nick.

He saw his brother exchange a glance with Delamere. Well, he supposed they must have seen it long before he had himself. It seemed Caro had been right. He had *not* known his own feelings. Though it looked as if everyone else had!

Lord Aymestrey was looking at him very hard. "You had better be speaking the truth, Weare."

Oddly enough, it was Apperley who said meaningly, "Actions speak louder than words, Aymestrey."

The man's glance came round to him. He was

frowning heavily, and Nick wondered whether he understood. For himself, he was itching to laugh. Had he been that obvious? He supposed he had. At the time, he had thought only of poor Friday, pitched into the water so unkindly! Whoever had done it, he thought he would have acted in precisely the same way. That it had been Hermione—and who else *would* have done such an ill-bred thing?—had offered the added spice of sweet revenge. He had the grace to admit that, unworthy though it was. The thought led inevitably to images of Friday in her woeful state, and he became all of a sudden impatient to be finished with this farce. He must see Friday!

"Sir, are you content to let this matter rest?" he demanded of Aymestrey, trying to keep out of his voice his wish to be gone.

"Yes, yes, my friend," said Mr Apperley quickly, laying a hand on his contemporary's arm. "You must see now that it will not do. Quite ineligible."

Aymestrey grunted what might have been assent, and roughly waved Nick away. "Leave me! Get away, the lot of you!"

Nothing loath, Nick thanked Apperley, who nodded briefly and signified his intention to remain with his other guest, and turned with alacrity towards the house, accompanied by Charles and Tony. The latter clapped him on the back.

"Well done, old fellow! My father would be proud of you."

"For the first time," Nick laughed. But there was no rancour in his voice. This time he knew that what he proposed for his future would meet with Lord

Weare's approval. If, that was, he could persuade a certain person into acceptance!

The doubt that menaced his peace was fostered by the discovery, when he finally ran his sister to earth in one of the drawing-rooms, that Friday had gone home with Lady Delamere. Caroline, unusually, was not in the least communicative, refusing to answer any of his questions directly. He was obliged to be content with her statement that Friday had been too upset by events to remain, and contain his soul with what patience he could muster until the following morning

So eager was he to see Friday that it did not occur to him that she might, a little past the hour of nine, be still abed. He blinked uncomprehendingly at Delamere's butler.

"I am talking of Miss Edborough, you know, Tattenhoe. Not his lordship."

The man bowed. "I am aware, sir. But no one has as yet been down to breakfast."

Nick's eyes brightened. "Ah, but she may be awake! Send someone up to tell her I am here, if you please."

A faint raising of the eyebrows gave Nicolas to understand that he had shocked the butler.

"Have no fear!" he said, taking advantage of the fellow's momentary weakness to step inside the house. "I have no intention of disturbing her *in* her bedchamber. Let her be told that I will await her pleasure—it if takes all morning!"

The eyebrows rose even higher, but Tattenhoe merely bowed again, saying, "Very well, sir. If you will step into the back parlour, I will request Miss Murdishaw to carry your message upstairs.''

"Thank you," Nick said, and walked briskly down the hall to the little room indicated.

He was in no humour to remember that this was the less frequented parlour, into which all undesirable visitors were shown whenever the butler wished to ascertain their welcome or otherwise from the master or mistress of the house. It happened that he and Delamere often used the place in their early youth to conceal their illicit potations from Charles's father. Its dark-panelled walls had deadened their inebriated giggles, and the old, worn chairs were comfortable enough. Since it was the Delamere's extravagant habit to have fires lit in all the rooms throughout the winter, it would certainly be warm enough to wait, as he certainly intended to do, for Friday to come down.

Reaching the parlour door, he grasped the handle and turned it, pushing it open. A gasp of surprise reached him, and within the room a figure shifted.

"Friday!"

She was standing before the fire, one hand grasping the mantel, the other hastily slipping the spectacles on to her nose. She had on a habit of blue cloth, rather more old-fashioned than she had lately been accustomed to wear, which seemed vaguely out of place.

But Nick was in no case to identify the reason. For her unexpected presence had sent a jolt through his veins. So strong was it that he could do no more than stand there, staring at her, his fingers about the doorknob still.

Friday was more than shocked—although her heart had jerked violently. She was horrified! Nick *here?*

At such a time! She had thought herself safely hidden away in this little back parlour while she waited for the summons she was expecting. Of all people, the last she wanted to catch her out at this was Nick!

Her pulse began a wild pumping and she stammered, "You g-gave me such a f-fright!"

"Fright!" he got out, stupidly echoing the word.

His glance, urged by that latent significance in her choice of dress, flicked about the room. On a chair to one side, a woollen cloak, carelessly flung down, caught his eye. Lying on top of it was a beaver hat. A frown creased his brow.

"What *is* this?"

He stopped as he noticed two portmanteaux standing neatly side by side next to the chair. A flood of emotion swamped his breast and the protest tore out of his throat.

"Where in *Hades* do you think you're going?"

"It is none of your affair!" Friday threw at him, responding instinctively to the passion she detected beneath his words.

"We'll see that!" he uttered gutturally, snapping the door shut. "My God, I'm *glad* I gave you a fright. You deserve one!"

"How dare you? Go away!"

Nick strode up to her, thundering, "*Where* are you going, Friday?"

"Don't shout at me!" she yelled back. "If you must know, I am going *home*."

He stopped dead before her. Incredulously, he asked, "To Finchamstod?"

"Where else? The coach will be here at any moment."

"But *why?* You *can't* go home, Friday. I won't let you!"

"Oh, won't you?" retorted Friday wrathfully. "Try if you can stop me!"

His eyes blazed suddenly, and he grasped her shoulders in a painful grip. "Try if you can escape me!"

"Let me go!"

"How can you do this, Friday? How *can* you?" he demanded, ignoring her command. "Scuttling off, without a word to anyone!"

"I am not scuttling off!" Friday declared indignantly, trying to pull away. How dared he come here and manhandle her this way? Under the spectacles, her glance flashed at him. "In any event, what has it to do with you?"

"It has everything to do with me, and so you shall find before you are a day older!"

"Let go of me, Nick!" she cried again, wrenching out of his hold. Matching violence with violence, she hurled her pain at him. "Go and bask in the arms of your wretched Hermione and *leave me alone.*"

Nick stared blankly. "Are you at that again? Friday, you must have taken leave of your senses! Haven't I *told* you, over and over, how I feel about that girl?"

"Oh, yes, you've told me," Friday uttered painfully. "And I was ready to believe you. For I had no reason to doubt you *then*. But it is difficult to refute the evidence of your own eyes, Nick. So pray don't *lie* to me any more!"

"Lie to you? I swear to God, Friday—"

"*Don't!* I can bear anything but *more* of your swearing and promises!"

Nick shook his head, puzzlement writ large in his features. What *was* the matter with her? After yesterday's fiasco, he should have thought his feelings were obvious. He studied her averted face, for she had turned away from him, fighting, he could see, with overwhelming emotion. If he touched her, would she go crazy as she had that last time? He did not know what he should do. But one thing he determined on there and then. He was *not* going to walk away this time!

He thought over what she had said, and found the anomaly. Evidence! There was no more thought of what he should do. He snapped into action, seizing hold of her again and turning her forcibly to face him.

"What evidence?"

"Leave go of me!" she ordered, struggling.

"No! *What* evidence?"

"You were *kissing* her!" Friday shouted at him, unable to help herself as the memory came hauntingly into her brain. "I saw you!"

Nick was so surprised that he did let her go. "You must be mistaken!"

"No, I am *not* mistaken," she told him angrily. "Do you think I am *completely* blind? Besides, I had on my spectacles. I was walking past the window yesterday at the Apperleys', and I saw it, Nick. You had the creature in your arms!"

He was frowning with the effort of memory. Good God, yes, he *had* struggled with Hermione! Perhaps it might have looked, from the outside, as if he was embracing her. Before he could say anything to refute the impression Friday had gained, however, she was off again.

"So you see, I *know*. And Hermione herself told me that you have been lovers—" her voice broke at the thought of it "—even when we were *betrothed*."

The green eyes lit with such a flame of anger that Friday involuntarily stepped back a pace.

"And you believed her!" he exclaimed bitterly.

Friday was at once conscious of doubt. But she *had* seen him holding her. And he had not even attempted to deny it. She was instantly on the defensive, and her anger rose again.

"I might *not* have done so had I not seen it for myself."

"What you *thought* you saw and what you saw," Nick said bitingly, "happen to be two very different things."

"That is what you say now."

"If you must know, the wench went for me with her nails and I was trying to control her. I am not answerable for what it looked like to you. And to suggest we were lovers—particularly during our betrothal! How could you believe me capable of such *base* disloyalty?"

"But she said—"

"She may have said it, but that does not mean it is true! And as for kissing her, why in the world should I wish to do so—*now?*"

"You wished to before. Why should anything be different now?" Friday demanded.

"Because, you idiotic, obstinate little fool, I happen to be in love with *you!*"

The world spun. Friday put out a hand to steady

herself and Nick caught it, pulling her hard against him. His arms encircled her, holding her up.

"Friday!" he uttered urgently. "This is no moment for fainting!"

Then his lips came down on hers. It was a kiss like nothing she had ever imagined! It was hard. And rough. And a flame of passion leapt within her to answer the need she recognised instantly. Her limbs closed against his own, and she felt a throb of desire that far outweighed anything in her dreams. Fire streaked through her, and her arms, which had slid involuntarily about his back, tightened unconsciously. The response that crushed her even more tightly to Nick's chest very nearly deprived her of breath!

But she scarcely noticed, for her lips had parted at an insistent pressure from his, and the velvet meeting within caused the most delicious liquid sensation to melt her limbs to jelly.

When at last Nick released her mouth, she felt herself sag as her knees began to collapse. But his hold did not relax, and she could feel his gaze burning fiercely into her face. Although she could not *see* it. For her eyeglasses were misted over and lying askew on her nose.

"Oh, *Friday*," he sighed, and a weak laugh escaped him. "My darling owl—only *look* at your spectacles!"

"How—can I?" responded Friday breathlessly, conscious of the feel of his heartbeat pulsing into her bosom over his own ragged breath.

His hand came up to pluck the spectacles away. "You can—do without them—for the moment."

Since he was so close, Friday could see that she

might very well do without them. Then she could see nothing again, for his mouth once more sought hers, depriving her almost instantaneously of awareness of anything save the utterly intense sensations that his kiss was arousing.

But the initial desperation of mutual longed-for ardour settled in a little, and he did stop kissing her at length. When the fluctuations of her pulse calmed sufficiently for her to be able to open her eyes, she looked dazedly up into his face, amazed at the tenderness she saw there. A tenderness that was so precious to her that she was suddenly afraid.

"Nick, am I dreaming?"

A frown crossed his face. The painful intensity of the question troubled him. "Why do you ask that?"

Friday's eyes filled. "B-because if I w-wake up again, I d-don't think I c-could *bear* it!"

"Don't weep!" he begged, cradling her closer. "It makes me feel like a monster. I've hurt you so *much*. I've been so selfish. I just—didn't realise."

"What d-didn't you realise?"

"That you loved me," he said with a frankness that warmed her heart. "But I have had time enough to think this last *long* day and night. I have hardly *slept* for thinking of it."

"Have you not?" Friday asked wonderingly, remembering her own sleepless nights. And, heaven help her, those *aching* nights filled with too much sleep!

He hugged her tight and spoke into her hair. "I remembered so many things, you see, my poor sweet love. What you said that *hideous* day about my Trojan horse. And the way you looked when I first put to you that *shameful* offer—so false of me! Oh, my darling, can you ever forgive me?''

Friday had never thought to hear such words. Her bosom was near to bursting, and for answer she pulled away a little and drew his face down so that she might kiss him—with a sureness, an innocent certainty that encompassed all the fervency, and more, of that first time when she had imagined she was saying goodbye.

''I remembered that, too,'' said Nick when he was able to speak again, as if he had read her mind. ''When you kissed me.''

Friday found herself blushing a little, despite the embraces they had just now shared. ''I have never been more ashamed of anything! I was so sure I had given myself away.''

''But you hadn't,'' Nick told her gently. ''How could you, to the fool I was then? I could not see it, Friday. Any more than I could see that I loved you.''

''But you *didn't*,'' Friday said forcefully, pulling away slightly. ''Not then. You most certainly did not.''

Nick nodded. His hold loosened and he slid his hands down her arms to catch at her fingers. ''Oh, yes. I loved you. I always have,'' he said, bringing her fingers up to his lips. ''It was that, as I have since guessed, that made Hermione attack you. I told her.''

''You *told* her?'' echoed Friday, amazed.

''I had to. I said, moreover, that I never *had* loved her, that I had *adored* you from the day we met— which is *true,* my bespectacled bluestocking, little though you may believe it.''

''But why in the world did you tell her such a thing?''

"I could think of no other way to get the wretch out of my hair," Nick said ruefully.

"Then that explains it," Friday uttered flatly. "She must have felt desperate. *That* is why she said that you had been lovers. She knew—she *must* have known—what would be the effect on me."

"Don't think of it any more," Nick advised. Then he gripped her fingers. "But thinking of it, Friday, she has been of *some* use. For if not for the farce of our betrothal I might *never* have discovered how I love you. I must be eternally grateful to my father for forcing me to offer for you."

"I thank you!" Friday retorted. "I, on the other hand, have been cursing him for *weeks*."

A little laugh escaped him, and he drew her closer for a hug. "Poor Friday! But only think if he had not put you through that hell—" He broke off, adding quickly as a shadow crossed her face, "Oh, I *know*, my darling! I have had time to recall—and mentally to *scourge* myself for them—every nuance, every gesture, every *word* in which you gave yourself away."

Friday grimaced. "So thoroughly?"

Nick kissed her forehead. "Have no fear! I had not the wit to recognise it, had I? Or perhaps I had. At the time I did not *wish* to recognise it. If my father had not done what he did—oh, my God, but it does *not* bear thinking of. Let us not think of it! I don't want to imagine a life without you...and the *misery* that would have been."

Friday heard this with the air of one bemused, unable to take it all in, to believe that this was indeed *life*, and not some figment of her tortured imaginings. She watched the frown enter Nick's eyes as she stared at him without speaking. Saw doubt coming in, and a troubled look that struck at the depths of her love.

"It *is* true, isn't it, Friday?" he asked anxiously. "I have read you aright? You do—at least you *did* love me! Oh, my God, don't say it's too late! Don't tell me my dullness has betrayed me." His hands came up to her shoulders again, and he shook her. "You *do* love me? Friday! Tell me quickly. *Tell me,* before I go out of my mind!"

Trembling a little, Friday's fingers reached up to his face and traced a path across his cheek. It was warm to the touch. *Real.* At last she began to be convinced. It was not another dream. This was actually happening. It was Nick standing here, begging her to speak of her love to him. Her body seemed to float, her brain was light, her heart...*free.*

"There is no pain any more," she whispered, and put up her face, closing her eyes in mute invitation.

The kiss this time was gentle. Nick mouthed her lips with a tenderness that brought a warm glow to her heart. She felt his fingers in her hair, a sensation so pleasant that she sighed against his lips. He drew away a little, opening his eyes to gaze into her own.

"Friday," he murmured insistently, "you still have not answered me."

She smiled. "About whether I still love you? Mine would be a poor sort of love if I did not."

"Well, *do* you?" he insisted, giving her a shake.

"Oh, Nick!" she cried, laughing. "When I have dreamed of nothing else since the moment we met? Of course I still love you!" A mischievous smile lit her eyes. "I do not know, however, that I can tolerate a *third* offer."

"I have no intention of making you a third offer," declared Nick. "You don't think I'm risking another refusal, do you? We will just be betrothed without it."

She cocked her head on one side. "Paris and Helen this time?"

"*No!*" he said vehemently. "Simply Friday and Nick. And if you ever dare to refer to me as one of your stupid Greek heroes again, I shall rip your Homer to shreds!"

Friday giggled. "I don't think I care any more. You may do so with my good will, Nicolas Weare, for I have no more need of dreams."

* * * * *

Harlequin Romance®

Delightful
Affectionate
Romantic
Emotional

Tender
Original

Daring
Riveting
Enchanting
Adventurous
Moving

Harlequin Romance®—
capturing the world you dream of...

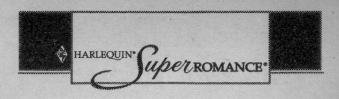

…there's more to the story!

Superromance.
A *big* satisfying read about unforgettable characters. Each month we offer *six* very different stories that range from family drama to adventure and mystery, from highly emotional stories to romantic comedies—and much more! Stories about people you'll believe in and care about. Stories too compelling to put down….

Our authors are among today's *best* romance writers. You'll find familiar names and talented newcomers. Many of them are award winners—and you'll see why!

If you want the biggest and best in romance fiction, you'll get it from Superromance!

Emotional, Exciting, Unexpected…

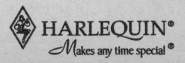

HARLEQUIN Presents

The world's bestselling romance series...
The series that brings you your favorite authors,
month after month:

Helen Bianchin...Emma Darcy
Lynne Graham...Penny Jordan
Miranda Lee...Sandra Marton
Anne Mather...Carole Mortimer
Susan Napier...Michelle Reid

and many more uniquely talented authors!

Wealthy, powerful, gorgeous men...
Women who have feelings just like your own...
The stories you love, set in exotic, glamorous locations...

HARLEQUIN Presents

Seduction and passion guaranteed!

HARLEQUIN®
INTRIGUE

WE'LL LEAVE YOU BREATHLESS!

If you've been looking for thrilling tales of contemporary passion and sensuous love stories with taut, edge-of-the-seat suspense—then you'll love Harlequin Intrigue!

Every month, you'll meet four new heroes who are guaranteed to make your spine tingle and your pulse pound. With them you'll enter into the exciting world of Harlequin Intrigue— where your life is on the line and so is your heart!

THAT'S INTRIGUE—
ROMANTIC SUSPENSE
AT ITS BEST!

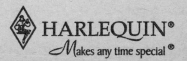

HARLEQUIN®

Makes any time special ®

INTDIR1

Harlequin® Historical

From rugged lawmen and valiant knights to defiant heiresses and spirited frontierswomen, Harlequin Historicals will capture your imagination with their dramatic scope, passion and adventure.

Harlequin Historicals... they're too good to miss!

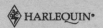

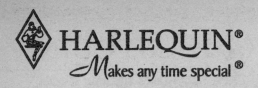
HARLEQUIN®

Makes any time special ®

HARLEQUIN®

AMERICAN *Romance*

Upbeat, All-American Romances

HARLEQUIN®

Duets™

Romantic Comedy

Harlequin®
Historical

Historical, Romantic Adventure

HARLEQUIN®
INTRIGUE

Romantic Suspense

Harlequin Romance ®

Capturing the World You Dream Of

HARLEQUIN®
Presents

Seduction and passion guaranteed

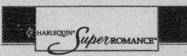
HARLEQUIN® *Super* ROMANCE®

Emotional, Exciting, Unexpected

HARLEQUIN®
Temptation

Sassy, Sexy, Seductive!

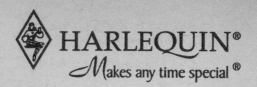

HARLEQUIN®
Makes any time special ®

Upbeat,
All-American Romances

Romantic Comedy

Historical,
Romantic Adventure

HARLEQUIN®
INTRIGUE

Romantic Suspense

Harlequin Romance ®

Capturing the World
You Dream Of

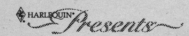

Seduction and passion
guaranteed

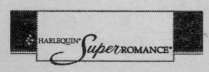

Emotional,
Exciting, Unexpected

Sassy, Sexy, Seductive!

HDIR2